A Dog in Sheep's Clothing

A. Sleeper

For my Dad.

ACKNOWLEDGMENTS

To Jessica Bottiglier, Elena Keener, Erica Jenkins and Olivia Hintz:

You've never shied from helping me write a story.

Thank you all so much.

"We have doomed the wolf not for what it is, but for what we deliberately and mistakenly perceive it to be – the mythologized epitome of a savage ruthless killer – which is, in reality, no more than a reflected image of ourself."

-Farley Mowat

"Hold on this will hurt more than anything has before
What it was, what it was, what it was
I've brought this on us more than anyone could ignore
What I've done, what I've done, what I've done"

-William Fitzsimmons

CHAPTER 1

The hospital room was dry and sterile. The countless flowers that sat in their pathetic bouquets which were supposed to be cheery and filled with goodwill were crisped around the edges as if they had been burned by a cruel kid who'd found his first lighter. The walls were a pale shade of salmon and the only redeeming feature happened to be the large picture window that took up almost the entirety of the south-facing wall. It opened up to a world of rooftops and the Potomac not too far away, glittering in the early summer sun as it had for hundreds of years before. Trees lined its edges, filled with the light greens of young leaves, shuffling in the breeze.

The harsh texture of the hospital chair's fabric annoyed him. The way the room smelled annoyed him. The fly sitting peacefully outside the glass of the window annoyed him. Tension built. Not in the room. Only in him. Everything went through his mind at once as if it were impossible for them to be separated. Colors melted into sounds. The hum of the radiator, the salmon on the walls, the blip of the heart monitor, the black of Avery's hair. He felt as though he were a balloon waiting to pop. As if all it would take was a needle and his entire body would simply burst with blood, intestines, brains, and bone. He tried to breathe evenly, but it was impossible. He tried to still his shaking, but found that to be impossible too. He needed to scream. He needed to pick up this stupid fucking chair and smash it out that window to watch it crash down onto the sidewalk and splinter into a hundred thousand little pieces of wood and tufts of stuffing. It wouldn't be enough. It would never be enough.

"Trent?"

His eyes lifted to the plastic and fabric of the hospital bed. The wires and tubes. Avery, his partner. "I'm here, bud." He couldn't tell if he was shaking from unreleased tension or trembling in fear. The idea filled him with rage. Another cause for shaking. Avery sighed through his nose past those annoying little plastic things that gave him oxygen. "Bad shape" was what Bentley, their boss, had called it. "Bad shape" was, in Winston's opinion, a mild way to put it.

He'd been stabbed in the abdomen three times with what looked to be a switchblade. While bleeding, he'd been tied to a chair and the bottoms of his feet had been cut cross-ways five times each to make it nearly impossible for him to run away if he did manage to escape. His blood had made a pool on the floor under him. He had burns on his neck and shoulders and down one arm from scalding water that had been poured onto him. Worst of it all... Winston took in a deep breath and then let it out when Avery put his hand out and he took it in his, squeezing gently. Worst of it all, his cheeks had been mutilated. What Detective Wilson had termed a "Glasgow Smile." The corners of his mouth now reached the edge of his jaw.

The damage was extensive. Permanent scarring was unavoidable. His partner would be different for the rest of his life. Physically. Mentally.

"Trent," Avery said again. He had his eyes closed. His speech was slurred from muscle damage and pain. "Dunn. Don...t. Go. Alone." The warning was a simple one. It had been given to him many times in the past and most of those times he had listened. Waiting for Avery to come with him.

"I won't be going alone."

Avery opened his eyes and his brows knitted when he looked over. "Who?" There were only a few options on the table. Either take Rayne Wilson or the newb rookie Ned Carter. Wilson was too nosy and Carter would get himself killed. Winston couldn't have either of them. He wouldn't be going alone.

"Don't worry about it, Avery."

That was an impossibility. If there was one thing that Avery could do, and could do well, it was worry about whatever hare-brained scheme his partner was up to. This time was a little different. This time there was vengeance on the table. This time Winston had taken out all the stops. There would be no jail-time for this killer. There would be nothing for this killer but suffering. More suffering than he could possibly imagine.

He was young. Lithe. Virile. He looked like an animal. His legs were crossed at the ankles and stretched out while he sat on the top of one of the park's many picnic tables, his heels resting on the table's built-in bench. The bottoms of his black *Toms* were worn almost completely through, the sides of them torn so badly that the color of his socks was evident through them. Other than his shoes, however, he looked good. He was a little dirty, his clothes a small bit frayed, and his hair cut in a do-it-yourself punk rocker spike-up that worked well with its color. Or lack of color. It was bleached fully white, the only hint to his natural color was his well-trimmed, jet black goatee.

Winston approached him with his hands in his pockets, looking around at all the distracted park denizens. It was a beautiful day. "You're up early."

"I'm not a raccoon," he replied, taking off his sunglasses and hooking them to the collar of his tight navy blue band T-shirt. Winston sincerely doubted that he'd actually attended any concerts. Without his shades, his eyes took on a slight squint but retained their icy emotion. He tried not to look into those eyes too much. He feared he might lose himself to some kind of rage or insanity. The non-raccoon stared at him, watched him avoid his gaze. "Winnie." His condescending nickname was only to get his attention. "If you really want me to find him, I need the reports."

"I have to make copies."

"I'll wait. I know what he did to your partner. More than what you

3

told me. He's different from the other one, Winnie. Still. Still rather the same, wouldn't you say?" He tilted his head. It was a tic that Winston had noticed a long time ago. He tilted his head as if he were listening to some inner voice. Or music. Or fucking audiobook. Winston didn't quite care. So he was fucked in the head. He was inclined to believe that somehow or another, they all were. He looked over at him. At his tattered shoes, at his muscular structure, at his bleached-out hair. Most people weren't as fucked up as Ren.

"I would say that all serial killers are similar in some ways and different in others. A prime example of a similarity would be that they...oh...I don't know. Kill people."

"Don't be stupid, Winston. Under that logic, you'd be a serial killer too." Ren gave him a shit-eating grin and leaned forward, uncrossing his legs so he could lean his elbows on his knees. "How many serial killers have you locked away, Winnie? Since the last time I saw you."

He blinked. "One."

"And how many have you killed? Maybe not you personally. Maybe your partner or your lackeys. How many didn't quite make it to their first hearing?" His grin spread and formed into a grimace that caught Winston's gaze. A single thought which came to him every time he saw Ren came to him again and with such force that he was caught staring. *He has too many teeth. He's got the mouth of a great white. My god he can't be human.* He was aware suddenly that he was trembling.

"Uh...A-Avery shot one. Self defense. Lots of paperwork. Another one threw himself off a bridge. There were...two other suicides. One shot himself. The other lodged a knife into a crack in his door frame and threw himself into it."

"Did you watch?" Ren was practically panting.

"I...I saw the one jump off the bridge."

"Into water?"

"No."

The giddiness in Ren's small laugh broke Winston's stare and he quickly looked away and then covered his eyes with his palm. Ren's voice broke through his attempt at solitude. The frost around its edges was palpable. "I don't think he jumped off that bridge, Winston.

Detective. I think... You know what I think. You're a little bit more like me than you like to admit. You can say that you're grateful you think like me sometimes because that means you can get a leg up. That means that you can create an understanding. But you have an ability, Winnie, that can make you more. You're scary. Because under that boy scout skin you're just an animal."

He couldn't argue. He didn't want to. Ren would be the only one who ever knew some of these secrets he held inside him. In a little pouch that had grown next to his heart. If it grew too big...he swallowed. If it grew too big it would swallow his soul. Then what would he be? Ren stared at him with cold, dark blue eyes, his grin gone. "Look, Ren. If you want to stay out here, then you need to stop antagonizing me. I don't need to be analyzed. Cut the Hannibal crap and give me what I want."

"What do you really want?" Ren teased, relaxing and leaning back on his arms. He opted to look away from Winston and squint through the bright morning sun to watch the mothers playing with their children on the playground.

"I'd like your word."

"On what?"

"I already told you before. Nobody gets hurt. Nobody gets hurt other than...him. That means his family, his friends, anyone working for the police..."

"And especially not *you*, right? Of course. I know you. You've got a safe deposit box set to be opened when you die. Probably going to let Naddy open it, won't you? Well, no worries, Detective. I'm sure all the arrangements you've made for your premature death at my hands will be for nothing."

"It's not just your hands."

Ren perked. "Then...?"

"If my death is ruled a homicide, they may open the box. In it is information regarding you and Tomi which may result in charges filed against her." The side of his mouth twitched. He could feel the rage emanating from his violent, frosty companion. "When we're done. You and I. I will take that information out of the box and destroy it. But only then."

"So if someone else kills you..."

"Consider it my safety net."

Ren growled, the sound much like that of an angry dog. "You want me to protect you. If someone else kills you, Winnie, I'll slaughter anyone who goes near her. Anyone and everyone. I'll make the term 'bloodbath' seem mild."

"I will not reconsider." The threat of his past lover's undoing seemed to do the trick. Winston hadn't been sure if Ren was going to feign uncaring or not, but it seemed that he couldn't. His connection to the tricky little blonde that had gotten him mixed up in Winston's old case three years ago was still as strong in his memory as ever.

Ren seemed to calm but it was simply a facade. Winston could see him bristle even more. "Well then," he hissed, "I guess I'll just have to keep you from meeting your maker. Don't make that harder by being a fuckwit. If I were your doctor, I'd prescribe going home and keeping the *fuck* out of my way." He jumped off the picnic table. "You're lucky I'm even going to still help you. Go make your fucking copies. I can't stand the sight of you."

As Ren was walking away Winston said loud enough for him to hear, "There's a train bridge over Newport Drive by the old park. Tomorrow. Noon."

CHAPTER 2

Avery was sitting up when he walked in the next morning. He was eating—or trying to eat—some breakfast. It looked as if all he was going to get down would be the apple juice. The angry redness of the wounds on his face made a lead weight tumble into Winston's stomach. The stitches were black and they stuck out, stretching the flesh of his partner's face into a disgusting, creepy, sardonic smile. He turned toward Winston with a stoic expression. The nurse left when she saw Winston's scowl.

"Wins...ton. I...am glad ...ou're here."

"Hey bud."

"Who ah-are -ou taking -ith -ou?"

Winston shrugged. "Nobody is quite as wonderful at interrogations as you are. Since you were the one attacked, I'm assuming that it's probably somebody we already interrogated. Does that sound right to you?"

"-es. But..."

"Well then there you are. I can ask questions just as easily as you can and I have a good ear for lies. I'll be fine, Avery."

"Don-" his partner shook his head, worry etched in his features.

"Hey, calm down. I'm not going alone."

"Who?" His voice was pleading and insistent.

Winston caved. Avery still had that knack for interrogations. That ability to make anyone crack. An insistence that was monumental. He could make God confess to driving Satan to Hell for making a bad batch of brownies. "A friend. Okay? He's...he's good at this."

"Damn it, Wuh-Winston." A small bit of drool made it through his lips and he dabbed himself gingerly on the mouth with a washcloth that the nurse had left. "-ou jusss can't be logical? Tuh-take Rrray-ne. He's a good det-tective."

"I'm not going alone. I'm not lying to you. He'll be just like my shadow. I buy him a new pair of shoes, it'll be good. We'll be fine."

Avery's eyes widened and he looked speechless, his mouth only gaping open slightly as the swelling was too much for it to open any further. If he didn't have his cheeks sewn shut his jaw might have fallen to the floor. Winston could feel the blood rush into his face and suddenly felt embarrassed by the way his partner reacted.

"C'mon bud, don't be like this."

"Not. Not w-worth it. Not worth it. Not worth it." Avery kept shaking his head. "Send him back. No more. No more deals. Jussst because it worked lassst time does not mean it will work again. This one is too smart. He'll kill him."

"Then what do we have? Just one instead of two? No losses here, Avery, we can do this, *there's nothing to lose.*"

His partner was silent and wouldn't look into his eyes.

"This is Ren's time to shine. I mean really shine. It's a game. He's always wanted a game like this. I have him hooked in. He has to help me." Avery still would not respond. "Come on Avery. I'll tell you everything. You gotta help us on this."

"I will...help -ou. But jusssst because I care about -ou. And I don' want...Tomi in trouble." So that's what it was. Avery was sore on the Tomi aspect. Winston wasn't worried. He had no intentions of dying young and especially not at the hands of a killer who took particular enjoyment out of slicing his victims into ribbons. Tomi, in his eyes, was in no danger of being exposed to the police for her past involvement with Ren. She was safely tucked away in a small town in western New York, carefully placed there for her own good. She was happy there, with a charming yet quiet older boyfriend who *didn't* happen to rip people apart with his teeth. Tomi was perfectly safe from harm.

8

"Thank you, Avery. Thank you. We're going to try our best. Ren's nothing but a dog. I'm just going to give him a scent and set him loose. There's nothing complex about it. All he needs is the chase. I'm just going to tell him which car." Once Avery's approval—tepid as it was—was gained, there was nothing to stop him. Nothing that could slow him down. He would find this killer. He would find him and he would make sure that Ren bit off exactly how much he was willing to chew.

Literally.

The old park had once been used for high school baseball games. It was unused and left to rot in the rain and the sun. The mowers that had once kept it looking trim and clean were all gone and long grasses and weeds sprouted up where the mound used to be. Vines climbed all over the tall chain link behind where the batter would stand. The swings were missing, long gone to vandals who claimed them as prizes. The paint on the rock climbing wall was almost completely gone—lost to the weather. An old building that once served as restrooms stood solidly in the middle of the overgrown field, now just a shelter for mice, raccoons, and spiders. It was a desolate place. No houses surrounded it. There was nothing save the end of a gravel street leading to its old dirt parking lot on the other side of the railroad bridge overhead.

Ren had been huddled above him, up in the support beams that criss-crossed under the bridge. Steel works that were designed to hold up tens of tons of weight at a time. He had been crouched up there like a spider, waiting for Winston with intense focus. Winston, however, was unsurprised. He knew of Ren's ability to climb into tight places with ease. He knew that Ren was able to be in trees and move from one to the other with speed and agility. He was a rural killer. He did well in urban decay.

Winston lit up a Marlboro and watched the spider come down, silent, and sure of himself. He blew out the smoke and smiled. "You're still too good at blending in. I think you killed more than I thought you did while we were apart."

Ren grinned. "Only a little. When I really got the itch. And I tried to do you favors. Didn't always work out but I tried to only kill *bad* people."

"Oh and you got to decide who was *bad* did you?"

Ren shrugged. "It's not like I had you to coach me. Would you like to know about them? I know you would. You're a little sick. You're curious."

Winston didn't respond.

"Kent Newman kicked a whore. Little did he know that the whore he was kicking was the one who'd been making me tuna sandwiches and coffee every day and dropping them off next to me when I was sleeping on the streets. She was such a sweet one."

"Kent Newman, huh?"

"I know his name. Impressed?" Ren put a Camel Blue between his lips and lit it with a match. "There was some fucker on the subway platform. We were alone. He was...on something. Crack or...something. I gutted him and tossed him under the train."

"Did he kick a whore?"

Ren shrugged again and looked away. "Maybe."

Winston snorted a little. "How many?"

"Wouldn't you like to know." He said it like a cheeky little ten year old who had just hidden where his favorite ball was. "But we're not here to talk about me and what I've done in the past three years. You know exactly what I've been doing in the past three years. Killing, walking, eating, and fucking. There are a lot of people who can help me do all of those things. You're one of them. Give me those files and tell me what happened the night tall, dark, and handsome got himself a date."

He handed them over and watched the killer flip through them, pausing at the photographs with an appreciative smirk. "About a week and a half ago. I was across town at a play. After it was over, I got a call from Avery. He'd had a thought about our killer. We discussed the case a little. When we were finished, we said goodbye and I thought that he had hung up the phone. I have this smart phone that ends the call whenever the other person hangs up so I don't have to press anything. Turns out that he had never hit the button to end the call. He'd put the phone down on the counter. I don't know why.

"A few seconds later, I could hear him on the phone. It wasn't pretty. He was being attacked. I stayed on the phone and tried to get him to talk to me, but instead of that, I think I just alerted our killer. He escaped before the police got there when I called them. Of course not before ripping my partner's face to shreds."

"And his feet," Ren mused. "Interesting. These...parallel lines. They're not so he doesn't run away. I mean, sure, that could be another aspect of it. But the others have parallel lines cut into them as well. This one on his thigh. This one on the top of his head. The CEO has his belly cut to ribbons." His black eyebrows popped up. "Although I would say that the attack on Avery-boy's face was atypical. He must have been angry."

He kicked a rock. "It was me. He was angry because I was still on the phone. Because he didn't have time."

"Well of course," Ren smiled. "Some killers are a little anal. They need five hours to get their rocks off. Fuckers are weird. How long did he have with Avery?"

"Maybe ten minutes to fifteen minutes, tops. The only thing that he really got to do was his stupid parallel lines. The water was already on the stove. Avery had been making himself a late dinner. It was all spontaneous. Everything else fits, but he was rushed. He needed more time. And I didn't give that to him."

Ren let him go silent and flipped through the files some more. "There's a list of the interviews in here right? Because I'm going to bet you fifty dollars right here and now that our killer has either been interviewed by Avery, or watched Avery interview someone."

The detective nodded his head. "My exact thoughts." He wiped a thumb over his lips and studied his killer. Blue eyes flitted back and forth over the lines and the photos. It was almost possible to hear the grinding of the gears in his mind. He wondered just how smart Ren was. He had always assumed that he was fairly intelligent due to Rayne's historically accurate profiling, but he had never actually seen Ren's mind work in critical thinking functions. It would be interesting now. Because now Ren was faced with hunting in a civilized place.

"He kills people who are in positions of authority or power. Could be out of resentment. Fear. Or just..."

"Just?"

"Boredom."

"Is that why you kill, Ren? Because you're bored?"

Ren mocked him. "Is that why you masturbate, Trent? Because you're bored?" He spat on the ground. "It's going to be a little hard for me to figure out who this killer is, bud. It's not like I can move in social circles very well."

"Let me do the talking. All I need from you is your sharp eyes and your protection. And in the end, I need him dead."

"Sure thing, boss."

CHAPTER 3

There was something about the whole affair that put butterflies in her stomach. She'd never felt as though she were in danger before. It was a new feeling. Their Victorian styled mansion just outside the city limits had always seemed like the perfect home, but now the empty halls lined with the scowls of past Kingsleys were too vast and solemn. They felt like tunnels in which anyone or anything could sneak up on her. She wasn't sure if she could be afraid of *things* as much as she was afraid of *people*. She had always been a level-headed girl in that regard. Never afraid of the boogeyman or the wolf under the bed or around the corner. No, she was much more afraid of things that were in reality. Burglars, kidnappers, mob thugs. They were all very real in her mind and all things that were to be feared on a basic level. She had never been afraid of things. Just people.

Now she wasn't sure what to think. It wasn't as if her uncle had been murdered by a person, but she also knew that it could not be a thing either. It had been a person who had killed him. But in such a manner...she closed her eyes. Such a manner was not something *people* did. There lacked sense. There lacked sanity. At least mob men were predictable. At least there were some things in this world that could be counted on. But this was different. This was awful. This was *torturous*. His eyes had been staring up at the ceiling in an expression of pure agony. The top of his head had been sliced from side to side in parallel lines. Made into ribbons of stringy flesh, colored by his blood. She hadn't seen it. It wasn't considered something that the youngest female Kingsley should witness. Her brother had told her after she'd asked. He had been short with it but went into enough detail for the deed to be considered horrifying.

Thank God for Sean. Her older brother might have had to catch her from fainting when she heard the news. He had been prepared. She remembered his face when they had come in the room. Sean and Father. Sean was pale and grim, his lips tight together as if he was holding himself back from crying. Strong Sean. He had stood beside Father when the news had come out that Albert had been murdered. Murdered in the most awful of ways. He had come to her side and placed a hand on her shoulder. As if he knew that she would feel faint. As if he knew that he might just have to catch her. He was her rock. He was what held her together. His calm demeanor and careful words always calmed her.

She started when the door to her room was rapped upon. "C-come in," she replied.

Sean inched into the room wearing a short-sleeved white cotton polo and a red sweater-vest she had bought him for his birthday the year before. His tie, which was tucked under the vest, was black. He always wore ties, even when he needn't. "I was wondering if you'd like to join me for tea in the garden?"

Sun would be good for her, but she wasn't sure if she was finished being quite afraid of the outdoors. "I don't know."

"Shannon," he sighed, "Don't be a bore. Please will you just come down and have some tea with me? Just on the patio even. Not even in the garden. Just right outside the door. You can't be afraid of everything. Besides, I'll be with you. With the two of us, no killer would ever be able to get by." He let his face fall into a lop-sided grin.

She couldn't help but be taken by it. "Alright."

Tea with her brother was an afternoon affair. She was the only one he really talked to and of course it was about things that she wasn't sure were any of her business.

"Well and of course he was thinking of wearing the Armani jacket with that awful Christmas sweater his sister had gotten him so I did the only thing I could think of. I burned it. He doesn't know it's missing yet, I think he completely forgot that he was even going to wear it. Hasn't mentioned it anyway."

She giggled a little. "You're lucky Steven is as flighty as he is or he might have figured it was you that got rid of it since you were the only one who made such a fuss over it."

Sean scoffed. "Lucky? Have you met his parents? He's lucky to have as much wit as he does with those two bumbling fools as kin."

Poor Steven, she thought wryly. He was the outcast of their group. There were five of them. Sean, Steven, Kyle, Ben, and Preston. The five of them often formed their own little rich boy *Sex and the City* grouping when they went to the country club to play a few rounds of golf and chat by the fireplace with brandy snifters clutched in their perfectly manicured hands. She tried to ignore her own nails and hid her hands in her lap. She'd been biting them. It wouldn't do. She tried to think of Steven again. Steven with his pouting lower lip and his slight lisp that annoyed Preston to no end. One might think the poor man would have fits over it if Steven thought to speak more.

All of them, aside from Steven, usually had the best of dress sense. They wore the perfect combinations of designers. Sean tried to dress her sometimes. He would buy her outfits and she would try to keep them all straight and together, but she was much too scatterbrained for such things. Still, Sean would deign to be seen in public with her just because he loved her too much to let her wallow in her bad fashion sense forever. He would carefully pick out shoes for her to wear and tell her exactly what would go with them that she already had. She wondered sometimes if he were gay, but dismissed it the next time she found a girl on his arm in his room.

The garden was beautiful in early summer. The buds on the trees had spread open to reveal fresh new leaves and the chill of spring had gone, leaving a warm summer wind that could blow easily through her thick auburn hair. She wasn't ugly. No. She certainly wasn't. One might even suggest that she was much like early summer herself. Not quite spring anymore being twenty-five, but still green as ever. She wondered just how badly home-tutoring had done her. She watched

Sean prattle on about inane subjects such as what kind of pomade Preston was utilizing and how it smelled. She had been left with nobody. No friends. No outside influences. Nobody except Sean. She wasn't quite sure what to say when his friends would come on to her. Of course she hadn't known that they were coming onto her until her mother's personal assistant (Mother simply called her the 'maid') had suggested that they were. Kyle did it most often. Giving her clandestine glances across the dinner table and playing with the hem of her skirt with a socked foot after he'd discarded his shoe under his chair.

She let her eyes wander over Sean's shoulder. She wondered what a man's touch might feel like. A feather-soft stroke on her shoulder. A man she was attracted to. A man she could see herself being sexual with. She could feel her face getting warm and she hoped Sean didn't notice her blushing. He was going on about Ben's latest romance so it wouldn't be too far-fetched for her to have flushed but even still she wished he would sip his tea and stop gossiping. Daffodils were cheerily swaying in the breeze. She wondered about the handsome detective who had given her such a warm glance in the lobby after he was done asking Father questions about Uncle Albert's murder. He was good-looking and seemed nice if not a little stern. She supposed a detective wouldn't make a very good husband in Father's eyes. She sighed softly. Sean didn't notice.

Eventually he did stop talking and sipped his tea so she let her gaze focus on him again. She smiled. "This was a wonderful idea, Sean. I'm glad you invited me. I'm glad you convinced me."

"Well if I can at least convince you to go outside, then perhaps I can get you to consider going to the gallery opening this weekend with me and the boys. There are four strong men to protect you there. Besides, you need to toughen up a little. So does Steven. We're going to get him drunk. It'll be fun. Just think about it, I think you'll love it."

"I'll consider it." It was really about time she let go of these silly notions. That there was something dangerous out there. The gallery opening would be at night. But she would be with Sean. And there would be all sorts of interesting people there. There always were at gallery openings. She wondered if the people she considered interesting ever considered her interesting in the least. Probably not. She was fantastically boring. Even to herself. She didn't even know how to knit. At least her mother knew how to do that. Perhaps she should go to the gallery opening.

Perhaps there would be something there that could make it worth going. Some fun for a change.

The drawing room was warm on account of the crackling fire in the fireplace by her over-stuffed chair. She had opted for the seemingly simpler craft form of crocheting, but her fingers fumbled with the single hook and the yarn. The book on her lap was supposed to easily show her how to do it, but its garbled mass of abbreviations confused her so she tried to only look at the pictures. Her chain had come out okay, but the first row of single crochets looked jumbled and awful. She was determined so she kept trying.

Her mother strolled into the drawing room with a book in her hand. A romance novel by the looks of it. "Goodness, girl, what are you trying to do? Such things are for old people."

She smiled. Her mother was only forty-nine but was obsessed with keeping herself young and good-looking. She still looked thirty and was convinced it was due to the latest snake oil concoction. Shannon knew that it was really just because of a slew of good genes. Looking at the scowling portraits in the halls could have told anybody that.

"Mother. Please. I have to have something to keep my hands occupied. I'm tired of reading. I read all the time."

"It wouldn't hurt you to take a walk or maybe...oh I don't know. Go out with your brother sometime. I'm sure Kyle would be elated to take you to the cinema."

"Is this a subtle hint that I should be considering parts of my brother's friend group as potential husbands? Is this just because I have no other male prospects?" She put the heel of her palm on her forehead and closed her eyes. She felt a headache coming on. "Mother, one of these days I'm going to find a man that is completely nothing like what you've ever dreamed of. Then you'll have more to wonder about than those silly romance novels you always read."

Her mother appeared hurt. "Oh well, maybe your love life, then will be sordid and filled with woe. It's all I could ever ask for." The sarcasm in her voice could practically soak the walls. "If that's what you want, it's better than being fifty and an old spinster."

"Glad I have your blessing, Mother." She poked the hook through another set of loops and tried again at her crochet project. Her headache was slowly taking hold. "I think I'll be going to that gallery opening they're having downtown. Gregory Studios or something or another. Sean invited me. And I heard that Father managed to send an invitation to that detective. He thought that since everyone would be crowded around in the same room, he might be able to do a little deducing. Like he's Sherlock Holmes or something. Imagine that."

"Fancying the detective, are you?" Her mother plopped down onto the settee and opened her book but didn't read. She was eying her only daughter over the top of it.

Shannon gave a coy smile. "He's not bad looking. A little snowy on top but I think that's more stress than age. He could only be in his early thirties."

"Only." Her mother giggled, "I suppose I shouldn't scold you on marrying closer to your age. I married your father when I was twenty-six and he was thirty-eight."

"Well then I guess I'll try my wiles on this detective then. I'm sure he's met other women in stranger situations. And goodness knows he'll probably want a friendly face in the middle of all that gallery madness." She thought her crocheting was getting better but she wasn't so sure. She studied the pictures again and decided that it wasn't. She would have to try harder. The fire shifted and she turned her attention to it. Her mother had gone into her book. She tried to imagine the way she might look at Detective Winston in the midst of the gallery and the crowd. She tried to imagine his responses. She was never good at flirting with men. She didn't know how. Of course she knew that she couldn't bother with imitating Kyle or even Preston, who was a little more subtle, because the ways that men flirted were simply barbaric.

She'd made up her mind. She would go to the gallery opening with

Sean. And she would try as hard as she could to link her arm with a man who could protect her.

CHAPTER 4

"Have you ever worn a suit?" If he were a dumber man he would have thought that he'd just asked that question to an empty room. But he wasn't dumb and he wasn't oblivious and he had opened the window just five minutes earlier.

"Maybe when I was six," was the reply from the fire escape. Ren eased his way through the open window and took his shoes off, shuffling in dirty socks across the hardwood and taking a seat on the couch.

"You know they design those fire escapes to be inaccessible to burglars."

"Oh. Makes sense why it was so difficult to get to it from the bottom." Ren shrugged. "Can I have some wine?"

"Sure." He opened the wine cooler and took out a Reisling, hoping Ren would appreciate a dry white. He seemed like the type to be alright with just about any kind of alcohol. "I was just wondering 'cause I've been invited to this gallery opening and it said that I could bring a guest and since I don't have Avery..."

"You want me to go with you to mingle around with the snots. No thanks. I'll keep myself low-key."

He laughed while he poured the two stemmed glasses full almost to the brim. "Actually, I was kind of hoping that you could wait outside and be my sanity. So if I have anything to relay to you, I could step outside, have a smoke, and shoot the shit. I can't stand these folks.

Avery was always so cool around them, like he grew up in that kind of weird-ass family."

Ren smiled when he reached out for the glass and Winston sat across from him in the Lay-Z-Boy recliner. "Just don't get yourself gutted while schmoozing up the suspects. Got anyone in mind?"

He shrugged. "Avery said that the killer wore a mask. Plus he was pretty konked out since he got hit over the head and he was in so much pain at the end. Said he saw a mask like...like a blacked out halloween mask so he couldn't even see his eyes. But he said his voice was younger and really angry."

"Wow Avery, real help," Ren rolled his eyes. "Although, it does tell us something."

"What's that?"

"He did think he had time but he wasn't taking any chances. He wasn't going to risk Avery seeing his face. Because he wasn't *sure* of anything. He's cautious, doesn't take chances. That means he's really smart." Ren's face contorted into a scowl. "But everyone makes mistakes."

"Do you make mistakes?"

"Of course." Ren dismissed the question soundly. "I make them all the time. It's not my fault that nobody really cares or picks up on it. I leave DNA everywhere. How can I not? I just commit murders in different jurisdictions and nobody communicates very well. Not my fault. And it's also not my fault that people can't handle the idea that someone could change their fucking hair color and grow a beard."

Winston smiled. "I'd recognize you anywhere."

Ren smiled back and met his eyes. "That's why you're my soul mate, Winnie. And by soul mate I mean arch nemesis."

"That's sweet of you, dickface."

"I told you not to call me that outside of the bedroom."

This was the point where Winston couldn't help but laugh. It was a deep belly laugh that hunkered down and helped itself to some refreshments while it was there. When he was finished, he had to wipe tears from his eyes. He took a few gulps of his wine and watched Ren grinning across from him. They sat for a while, sipping from their glasses, comfortable in their self-imposed silence. He hadn't felt this way for a long time. That he could be completely at ease in silence. He hated that it was with Ren. He hated and loved it. He felt a bond. A connection. An *understanding*.

With a killer.

"So where am I getting this suit? And when and where is this gallery show?"

"You're about my size. I'll lend you one. It's on Mayfair Street. I'll take you, it'll be no problem. Don't worry about it."

"Can I smoke in here?"

"Let me light a candle first."

After the candle was lit, Ren started smoking. Camel Blues. He was so predictable. For some reason it wasn't out of the question for Winston to be sitting in his own living room across from a man who was fully willing and able to eat—or at least bite, people to death. He looked so young. It was funny, he thought, that he should look older from the amount of stress that Ren had put him through over the years and yet the killer himself couldn't look a day over twenty.

"How old are you, Ren?"

He was still grinning and added a wink for good measure. "Old enough."

"When I finally get you, I'm adding a charge of statutory rape."

He chuckled. "I'll pretend to be surprised."

He put down his wine glass on the coffee table and leaned forward, putting his forehead in his palms and groaning. "Oh my Lord. My fucking partner is in the hospital recovering from getting mutilated and I'm laughing and screwing off with you. Of all people, you."

"You don't have to feel bad," Ren sipped the wine. "We're not friends."

"But..."

"Don't make yourself feel bad just because your partner's been beaten over the head and stabbed a few times. That fucker's on enough morphine to make a junkie jealous. He's in no pain and is probably having the time of his life just staring at the ceiling."

He sighed and let the side of his mouth rise in a tiny smirk. The thought of Avery high as a kite amused him.

"Any chicks at this shindig?"

"Where are you going to fuck them? Some cheap motel?"

He snorted, "You said they were snotty. Hopefully their sugar daddy's been paying for a good penthouse or something. Back to their place would be what I'd hope for." He forced a falsetto. "Would you like to come in for a drink...stud?"

Winston couldn't help it. He laughed again and settled back into the comfort of his recliner. Staring at the man across from him, he lazily grinned. "Have you eaten anything?"

"Whatever I can find."

"Raid the cupboards. I'm going to bed." He didn't forget to lock the bedroom door behind him and when he awoke the next morning, the apartment was empty, the window to the fire escape closed tight.

There were people everywhere. They were all dressed up. Of course, that depended on one's idea of "dressed up." Some of them looked like they were supposed to be at the circus. Or they escaped from it. A few had pink or green hair. One was hardly wearing anything at all and what she did have on was neon in color, strappy, and Shannon wasn't quite sure how in the world she even got it on. Double sided tape was the answer that she had settled on when she finally saw the detective out of the corner of her eye. He was standing in the corner of the largest gallery room with a little plastic cup of punch clutched to his chest. He was eying everyone as if they were mice and he were the hawk; yet still he looked nervous.

She made her way over to him. "Detective." She tried to smile what she thought was a disarming smile, but he didn't look very disarmed. "It's good to see you here. Are you enjoying the art?"

He lifted his gaze and looked at all the art pieces with disinterest. "I'm not much of an art lover."

"Well, that's alright, sometimes it's more entertaining to watch all the people in an art gallery. Everyone is often so odd. I love it. Art has a way of bringing things out in people."

"Right." He was being short with her. Clipped. She could try to get him to open up to her, but she felt like she wouldn't be able to do it here. This was not his element. He was uneasy. Where was that cool cucumber of a partner who used to be with him?

"You don't seem very interested in them either."

He sighed. "I'm sorry. I'm...I just need a cigarette."

"Oh," she wanted to offer to go outside with him. But outside was dark. Outside was wet from the last rain. But...he did have a gun. He could protect her. He could try. "I...I will go out with you. I need some fresh air anyhow. All these people in a room together makes it stuffy."

He gritted his teeth. "I, uh. You should stay inside. I mean, there are a ton of people smoking out there, it's hardly fresh air." The detective appeared nervous. Maybe this was her in.

"Nonsense." She grinned while she led him to the door and relished the cool night air and humid breeze. She tapped down the concrete stairs with him at her heels and swung around the railing at the bottom, turning and watching him light up a cigarette while he descended.

He took in a long drag and then let it out, watching her with keen eyes. "You're Shannon Kingsley. Niece of one of the victims. I don't think we interviewed you."

"There's really no need. I don't know anything. I didn't discover the body and was just as blind-sided as everyone else. But I wouldn't mind being interviewed by you, Detective." She hoped that sounded flirty. Her strapless dress did nothing to show off her bosom and it was too late to try to adjust it. "Although I don't know what I could tell you."

He nodded and looked over her shoulder for a few seconds before she felt a presence behind her. From nowhere, suddenly beside her, was a man. Younger than Winston. He appeared dapper and his suit was neatly pressed and very clean. It fit him well. His hair was pure white but artificially so and was styled to create a modern, messy look. He was well-groomed as well, with a carefully trimmed goatee that was in stark contrast with his white hair. His dark blue eyes under equally jet brows were striking.

"Miss, this is Adrian Woods, he's a friend of mine. Doesn't like stuffy rooms either."

"Charmed." Adrian smiled, holding out his hand.

She placed her fingers on his and he gave them a curt peck. "You are Detective Winston's friend?" A strange thought occurred to her. They were gay. Disappointment flooded her and she shrunk down into herself. She felt her cheeks flush. Now she was stuck outside with them.

"'Friend' is an over-estimation of what we are. We're not that close." Adrian was giving Winston a tiny scowl. "We're just close enough that I'm his back-up plan when his other friends desert him."

Shannon smiled. "My brother has a name for those people. The people you keep around so that your social events are never boring but have just the right amount of tension. You take them to places where you think you're not going to have a good time. This is a good place to take those people." Adrian warmed to her while she spoke. "Frienemies."

He chuckled. "If there was ever a word for Winston and I, that would probably be it."

Winston snorted and then nodded a little with his eyebrows perked up.

Shannon turned so she was facing Adrian a little more. He was calm and seemed content. Nonthreatening and yet she could imagine a strong body underneath his suit. He could probably hold his own in a fight. Could probably best Winston. "What do you do, Adrian?"

"I'm a consultant. Boring stuff, wouldn't interest you. It hardly interests me. I'm more interested in you, Miss Kingsley."

She could hear Winston mutter a bit but she was much to distracted to wonder why.

More blood flooded her cheeks. "Oh. I don't do anything. I've been trying to learn how to crochet, but I haven't been able to catch the hang of it yet. The book is very confusing."

Adrian didn't seem bored by her but only more interested, his dark eyes intense in the soft light from the yellow street lamp above them. "Maybe you need a more hands-on approach to learning. Maybe you just need someone to teach you how."

"Re— Adrian..." Winston growled.

25

"I'm just trying to be helpful," he chided Winston.

Shannon nodded her head. "Do you know how? It would be very helpful if someone could teach me; I'm such a klutz with it right now. How much would you charge for a lesson?"

"No charge. Other than..." He looked up at the street lamp for a second then back down at her. "A date."

Winston coughed. "No, no, no, no, no. No dates."

She smiled and covered her mouth with her hand. "Oh my goodness."

Adrian scowled, "Stuff it, Winston. You're just jealous." He turned his attention back to her. "Your crochet career will boom. I promise. Just dinner." His body language and expression pleaded with her. "Nothing to lose. If I'm a complete bore, you can just sneak out the back way. I'll be paying the whole way, no matter what." He tilted his head and looked just above her head for a few moments as if he were listening to beautiful music. When he came back down, he gave her a wide warm close-mouthed smile. "I promise not to pick a restaurant that doesn't have a back exit to sneak from."

"I suppose I'll just have to say yes when you put it that way."

Adrian passed a smug little smirk to his friend, or so she should think, frienemy, and then came back to her with a genuine beam. Winston was glowering at him.

"Thank you very much Miss Kingsley."

"Shannon."

His smile got warmer, but something seemed off in her mind. There was something not quite right about his eyes. They were still frozen, she thought blankly. His smile was warm, but his eyes were just like ice.

"Shannon," he murmured.

She felt goosebumps on her arms.

CHAPTER 5

"I heard," Sean drifted into the drawing room, "that you agreed to go on a date. And fancy it's not with Kyle. He's been trying to woo you ever since last year's Christmas party when you got a little flushed in the face from the Chardonnay." He stood by the fire and watched her while she read the last paragraph of the chapter in her mystery novel. When she looked up, he continued. "Pray tell, who is this mystery man you've agreed to spend an evening with?" His brow was arched.

"A Mr. Woods. I met him at the gallery opening. He seems a decent sort." She decided to leave it at that. Her brother wanted all the gritty details but she could only let him have so much or he would ruin him for her. He would go in and out with all his faults or presumed faults and it would create a mess in her head. Not that she had many gritty details to share about him. Other than his gorgeous little close-mouthed smile and his deep, almost gravelly voice, there wasn't much she knew about Adrian Woods. He knew how to crochet. That was one thing.

Sean fiddled with one of Mother's snow globes that sat on the mantle. He twisted it a little so the glitter inside floated at the bottom and swirled a little around the plastic colorful dolphin inside. It was well-known that Sean hated all the nick-knacks that littered the place, although he had never actually said anything out loud. "Mr. Woods. I don't think I noticed a Mr. Woods at the show. Although I have to admit we were having a rather good time getting Steven to drink more of the punch." He snickered. "Kyle is quite put out that you have a date."

She put her bookmark inside her book and put it down on the little table beside her. "Well, he never actually asked me out on a date before. I don't know if he has any right to be put out by it. He just wasn't brazen enough to actually ask."

"Is this one brazen, Shannon?" Sean looked like he might want to tip the snow globe off the mantle. He was staring at it. Contemplating it. Like he wanted to know what would happen if he did it. "Is he rash?"

"He might be."

Sean nodded and took a breath, breaking his concentration on the snow globe and blinking a few times as if to dispel the idea of breaking the thing. "Well, if this dinner thing goes well then you should most certainly invite him to dinner here. I'm sure Leslie could cook us up something special for a nice dinner to meet our family."

"Oh," she smiled, "Perhaps he could bring Detective Winston. They are friends."

"Are they?" Sean perked up, "Good. Father would love for the detective to root out our family secrets in some strange attempt to find Uncle Albert's killer. He's all about those strange tales of horror and mayhem and I'm fairly certain he's not of a mind that our family has many secrets to hide."

His sarcasm had not been lost on her. "Oh Sean, please. I'm certain that if anything comes to light about your love life or anything strange about our family, the detective will keep it hushed as best as he can."

"And this Mr. Woods?"

She paused. "I'm sure he has the ability to be bought if you truly are concerned."

He grinned, "That's my girl. Throw money at your problems."

She pouted. "Mr. Woods is not a problem yet. Wait until my date is through and then you can consider him a problem if you wish. I will simply consider him a distraction from all this horrible business. Then maybe I can get a little better sleep at night." She picked up her book again and flipped to the right page in order to stop Sean from talking to her. It didn't quite work. In fact he moved to just in front of her chair so she pulled her legs up and curled into a comfortable position while he stood with his arms crossed and his brows knitted.

"You're not worried at all?"

"Of course not. About Mr. Woods? Why should I be worried?"

"A ruthless killer randomly slaughters your uncle and you're out meeting men? What if he targeted you?"

She rolled her eyes. "Did I not just say that he was friends with the detective who's in charge of the case? The detective who supposedly has this amazing history for tracking down murderers?"

"It would be the perfect cover. Friends with the very detective that's pursuing him."

"That's stupid, Sean."

He put up his hands as if he were defeated. "Fine, Sis. It's stupid. You're right. All of this nonsense with Uncle Albert has made me just a little paranoid. I feel like there's someone out there who's just waiting to do the same thing to me."

"Have you told Nunk?" The family shrink had been in their employ for many years. She was sure that she might be the only one who even bothered to tell the calm old doctor the truth.

"Of course I told Nunk. He just...he just nodded. I think everyone in this house thinks that very same thing. That we're all being watched by some psychopath. All of our schedules are mapped, all of our movements are recorded, everything we've ever done. I just want to break the monotony. Do something out of control." He shook his head and gritted his teeth, uncrossing his arms and turning away from her. "I might need to go away for a while."

"But the detective said..."

"I know what the detective said. Once this business is over. Once everything calms down. I think I'd just like to take a drive. Maybe out to California. Maybe I'll find some peace there. From all of this madness here."

She wasn't sure but something in the sound of her brother's voice told her that he wasn't just trying to get away from all of "this." He was only trying to run from himself. She looked down at her book but it could have been written in Japanese for all she could pay attention to it. Sean didn't say anything more but he made a sharp movement and snatched the snow globe from the mantle and stomped from the room. She watched the door close behind him and latch. The only sound was from the fireplace beside her.

Somewhere inside the house—glass shattered.

A thousand tiny drops of dew glittered across the empty field next to a dark basketball court. Smoke rose from his lips in languid curls, dissipating slowly and evenly into a milky starlit sky. His shoes scraped on the pavement while he walked the perimeter of the blacktop, thinking. All the families of the victims, the Kingsleys, the Houseals, and the Haleys, had been investigated. The coworkers of all of them had been interviewed. Their secretaries. He'd made a list of the people they'd talked to. It was sitting on his desk. He had crossed off names for those who had an alibi for two or three of them. But not those who only had an alibi for one. They would think that one was enough, would they not? And one would be easy enough to fake.

His list was still too long. It had always been too long. But at least this time he had a lead. And he would try to figure it out. His killer killed those with authority or power. One was a CEO, another a high-powered banker, and still another was a politician. Had they wronged the same person in different ways? Had their companies? Or was this personal? Did the killer know them?

He took in a long drag from his Marlboro and let it out again. There were a thousand different possibilities. Not one single worker ever worked for all three of them. Not even two. The worker angle was a bust. He tapped his foot on the pavement. He could work under the assumption that they'd all been killed by a random killer. One who had merely seen them as pillars of their communities or businesses and targeted them specifically for the mere purpose of creating havoc. He should work all theories. Look over the interviews carefully. And he might give serious thought to renting out his couch to a certain *Rottweiler*.

He put a thumb to his lips and watched the orange tip of his cigarette burn against the dark of the night. Crickets chirped for a small time and abruptly stopped. Winston's ears perked.

"Avery said that you came out here to think sometimes."

He turned and nodded. "It's quiet."

Detective Rayne Wilson looked back at him with solemn brown eyes. He had his hands tucked into the pockets of his track pants. "You appear to be a little puzzled. Is there something I can help you talk through? I mean, since Avery doesn't do much talking now—not that he really ever did." He shrugged. "Maybe you just need to get it all organized."

The side of his mouth raised. "That's nice of you, Rayne. I know you just want to help but you've gotta know that I'm in a bad place right now."

"I know. But then again, Trent, I've been under the impression that you've been in a bad place for a very long time." Rayne tilted his head to the side. "You're not like us. You don't investigate things or people because you want to exact justice or do something good. You're not interested in being a positive force."

Winston narrowed his eyes. "What am I interested in?"

The other detective pushed his lips together and studied him carefully before continuing. "You've got a vendetta. Not just for this one. This one is understandable. This one could drive you mad."

"Already there," he interrupted.

Rayne went on unconcerned, "You like to win."

"It's not a game."

"Don't lie to me."

There was something deep in Rayne's words that stopped him. He glared. If he would have tried to speak, he would have sputtered. He could have spit with his cold fury. It wasn't Rayne that had made him so angry.

Rayne met his glare with a disinterested gaze. "I can help you win, Trent."

"I don't need your help."

"The offer is on the table, though. It's for you. Because I know you're not doing this for the next victim or the families or the children. You don't care about them. You care about you and yours. And I can help you with that."

Winston chewed his bottom lip, then replied, "If I ask you for your assistance then I require one thing."

"Which is?" One dark brow rose.

"That you only get as involved as I want you to be. No more. Ever."

Rayne nodded. "I understand."

"You can't."

"You have a dark side."

He looked down at his shoes and then up again. He wasn't sure how to reply. It didn't matter.

"I know you have a dark side. And you have secrets. You and Avery do. I'm not interested in them. I don't want to know everything about you, Trent. I just want this guy to pay for what he did to Avery. He's my friend too, you know."

"You read the file?"

"Yes."

He thought for a moment and then stamped out his cigarette, watching the crushed filter try to expand again after he'd smashed it, moving slowly like a dying man. "Tell me what you think."

"White male, possibly between the ages of twenty to thirty based on the types of physical demands that some of the scenes would require for escape or access. Especially Avery's apartment. He's smart. He's careful. He's also choosey. He's picky. I'm thinking he has some kind of attachment to the victims. He knows them. He might be part of their social circle."

Winston took in a deep breath. "Because he knows their schedules?"

"Exactly. He knew exactly when to strike."

"And Avery?"

"I think Avery was different. He wasn't like the rest of the victims. He was an impulse buy, if you know what I mean. He didn't spend as much time researching him, watching him. He didn't *know* Avery. It was planned, but not quite as well. Still very good. If you hadn't been on the phone..." He shrugged again, his hands still in his pockets.

"If I hadn't been on the phone, he'd be dead."

"Yes."

"Why does he kill who he kills? Why the powerful? Why the authority figures?"

Rayne sighed. "I don't have that one yet. I'm not perfect."

32

"Do you think..."

"Mmm?"

He took a step toward Rayne but stopped as if before him was a brick wall. "That we're...in danger?"

Rayne looked around them at the glittering meadow and rustling trees. A swing set was barely visible far away in the moonlight. Somewhere in the city a siren sounded, warbling across the landscape. "Right now?" he murmured.

"Yes. No." He shook his head. "All the time. Everywhere I go I feel like I'm the next one. That it's my apartment he'll be hiding in. I don't have an Avery on my phone. All I have is..." *Ren. The Roanoke Rottweiler, serial murderer extraordinaire. Hero to whores.* "Nobody."

"Would you like a long distance baby monitor? That way if I ever hear you getting murdered I can call the police."

"You're joking."

"Just trying to get you to lighten up. It's good to be a little paranoid, but don't let it destroy your life. There's a reason he chose Avery instead of you and don't tell me it's because Avery did the talking in the interviews. I know what you do while he's interrogating. You stand in the doorway and watch. You're just as intimidating."

"But not as..." He suddenly focused clearly and the answer hit him. "Not as predictable. Avery's predictable. So if the killer chooses someone else outside of his social circle, they should be predictable and easy to follow."

Rayne agreed, "Yes. Now if only the killer were easy to predict."

"He might be. Do me a favor. Go home and get a good night's rest. In the morning we'll map out a web of friends for the victims. We'll see who's a common friend, including family, and go from there."

Once Rayne had gone, Winston walked back to the black Ford Fusion and sat on the hood, his heels on top of his bumper and his knees supporting his elbows while he leaned forward and smoked again. He didn't bother to turn around when he sensed a presence behind him. "Get off the car, you'll scuff it."

A slight shuff of dirt to his right told him that Ren had followed his order. "I could have been your killer. You weren't even concerned. Aren't you afraid of death, Detective?"

"I wouldn't have this job if I were afraid of death. That would be stupid."

"So his name is Rayne?" Ren came into Winston's sight and sat in front of him on the ground with his legs crossed.

"Rayne Wilson. He's a good detective. He did the work with your profiling."

Ren shrank and appeared peeved. He stared at one of Winston's shoes and rubbed his chin with his finger.

"Intimidated?" Winston teased, grinning. "What he said was true."

"I'm aware. If it weren't, I'd be either dead or in prison. But Rayne doesn't have such an affliction. He's got this annoying thing called a moral compass. He's out for good. For justice. Some universal justice that he's been raised to believe is the only real thing in this whole world. Which of you two do you think will be able to think in broader terms?"

Winston didn't respond.

"You've got a moral compass too. It just got knocked out of calibration a while ago. You're better for it."

He hopped off the hood of his car. Ren didn't flinch or cringe. He just watched. Winston crushed another cigarette butt under his toe and walked toward his car door. "When's your date?"

"Two days from now."

"You'll have to borrow some clothes." He reached into his pocket and pulled out his keys. "Meet me at my apartment. Mr. Woods needs a better wardrobe so he can schmooze with Miss Kingsley. The killer could be part of the victims' social circle. Miss Kingsley is the niece of—"

"The fat one. I know."

He opened his car door. "Thank God you can at least *pretend* to be civil in polite company." With that, he got in his car and turned it on. The lights illuminated the ground in front of him, Ren nowhere in sight.

CHAPTER 6

It was around six o'clock and they were sitting in a small secluded booth at a restaurant she didn't catch the name of. It was decorated divinely with cream walls and cherry wood accents. She was inclined to believe that the edge of the table was actually gold plated. A chandelier hung from the vaulted ceiling and sent tiny specks of crystalline light floating over the diners in an array of transient glitter which she found amusing to watch.

His cold blue eyes were on her and she avoided them purposefully. Leslie, their cook, had said that it was only by playing 'hard to get' that men truly appreciated the chase. Let him chase, she had said, let him see that you're worth fighting for. His tiny little smile almost distracted her from her cause. She couldn't help but look at it. It was wonderful. For all the ice in his eyes there was fire in his smile.

"What's your middle name?" he asked with a little narrowing of those cold eyes. Curiosity bubbled in them.

"Claire," she responded. "And you?"

"Ringo."

She giggled, "Is that true?"

He nodded his head with a small grin. She flitted her gaze away from his mouth for just a moment then allowed herself to move it back again for the sake of propriety. He had a strange quirk about his grin. Something disconcerting, but she couldn't tell just why.

She continued, "Well, I suppose you don't want to talk about work. Men never do. Do you have any family?"

"Not close. My mother lives down south. My father passed away and I have no siblings."

"Friends?"

He shrugged one shoulder. "Here and there. Most of the people I encounter are just acquaintances, but I have a few friends."

It was her turn to grin. "Most of them are women, I assume."

"How did you know?" He sipped his tea.

"You don't seem like the type to have many friends, and if you did, I think they would have to challenge you. I think women would do a better job of that than men."

"Perceptive," he noted. His shoulders were not tense, in fact, he seemed perfectly at ease in a situation that would completely destroy some men. "Would you be my friend, Miss Kingsley?"

"Please call me Shannon."

"Shannon...?" He raised an eyebrow to signify that he was still awaiting her response.

"I'm not so sure if I'm interested in being your friend, Adrian. I think I'm more interested in being something else entirely." She tried to lower her eyelashes, dark with the mascara that Leslie had applied earlier in the evening. Her make up was supposed to be subtle enough that he wouldn't quite notice when she wasn't wearing it—which was more often. But she could see it. It was so dark. She hoped it was seductive.

His smile told her that it was. "Well, that just might be the best news I've heard all day. All month, even."

"Now that we have that out of the way we can get to the serious business."

"Which is?" He appeared amused.

"Your favorite color."

"Red. And yours?"

"Purple."

He nodded. "A good choice."

"What's the bravest thing you've ever done?"

He looked down at his tea and then sipped it again while he

contemplated the question. "I would suppose that the bravest thing I ever did was to leave home. What about you, Shannon? What's the bravest thing you've ever done."

She blushed. "It's going to sound stupid."

"Nothing's stupid."

She fidgeted. "This is it."

He chuckled. His smile was radiant. Her heart was skipping beats. "Shannon." She wished he would say her name again. "That isn't stupid."

"It isn't?"

"No. I think it's wonderful. I can only hope to inspire more bravery from you."

She fiddled with her fork and wondered when their food would be coming. She hadn't noticed that they'd been sitting there for a little while. And all they had consumed was tea. He wasn't even trying to get her drunk. He wasn't after her for sex. *That's ridiculous,* she thought, *All men are out for sex, this one is just a little more patient.* "Have you ever been close to dying?"

His eyebrows raised.

"I'm sorry, that's such an odd question. I—"

"No," he said, putting out his hand to stop her. "Don't retract it. I'll answer it." He frowned down at his tea and was thinking. "I have been close to dying. But I suppose none of us really register it at the time as being a near-death experience if it isn't slow like cancer." He paused then started again, "My family lived on the ocean and I used to swim in it every day. When I was ten years old I was swimming and I was sucked out into the sea by a rip current. I didn't know what was happening. I knew about rip currents, but it failed to dawn on me and suddenly I found myself far from the beach alone."

"What then?" she whispered.

He tapped his lips with one finger. "My father swam out and put his arm around me and somehow took us both back to shore. We were a ways down the beach when we came to shore and I remember being very tired despite him being the one who had done most of the work."

"Were you and your father close?"

37

His eyes met hers and a darkness filled them. "Not...particularly. Although I'm more like him than I would ever hope to be. It's a curse."

"But he saved your life."

He blinked and the darkness fled, but the frost remained. "And I'm sure I've saved a few in my time."

"Well, I don't think I've ever been close to dying." She tried to lighten the mood with her tone. "I'm such a homebody that there's nothing that ever happens to me that could be considered dangerous. I'm a little boring, I suppose. I've never even fainted in the shower or slipped at all. My father thinks I'm like some delicate little flower." She fidgeted a little. "Maybe I am. Maybe I just need a protector."

"Or maybe..." he grinned. There was mischief in it. "You just need a little adventure."

Their food arrived before she could respond.

"So tell me how your date went," Mother stated. It wasn't a request. It also wasn't a suggestion. She sat with her legs tucked against her on the settee, her book beside her. She was staring into the fire while Shannon tried to remember the way Mr. Woods had shown her to put the hook through the loops. She was doing so much better thanks to him. She would have to formally thank him in some way. Perhaps a card. Mother was scraping one nail against the fabric of the small couch. She was getting impatient.

"It went well," she responded, putting down her work and glancing over at the mantle over the fireplace. She wondered how long it would take for her mother to notice that the snow globe with the tacky dolphin in it was gone. There was a blank spot on the mantle where it had been. "Dinner was fabulous and he's a charming man. Afterward, we sat in front of the theater and he showed me how to crochet better. He even showed me different kinds of stitches. I'm thinking of asking him how to do a circle next."

Mother's mouth seemed to make a perfect 'O' shape. "So you *do* expect to see him again. Well, this is very exciting. We should select a museum for you two to peruse. Natural History, perhaps?"

"Mother, don't go out of your way. I'm sure he'll call on me soon and he'll probably have his own idea for a date."

"You didn't kiss him, did you?"

She almost scoffed but remembered herself and merely sniffed. "On the first date? Mother, how do you think you raised me? He was a perfect gentleman."

She pouted. "You know those rules were meant to be broken. How on Earth are you supposed to know he likes you if he doesn't at least *try* to kiss you? How boring. No wonder he knows how to crochet. He sounds dull."

"He's not dull, Mother. He's just different. I think you'll take that back when you meet him. He's perfectly interesting. His favorite color is red. A dull favorite color would be blue. Especially in a man. Red is a color of action." She smiled at her mother and caught her attention fully. "Do you know what he said to me?"

"What's that?" Her mother sounded almost uninterested after she'd determined him dull.

"That perhaps all I need is a little more *adventure*."

At this her mother perked.

"How'd it go?" Winston's face was half full of Italian sausage when Ren slid in through the open window still in Winston's immaculate suit and tie.

"You know, you might consider giving me a key."

He decided not to answer that one. "Is she your perfect sugar momma?"

"You might be my perfect sugar *daddy* with all this food in your cupboards." The young killer eased his way around the couch with his eyes set on the pantry.

"You were just out to eat."

"That place couldn't feed a squirrel with their portion sizes. Whatever happened to really fat people living in America?"

Winston rolled his eyes and took another bite of his sausage, chewing while he watched Ren sift through the goodies. He didn't much mind when the younger man settled on a bag of chips and an almost-full package of Oreos. "You didn't answer my question."

"Sure I did," he answered, sitting across from him at his kitchen table.

"You answered the second question. Now answer the first."

"It went well. She's very sweet. Very innocent. Not many friends. Kind of a home-body. She's looking to break out it seems. Responded very well to me. *Definitely* sexually repressed."

"She's rich, of course she is. Is she happy?"

"She's mildly discontented."

He nodded. So that was how it was. That was how they would get their in. His in. He eyed Ren. He wondered what exactly Ren thought of all this. All the business of getting into the family by way of romantic involvement. It had occurred to him that it would have been easier if it had been him. She had been hitting on him. Clumsily but still with focus. He swallowed. It would have made him an easy target. Now he was at a distance. He was still in. Well as "in" as Ren would allow him to be in any case. "When's the next date?"

Ren shrugged, "When would you like it to be? You're the captain of this ship. I don't care when it is, I simply care *that* it is. She seems like a really nice girl."

"Oh, you know, because you're totally into those nice girls." He had tried to sound sarcastic, but by the end he wasn't sure if he was. He decided to take a sip of his soda before he made an ass out of himself accidentally.

Ren didn't seem to even hear the smart-ass response. He was busily pouring himself a glass of milk and settling down to eat probably the whole package of Oreo cookies.

"Have you been checked for any STDs?"

Ren had just poked two cookies at once into his face and looked up at him like a comical little chipmunk with wide blank eyes. Winston supposed that it meant "no." He chewed slowly.

"You should probably find a free clinic since I assume you've been screwing everything with a pulse in these past three years."

He swallowed. "That's offensive."

Winston raised a brow at him.

"I'm perfectly capable of controlling myself. I'm a killer, not a rapist. And it's hard to find women who will fuck a drifter. Life isn't a porno clip, as much as we wish it were. I'll get myself tested if that's what you desire. But after all my results come in clean that's *not* a free pass into my ass, faggot."

He chuckled and watched Ren dunking more Oreos into his milk and stuffing them in his face. There was something about him, sitting at this kitchen table, that seemed very right to Winston. A few years ago, he would have been outraged at the idea that some serial murderer was sitting at his table. Even more so at the thought of Ren. Ren, who had gotten away. He touched the scar on his collarbone where he'd been bitten and torn. It rather looked like a shooting star if one had an open mind. He remembered what it had felt like. Remembered what Ren had looked like. He wondered if he had tasted good. The younger man had had an advantage then. He had chosen where to strike. He had chosen for Winston to live.

When all the Oreos were gone, he chugged his milk and licked off his fingers in a boyish manner, raising his gaze to Winston and appearing if not happy at least contented. He quickly noted that Winston was lightly rubbing his collarbone. "You almost got me that day." He smiled a tiny cat's smile.

"I would say that rather *you* got *me*." Winston returned the smile. "I'm the one who ended up in the hospital."

"You broke my nose." Ren ran a finger down the bridge of his nose. It wasn't obvious that it had been broken, but Ren at least knew where the fracture had been.

"Tomi nearly caved in my skull."

Ren scoffed. "Prove it."

Winston glared at him and was delighted when Ren shrank down in his seat a little bit. He lessened his glare, the lesson learned. There wasn't much Winston didn't know for sure about Ren and his relationship. "Where have you been sleeping?"

Ren shrugged. "In that park."

"The couch is free. I'm gonna go read and go to bed."

CHAPTER 7

She was relieved to see him. He was standing in the doorway with that radiant little smile and both of his arms full with two bouquets filled with daffodils, lilies, and tulips. One he handed to her.

"Well goodness, who's the other one for?"

"Your mother," he responded without hesitation. "She is most certainly not the woman I would like to be my enemy in any case. Especially in attempting to woo you."

She giggled and her face turned hot. "Woo me? Is that what you're doing? Oh, I hate to give it a name." She ushered him in and led him into the drawing room. "Wait here, I must get these into a vase and get my mother so she may accept these from you personally." She scurried off and after giving the flowers in her hands to Leslie, who was very excited for the man in the house, she went off to find Mother.

Her mother was ecstatic. She swept into the drawing room ahead of her daughter as a commanding presence and accepted the flowers gracefully and with perhaps the most pleasant demeanor she had ever seen her mother display. Mother was so happy indeed that she even kissed the poor man on the cheek. Granted, it was just a small peck and he seemed to take it in stride, but Shannon was almost mortified. She kept her thoughts in check by forcing a blank smile onto her face. Her mother held the flowers to her chest as though she were a movie star who'd just been given an Oscar.

"Oh, you are just the sweetest young thing, aren't you? You're a dear, that's for sure. Oh, Leslie is cooking up wonders in there for us all. Thank you so much for coming tonight, it's so good to have company and I'm so sorry that our eldest couldn't be here. He has a golf event he had to attend to. Something he couldn't get out of. A tournament or something of that nature. Goodness knows what children *really* do when they say they're out golfing."

Adrian chuckled at that and was visibly thinking about what to do with his now-empty hands. Shannon took pity on him and ask him to sit, motioning to the settee. When he did, she sat next to him and she took his hand in hers. Knowing what to do with one of them was enough, she thought. Mother sat in the overstuffed armchair across from them, the flowers across her lap like some colorful babe.

"So Adrian," Shannon murmured, capturing his attention. "Are you a fan of lamb?"

"I'm a fan of just about any food."

Mother giggled. "Just like a man to be enraptured by any and all food."

Adrian's cheeks were a little redder than Shannon expected them to be so she decided to change the subject. "Well, Adrian is a consultant. But he thinks that's boring. Perhaps we should define him with his hobbies. Tell us your hobbies then?"

He nodded very slowly and thought for a moment. "I um. I like to...paint. But. Mostly splatter paint. I like the...randomness of it."

"And of course you crochet."

"Yes. Of course." He cleared his throat. "I'm a big fan of nature too. I really like hiking." This seemed more his element. "I like being outdoors. I'm not much of an indoor person. Getting all muddy is a pretty good day to me."

She nodded. She couldn't imagine herself getting muddy but it didn't sound all that unpleasant. She tried to think of a time when she was dirty, but couldn't get further than a day she had gotten jam all over her hands and face. The best thing about people, she supposed, was that they were washable. 100% washable even. She squeezed his hand and he squeezed gently back, letting the side of his mouth slide up. She hoped it had reassured him. He was so nervous.

He continued, "I'm not much of a sportsman. I can do some things and not others. I hope that's okay."

Mother chided, "Of course that's okay, dear. You're just a little quirky. That's all that is. Shannon here is a little quirky herself. A terrible party planner. She'd much rather read a book than go to any garden parties. Not much of a social butterfly. I'm surprised she went to the gallery opening with Sean. Goodness knows, it's fantastic that she did. She met you after all. Tell us how you know the Detective."

"Oh, hah." Adrian gave a full-blown smile. She'd never seen it before. A thought suddenly came upon her. It was a silly thought, but still the same it filled her with a nameless dread. *He's got too many teeth.* She shivered a little. He didn't seem to notice as he continued, "Trent and I knew of each other for a while through people. Then out of nowhere we just found each other. It was...kinda fate. We worked on some stuff together. I helped him out with a few professional things and here we are. Just orbiting around each other." He shrugged.

Shannon took a breath and calmed the anxiety in her chest. "You're like planets, then."

"Yeah." He had gone back to his gorgeous little smirk. She felt better about that smile. "Just like planets."

When Leslie shuffled her way into the room and announced that dinner was ready, she passed a cursory glance over toward Shannon and lifted her blonde brows with approval of her choice in men. Her thin, pale lips curved a little into a soft grin and she nodded when Shannon was able to catch her gaze on the sly while walking toward the dining room.

Leslie was a pale woman of Nordic descent with a keen sense for taste and a wonderful set of skills in the kitchen. At just shy of thirty, she far surpassed all of the old cooks that Father had hired in the past. Her home-styled cooking was much better than the dishes made by the wrinkled old French cook they used to have. Plus, Shannon much preferred to talk to Leslie while she worked, sitting on one of the counters while the woman spoke of her past and the latest tales from other families' servants. Leslie was her main source of information as she could not yet function Father's computer and did not have the courage to attempt to use Sean's. Leslie was the one who had taught her everything.

Especially about sex. Her cheeks turned rosy and she hoped that the dim lighting of the dining room would hide the shade from Adrian. She sat in her chair and watched him sit across from her. He wasn't looking at her. He was eying Father's empty chair at the head of the long table. When another door opened and he emerged, Adrian's eyes snapped away and he stared at his blank egg-shell colored plate. She tapped his leg with the toe of her shoe and caught his attention, smiling at him. He gave a tentative smile back. He was *far* out of his element.

"Good evening everyone," her father murmured. Shannon's heart filled with no small amount of pride. She hoped her father would impress Adrian as much as she hoped Adrian would impress her father— much as she doubted the latter. Her father was a renowned professor, known for his research of bird species in sub-Saharan Africa. His works were widely published and known by many in the science community. He had spoken at conferences around the globe and spoke three languages fluently. More importantly, he was unimposing. That was Shannon's favorite trait of her father's. He had a thin frame and wore thick spectacles with sharp eyes behind them. He had a knack for listening and another knack for being unequivocally right in all arguments. He gracefully sat in his chair at the head of the table, placing his cloth napkin in his lap without making a single motion to indicate that he had even noted Adrian's presence. Shannon knew he had.

"Mr. Woods," he stated after a slight pause. "I'm glad you could join us today. Allow me to apologize for my son's absence."

"It's alright."

Her father took in a small breath. "I understand you know the detective."

"Detective Winston, that's correct."

"And you are aware of what happened to his partner?"

Adrian nodded. "I am aware."

Her heart started to flutter. Nobody had told her anything about Detective Winston's partner. Their faces were rigidly serious.

Something awful? Something horrific? Her father's brows knitted.

"I do not want you to be in danger, Mr. Woods."

Adrian's face hardened further. "I understand, sir. I have taken that under consideration. I do not feel that I am a threat to the killer, whomever he should be. I have no interest in such things but if I do happen to run across information, it is my obligation to alert the authorities."

"I agree, Mr. Woods. You are under obligation. If I were you, Mr. Woods," her father briefly glanced at each of them in turn then returned his stare to Adrian, "I would reconsider ignoring 'such things' as you called them. 'Such things' have an effect on all of us and I would as soon capture the killer as Detective Winston would. Consider what I have said carefully and keep a watchful eye."

Adrian nodded, his expression determined.

"Now that is settled." Father gave them all a bright smile. "On to supper."

The rest of their dining experience was relatively normal, but Father's words were sticking in her mind. It had been the first time Father and Mr. Woods had met. After supper, they had all retired to the drawing room where Mother was fiddling around with the piano and she was sitting like a little doll next to Adrian who was conversing with her father. It seemed that they had taken to each other. Adrian asked many questions about birds and her father answered them. He was very good at answering questions and appreciated curiosity. Adrian would do well, she thought. He was just inquisitive enough to make Father happy.

When Father got up to smoke his cigar outside, she and Adrian had a moment to themselves, watched over by her slightly distracted mother across the room, of course.

"My father likes you," she whispered.

"And I'm glad of it. I think he wants me to...observe."

"Observe what?"

"Not what—who." His expression was grim. "I think he wants me to observe your family and friends. Odd, isn't it?"

"Well I suppose that makes sense." She murmured. "Uncle Albert was his favorite brother. He has three. Albert was the eldest, my father the second eldest."

"Tell me about Albert."

His soft gaze lured her and she simply spoke without thinking. "He was a...a larger man. He worked at a big company. I think he was the president or something. He didn't talk about work much when he was with family. He was just Uncle Al. You know?"

Adrian nodded.

She shrugged. "I suppose you're looking for any reason for his murder, but I'm not much for grudges so I don't really have a mind for speculation."

"What about memory? Do you remember anyone being angry at him or him being angry at anyone else?"

"Angry enough to kill? No. I mean of course he and his brothers didn't always see eye-to-eye, but that was always resolved readily."

"Do these other names ring a bell to you Shannon? Mark Haley and Benjamin Houseal?"

She frowned. "Mr. Haley is a city council member. He's friends with father. And if I recall correctly, there is a Mr. Houseal at Father's club who golfs with my brother."

"Used to golf." Adrian's mouth was a tight line.

She suddenly felt breathless and put her fingers over her mouth. "So that's why father wants you to observe. All the victims are...are tied to the Kingsleys somehow."

"It might be the wrong direction. It might have nothing to do with it at all."

She hugged herself. "I...I don't know. I'm so...I'm so out of the loop. I'm the littlest Kingsley. They keep me out." And she had been grateful for it. Of course now she wasn't so sure about being grateful. Now that the killer was in her own back yard. "Adrian," she could feel tears in her eyes and she was sure he could hear them in her voice. "I don't want to be scared."

He gently took her arm from her and held her hand. He kissed her palm then earnest dark blue eyes met her soft green ones. He whispered, "I won't let anything happen to you, Shannon." His next words would come to mean the world to her. "I *promise*."

"You know it's difficult to find you when you want it to be," Ren stated.

Winston whirled around and saw him appear from the other side of his car.

"Are you insane?" Winston spat. "If you were seen in here, there's no way you'd escape." He made a wide sweeping motion with his arm to indicate the entire above-ground parking complex. He was right, too. Winston was parked on one of the upper levels. There was no way he could jump from it and getting out the exits would be impossible if they had been blocked by the fuzz.

"I'd find a way."

"You'd break your goddamn legs. Get in the car."

He did as told. He was fingering the leather front seat between his legs when he spoke again. "I couldn't find you. So I searched. Found your car. Figured where you were. Did something happen?"

"I was left a note."

"From the killer?" Ren was suddenly intrigued.

"It was slipped under my door in the night. I suppose it's not hard enough for people to find where unlisted folks live. Of course, it's probably easier when you're part of a high-powered family." He left a small silence after that statement so Ren could soak it in. Then he would state his intentions. "I'm going to take Rayne with me and interview the Haleys. You can come if you'd like, but you'd be out of place."

"What did the note say?"

Winston rummaged around in his suitcase for a moment before handing Ren a white piece of paper. "I made a few copies. You can have that one."

It was hastily made with blocky font.

Detective Winston,
Your search is at an end.
Continue and condemn your friends.
I am watching you, Detective.

"What a fuck," Ren mumbled before belching rather loudly in the cramped Fusion.

"Tacos?"

"Burritos."

"If he's watching me then he would know just how involved you are. I think it's just a scare tactic. Has anyone let on at the Kingsley household that they know you're involved with the case?" He started the car and popped it into reverse after rolling down the passenger's side window to air out the stench of half-digested burritos.

"Mr. Kingsley, the professor. He implied that he wanted me to snoop. He's got an odd mind, but I kind of like it. He's interesting."

"He's a smart man. He's won prizes for his work in Africa. But he's not our killer. He was speaking at a conference in Memphis the night his brother was killed. Hundreds of miles away. Not that I could really find a motive for him anyhow, despite his knowing all three of the victims."

"He's very intelligent. He might just have a way of hiding his grudges," Ren suggested, watching the world pass by outside the window. "And what if he had a partner?"

"He's too smart for that. He'd have to kill the partner in the end in order to tie him up. Loose ends and whatever. Rayne's thinking that the killer is probably not as high up in a pecking order as the victims. That he might be envious."

Ren shrugged.

"Have you met the brother?"

"Which brother?"

"Shannon's brother Sean."

He shook his head and scratched the top of his bleached white hair. "No. He was at a golf thing so he couldn't make it to dinner."

"He's got four friends. If you could observe the five of them, that would be wonderful."

"You think it was one of them?"

"I don't think anything right now."

He was just about to flick on his turn signal to journey down the dirt road toward the old park when Ren blurted, "We're being followed," as if it were the most wonderful thing that could have been happening at that moment. As if he had just been given exactly what he wanted for Christmas. His smile was gigantic and horrifying. "Oh, do go into the park, Winnie, I want to have some fun."

"No," was Winston's curt reply and he continued on. "We're going to a public place and we're going to have lunch and we're going to be sneaky."

Ren wilted. "Fine."

The diner that Winston brought them to was cramped, with booths lining either side of it and a breakfast bar in the middle. He'd chosen it because it was also lined with windows. It would be easy to capture whomever had been following them as long as that person was willing to be a little daring. "A booth in the corner if you can," he told the waitress and he flashed his I.D. It was usually enough for a person to give what was necessary.

She nodded and studied the two of them out of the corner of her eye as she set up the table. It was a normal reaction. She was wondering if she would have to duck back behind the counter or into the kitchen if shooting started. That's what they all wondered when the badge was flashed and no questions were asked. He scratched his head and watched out the windows. It had been a little dark blue Volkswagon Jetta. He theorized that it would possibly take a few passes around the block before it bothered to stop in. When the waitress came back with her pen in hand, he ordered pleasantly and Ren did the same.

They were silent, watching out the windows carefully.

The waitress disappeared.

"Any plans, Boss?" Ren asked.

"None in particular. Just be subtle."

There was an old man at the other end of the diner within viewing distance who could probably be relied upon as a witness if the need arose. Winston didn't foresee the need arising but he was comforted by the man's presence. He didn't bother to look up when the bell above the door jingled. A shadow fell over the table.

Ren visibly paled.

She curled her brown hair behind her ear and her stance shifted so her hip popped out and one of her legs went slightly slack. "Guys. I'm sorry but...I saw you and I wanted to talk to you. I didn't know if I was going to be able to find you again and it's quite important."

"Miss Kingsley." Winston blinked and then motioned to the booth seat next to Ren. "Why don't you have a seat?"

She was flustered. Her cheeks were pink and her big green doe eyes looked puffy as if she hadn't gotten enough sleep or she had been upset. Her hair also had parts that had been wind-blown or out of place and her brows were arched into a frown. She sat next to Ren and placed her bag by her feet. No doubt a real Coach or Gucci. She didn't seem to mind that Ren was clad in a tattered sweatshirt and jeans with dirt streaking his face under his eye and across the bridge of his nose.

"Detective I just...I have just had this awful feeling. My father is acting so strange. I think he's trying to locate the killer himself."

"Are you sure?" Winston asked with his brow cocked.

She shook her head. "No. No, I'm not sure. But it just seems like it. He's suspicious of everyone and he asked Adrian to...to be on the look out. Tell him, Adrian." She turned to Ren and he nodded at Winston quickly. "He knew all the victims and I think he has a hunch. You should talk to him. I don't want anything to happen to him. I don't want him to be hurt."

"Don't worry, Miss Kingsley." Winston smiled at her and tried to look sincere. She was obviously upset and she wasn't quite as oblivious to everything as he had thought. He flashed a glance at Ren who was failing at not staring at her. He narrowed his eyes at him while Miss Kingsley sipped the water Ren had offered her. "I'll address your concerns about your father."

"Thank you," she breathed. She looked up at Ren. "Adrian, I was wondering if you would like to join me for lunch tomorrow afternoon. My brother will be there and I do want you to meet him. He means the world to me and it's very important that you meet him." There was anxiety under her voice. She was afraid they wouldn't get along. The side of Winston's mouth turned up. What he wouldn't give to be a fly on the wall for *that* particular encounter.

"Of course, I'm not doing anything. I would love to join you."

She breathed a sigh of relief and then picked up his napkin, wetting it with the water from the glass and then turning to wipe his face with it. Winston chuckled when Ren allowed her to clean his face. The killer shot him a dirty look in response.

She was unperturbed. "I think we're going to have egg salad on the patio. Do you like sweet tea?"

"I love sweet tea."

"I'll make sure to make tea then." She nodded. "I'm sorry; I'm in your way. I can tell. You two have something you have to discuss and I'm in the way. I'll, um—I'll go then. I just had to get that out. I'm sorry. I'm just a little scatterbrained today I think." She poked her head a few times with her finger and then got up, pulling her bag out from under the table and waving awkwardly at the two of them, only leaving after Ren had given her a little wave and a tiny kitten smile.

"You're disgusting." Winston grinned.

Ren rolled his eyes. "I'm sorry, but if you don't want a piece of that fine ass you have to be a faggot." He frowned down at the table and then up at Winston. "You're not gay are you?"

"Worried if you're offending me?"

He shrank back in his seat.

"I'm not gay."

"So where's the broad?"

"What broad?"

"The one you've been hiding from me. Are you afraid I might steal her?" His teasing demeanor was back and he grinned like the devil he was.

"No broad."

Ren put his palms up. His expression screamed, *What the fuck, man?*

"My work is too dangerous for there to be some woman who's constantly worrying about me." He tapped his finger on the top of the table. "There was a girl once. That was back when I was working on your case for the first time. Grace. She was nice."

"What happened?"

"You did."

Ren was still grinning. "Sorry."

The waitress clunked down their plates in front of them, unamused by Ren's grin. She said nothing to them but took Ren's water glass for a refill.

"No. No you're not." He scratched the back of his head. "Anyways, I was still willing to give it another go, but she said that I wouldn't change and that I needed to re-think my life and my priorities before she would consider going out with me again. Obviously *that* never happened." He paused and looked at Ren who was eating his sandwich but still paying attention. "Are we having a bro moment? Because we are *not* bros."

Ren put up his hands and said, with his mouth full, "No, no man. Not bros. We're not having a moment either. You're just letting me know what's up. It's chill."

He put his face in his hands. "My God. She thinks her father is trying to find the killer, you're out to fuck her, and I'm...what the fuck am I doing? Condemning my friends."

"You can't condemn your friends, as far as your killer knows, *I'm* your friend."

He looked down at his BLT. Ren was right. He was Winston's only "friend" who would be available for murder. Rayne was hardly involved, Avery was heavily guarded in the hospital, Nadine was safe in North Carolina, and he didn't have any friends. All he had was poor, unsuspecting Mr. Woods. A joke at the least. Ren was asking him to disregard the note. He would be on his guard. He would be suspicious. The killer was much too obsessive to simply kill on a whim. Or so it seemed. He had gotten a little more daring when he had gone after Avery. Perhaps he was willing to do so again. If it meant making Winston a little angrier. If it meant making Winston a little less sedentary in his methods. He felt his left eyelid twitch with rage. Ren would make it worth it. That had been his promise.

CHAPTER 8

Somewhere, a clock struck midnight. Twelve gongs from the ancient clock reverberated through the house, bouncing off the walls and moving behind the tapestries as shadows of sound. The early summer night was chilly and a breeze brushed over her shoulders from a cracked window. Goosebumps rose on her arms. She couldn't remember how she got here. Standing in the wide front hall with her bare feet on the cold hardwood. She was facing the double front doors, their towering frame ominous in the dark. She hugged herself. Somewhere behind her, the floor creaked.

She turned slowly but couldn't see well through the darkness. She squinted. The floor creaked again.

"Huh...Hello?" she mumbled. She tried to take a step toward the noise. It was her own house. Her father's house. Nothing had ever happened to her here. Why did her heart race? Why was she about to run out the front door into the night? Why did *outside* seem safer? She took two steps back toward the doors. "Puh...puh..." She didn't know what she was trying to say. She could feel tears in her eyes. There was movement down the hall. Or was there? She couldn't tell. Her heart was beating so fast. Did something move? Again? She backed up further. Her back hit the front door and her hand found the cool cherry wood. "Ooooh," she made the sound from a brisk release of air from her throat. A small panicked noise as she groped for the doorknob.

There was a rustling in front of her. Feet on the carpet that started just a few feet from her. She opened her mouth to scream.

"Shannon?"

It caught in her throat and she let out a large whoosh of breath. She leaned all her weight against the door and slid down it, her butt hitting the floor harshly. Her tears spilled.

Her brother rushed to her side. "Shannon, whoa. What are you doing downstairs?" His soft voice comforted her and he took her into his arms while she let loose sobs that racked her body with their force. "Shhhh, my god, you're shaking." He held her close. He was in his Pjs, just as she was. "Shannon," he murmured. "It's okay. I'm here now. You're okay. You're okay."

She nodded and attempted to control her breathing. She gulped several times before she could form words. Her cheeks were wet with her plentiful tears. "I don't...I don't know how...how I got here." A few more sobs escaped her but she felt that they were the last so she tried to wipe her eyes with the heel of her palm.

Sean petted her hair with a gentle hand. "It's okay. Love, maybe you were sleepwalking? We'll have to tell Nunk. That's very uncharacteristic of you. Do you think you can stand or shall I carry you to your room?"

She shook her head. "I think. I think I can walk."

He helped her stand and climb the stairs. He held her steady while they walked to her room. He held her hand as she got in her bed. He even tucked her in and fetched her some water. His soft thumbs wiped away any stray tears and his warm smile calmed her fluttering heart. "Would you like me to stay? I can sleep in this chair." He motioned to the overstuffed chair in the corner.

"No Sean. That's ridiculous. You'll ruin your back. I'm fine now."

"What if you get up again? Someone must stop you. Who knows what you would have done if I had not heard you going down the stairs?" He touched her hand.

"So put bells on my door knob. If they ring and wake you then you must come rescue me again."

He sighed, resigned. "That is acceptable, I suppose. I'll find the

Christmas bells mother puts on the front door. Get some rest. Remember, we have lunch with your Mr. Woods tomorrow."

She put her hand over his. "I hope you like him."

"I'm sure I will be head over heels for him. Figuratively, of course." His wide smile reassured her and she closed her eyes.

She slept.

He was wearing a dashing navy blue sweater with the collar of his shirt just peeking out and the top of an equally as blue tie in evidence as well. His hair was artfully arranged in a messy chic and he had on very nice khakis. He looked much better than he had the day before—she'd tried to not notice how dirty he had looked. How ratty his clothes had been. He had that disarming little smile in place and she managed to forget the smears of dirt that had been on his face. He had willingly allowed her to wipe them off. That wasn't so bad. Complacency in a relationship. Is that not what Mother called it? He was not submitting. He was merely...humoring her. He was satisfied. That's what she thought.

There was no dirt to wipe now. He was perfect.

"Shannon." He greeted her and grasped her hands in his very warm ones. "How are you? I'm sorry I wasn't very warm yesterday."

"That's okay. I wasn't myself either." She led him through the house, down the front hall and through a small door that led to the kitchen. From the back of the kitchen was a sliding glass door that led out to the garden. He held her hand while she guided him down the stone path toward the patio. "I hope you don't mind eating out here. It's just so warm and beautiful this time of year." She admired the brilliantly colored flowers that were blooming on either side of them as they journeyed through the garden. "I'm very much fond of the flowers that are planted here. Although secretly I rather like the flowers that grow from the weeds. Forget-me-nots are so beautiful."

"Forget-me-nots," he mused behind her in a soft voice. "They're wonderful."

They reached the patio where Sean sat, reading his newspaper. A cigar was jutting out the side of his mouth as though he were just born to smoke them. He folded the paper and dropped it to his side while he stood. With the cigar in between his fingers of his left hand, he held out his right toward Adrian.

"Mr. Woods," he started as they shook hands, "Sean Kingsley."

"Just call me Adrian if you please." His smile was disarming. Sean's was equally as charming.

"Just Sean then. Please have a seat Adrian, it's great that you could come visit us today. I know you're probably very busy."

"Well when something's important to you, you manage to find the time for it." He gave Shannon a warm look and she could feel her cheeks flush.

"I know what you mean," Sean stated. "I hope you don't mind, after lunch, my friends are coming over for coffee and cigars. You're welcome to join us if you'd like."

Adrian looked at Shannon and she responded, "That's up to you. I take tea and just listen to them talk. They're rather hilarious when they want to be. I'm a watcher, you know. I think I might crochet a little."

"Then I would love to stay." He grinned at Sean. It was that grin that had made her doubt him. She watched Sean's face carefully for any of the unease she had felt from Adrian's mouth.

He displayed none. In fact, he seemed even more taken with her new beau. "Grand. Simply grand. They'll think you're great."

It was then that the sandwiches were brought out and they ate in relative quiet. Adrian's keen eyes were studying the back garden. The multiple types of flowers stood out against a vivid green backdrop. It was beautiful in early summer. Shannon felt a swell of pride in her chest for her home and her garden. She wondered where Adrian had lived—if he had possibly been as lucky in his economic status as she had been.

"Adrian," she started before tapping her napkin against her lips. He looked up with an odd expression, as if embarrassed. Did he always look like that when he ate? She couldn't remember from the night at the restaurant. "Tell me about your family."

Sean leaned forward and sipped his iced tea, the ice tinkling against the glass.

Adrian thought for a few moments before starting. "Okay. Um. I suppose I can do that. Uhm. My father is deceased, my mother is insane, and I don't have any siblings."

There was a silence over the patio. None of them spoke. The birds chirped above them in the trees.

Adrian took a bite of his sandwich and stared down at his plate while he chewed.

Sean was the first to speak. "That's just awful. I couldn't imagine not having any siblings. Shannon is the closest thing I have to a best friend. Did you have a best friend at least?"

"I did. He lived next door. We lived on the Outer Banks and his beach house was next to mine. His name was Teddy."

She breathed a sigh of relief. He had lived in a beach house. One of those gigantic behemoth mansions that lined the banks of North Carolina. He had been well-off. Or at least his family had been. "Was it very long ago that your father died?" she asked him.

"About six years ago, I would say. He was murdered."

Her back stiffened and her heart dropped into her bowels. She felt cold. A sudden fear gripped her and she wasn't sure if she could speak.

Adrian leaned forward and put a hand on shoulder. "What's wrong, Shannon? You're trembling."

"I..." she tried, "I'll be okay. I just. I'm not used to all this mayhem. What an odd thing. To be surrounded by murder."

He chuckled. "Hardly that you're surrounded."

Sean was leaned back again with his tea in his hand. "He has a point, Shannon. You're hardly surrounded by murder. Uncle Albert is one thing but Adrian's father is another. You're not surrounded by murder, sister, you're just a sheltered girl. Nothing wrong with that. Murder happens in the world and there's not much to be done about it. Did they catch whomever killed your father?"

Adrian shook his head. "No."

"Pity. The bastard's still running amok, I bet you."

He shrugged. "Well, it was no great secret that my father was in rather deep with the mob so if that was involved..." He trailed off and picked up the toothpick from his sandwich and poked it into a piece of crust.

Shannon rubbed her hands over her forearms in an attempt to dispel the awful coldness she had felt. It was stuck inside her like a spider's web. She could feel the discomfort deep within her body. Her belly, her chest, her head, as if a massive arachnid had spun it long ago and she was just now discovering it. As if it had been built in some chamber of her heart and released at the thought of murder. Oh, such an unpleasant thing. Such an unpleasant existence to have experienced something so terrible.

Sean and Adrian went back to a complacent silence, eating and sipping their iced tea as if they knew one another and needn't speak.

She had to break it. "Did Detective Winston say anything about the case?"

Sean sighed, "I thought you *didn't* like to talk about murder?"

She stuck her tongue out at him and then turned back to Adrian, who was giving her a little smirk. She blushed. It was then that three of the four of Sean's friends sauntered in. Preston, Steven, and Kyle. They appeared through the brush without fanfare or sound and all were appearing rather contented with themselves. They approached the table while Adrian spoke.

"Apparently, Trent got a little love letter from the killer. He didn't say what it said. He's a little bit of a loner, that one. Sometimes I have the thought that I'm his only friend. Other than Avery, I suppose, but even Avery thinks he's a little too independent in his methods sometimes. He's an odd character. You never quite know what he's thinking. Very unpredictable."

"A strange bird?" chimed Preston. "Sounds like someone fun." His wide smile was from ear to ear and he picked up a strawberry from a bowl on the table and popped it into his mouth. "Why don't we have this detective over for drinks or something?"

Steven visibly paled and mentioned in a soft voice, "But detectives are only good at one thing. Snooping. And what if...what if he snooped into something that we didn't want him to snoop into?"

Adrian's brow popped upward. Shannon noticed. She also noticed that Sean had noticed it as well.

Sean put his feet up on the chair that Steven had been about to sit in. "Dear Steven, that notion is perfectly ridiculous. The detective would keep any and all of our little white secrets alone. He might only know how to do one thing but he's also only *after* one thing. There's no reason for him to oust any of your sordid affairs. Not that you've had any."

Preston leaned against the solitary chair with Sean's feet upon it, edging Steven out of the way with his shoulder. He was eying Adrian with a curious gaze. "So you're the fella whose been wooing our little Shannon. Well, I'm willing to sell her...for a reasonable price."

Adrian grinned. "Oh yes? Sell her?"

Sean leaned forward and addressed Preston, "As if you have any right to sell her, she's my sister. And I say the price on her is a nickel." He put his hand out to Adrian with humor and heck, if Adrian didn't reach into his pocket and find a nickel. He pressed it into Sean's palm and Sean examined it as if he were examining a Spanish gold piece allegedly found at the bottom of the sea. "Well that's that then. You're the proud owner of a new woman. You'd better treat her well or I'll have to repossess her."

"No worries," Adrian replied. Then he winked at her.

Shannon's face was blank and she was unamused by the act of Adrian buying her. "For the love of Pete," she started, "What in the world would make you men think it was alright to go about buying and selling me as if I were some kind of slave?"

Her brother frowned, "Goodness gracious, Shan, it's just a joke. Don't be so sensitive."

She stared at Adrian for his reaction. She wasn't expecting what he said.

"I apologize, Miss Kingsley."

He *did* look sorry, she thought. It was in the way his mouth was tipped downward in the corners just so slightly and the way his shoulders had drooped. He had just been trying to get her brother to like him. He'd just been trying to fit in. She felt a little bad for putting him on the spot. But then again...not too bad. He'd learned a lesson, after all.

"I forgive you. But remember this, Mr. Woods: I'm priceless."

His grin was back and she couldn't help but allow him a small smile

61

in return.

It wasn't long before there were cups of coffee on the table and Sean had passed around several cigars. Adrian took one as well and puffed along with the rest as they joked about their days. Kyle was conspicuously quiet throughout the afternoon and of course she knew it was because he was coming face-to-face for the first time with the man who had been brazen enough to actually ask her out on a date. She studied him for a few moments while he was listening to Steven tell a very lame joke. He had a stronger jaw and chin than Adrian did and his nose was a little straighter. His eyes were chocolate brown and his hair was light chestnut. He didn't have freckles like Adrian did. In fact, they seemed rather opposites. She amended that in her mind. They weren't completely opposite. They were both strong. Kyle was strong in a man-like way. Adrian was strong in a smooth, sleek, *animal* kind of way.

They laughed and sipped their coffee and smoked their cigars. She took to her crochet project and watched them like she had said she would. But she noticed him looking at her. Sly little glances like he would rather be with her alone. She suddenly felt naughty, wishing that they could be by themselves. What would he do? Would they just talk? Or would he kiss her? She tried to imagine his kiss. Eager. Giddy. Experienced. She'd only been kissed once before by a boy. His name had been Arthur Hammson and they had been fourteen. He'd taken her to a movie. Their first date. He'd gripped her upper arms hard while they stood on her porch and had mashed his lips into hers.

She sighed and lifted her eyes to Adrian again only to find herself making eye contact with him. As surprised as she was that he was looking at her, she couldn't help but smile at him. He responded with a warm little smirk. A devilish kind of expression. He was doing it on purpose. Making her feel odd things. The man was demonic, she thought.

The idea was not entirely unpleasant.

Sean's voice broke through into her consciousness. "Steven, what possesses you to think of these things?"

He shrugged his shoulder pathetically and scratched his forehead. He was the least attractive of the five of the friends. His eyes were a little too close to one another and his hair was a dusty shade of brownish red. He didn't dress very well. Hardly that Shannon could fault him for that, but the rest of them had. His lower lip pooched out a little bit with a slight under bite that made him seem perpetually pouty. He had suffered much at the hands of her brother and his other friends and yet he did not seem to be angered by it. He simply took it in stride. They were all he had. He would accept them for all their teasing and their bullying.

There had to be a runt of the litter, she supposed.

She jumped when she felt warmth on her knee under the table. Adrian wasn't looking at her. She settled herself and was glad that nobody had seen her jump. His hand was touching her knee, his warm fingers tickling the delicate, sensitive flesh on the inside. She almost lost her breath. It was most definitely not something accepted by etiquette, but why couldn't she feel indignant about it? She should. She should slap his hand right off of her. But she didn't. Butterflies fluttered around in her stomach and she swallowed. Nobody could see his thumb going back and forth over her skin under the dark red tablecloth. The boys continued with their conversations as normal. Adrian even contributed.

She didn't know what was being said. She couldn't pay attention to it. Not when his fingers were putting butterfly kisses over her flesh. Were her cheeks red? She was lost in his touch. She lost her breath and an odd feeling sank deeper than her stomach and for certain she was turning a deep shade of scarlet.

All thoughts of the conversation were washed from her mind and there was nothing but her body and Adrian's errant hand. It hadn't moved from her knee. It wouldn't. *He* wouldn't. She knew that at least. But God, somehow she wanted him to. His palm pressed against her skin fully and his fingers stopped their movement. It was time to regroup herself. When he caught her eyes again she was struck by his shamelessness. There was Sean's answer. He was most definitely bold. Brazen. Reckless. *Wild*.

The warmth on her knee left abruptly and she looked up and around. Her father had entered the garden with a book in his hands. He looked disappointed to find the ruffians carrying on in his favorite reading spot. Resigned, he approached the table to a multitude of "hey pop"s from all the boys. Adrian stood and shook his hand before sitting back down next to her.

"Well, I suppose I won't be doing much reading out here," he sighed. "But it is good that you are here, Adrian."

He tilted his head curiously.

"In a few weeks my niece, Shannon's cousin, will be getting married. I don't want to step on any toes, but I was hoping that you would accompany Shannon to the wedding and the reception."

"If she'll have me, I'd love to escort her." He turned his eyes to her. "Would you want to go with me?"

She fanned herself discreetly with her hand, pretending to consider it hot outside to hide her embarrassment. Her voice was trembling a little. "Yes. I'd...I'd love to go with you."

Her father didn't notice. He was much too interested in the thought he'd had about Adrian. "I was mostly hoping that you might observe the family. As they will be all together at the wedding. I can give you a list of people that you might wish to speak to. Discreetly of course."

"You couldn't get an invitation for Winston?"

Father chuckled. "Getting a wedding invite for a detective is a little harder than it might seem. It's easy to get you in. Your friend actually contacted me this morning, dropping subtle hints that he's gotten a few good ideas and to stay out of his investigation for safety reasons. But this wedding is an opportunity for him and he'll miss it without my help. Of course, it's rather difficult to convince a bride that a detective meant to snoop into the family would be a good idea at her wedding."

"That's why you need me." He turned to her. "You don't mind having me as your date, right? I mean, even if I'm snooping?"

"I don't mind at all. I'm sure I'll be able to distract you occasionally anyway."

They smiled at each other and her father smiled as well. She wasn't so sure about Adrian going to this wedding in order to snoop around for some kind of cold blooded killer, but she was also certain that Adrian was a little more than met the eye. If he agreed to a scheme like this, he probably had a little more grit in him than your average... She bit her bottom lip and looked around. Her eyes fell on Kyle. *Your average rich snob*, her brain mumbled and she had to acknowledge the thought. Adrian was definitely not the average snob. He was wilder than that. Wilder than her brother's friends who found their fair share of fun at the bottom of a tequila bottle.

Adrian was a little bit more *something*.

CHAPTER 9

"I knew about the wedding." Winston was sipping a glass of whiskey on the rocks, relaxing in his arm chair with a book at his elbow and a serial killer lounging across from him on his couch. "Did anything else happen? You said his friends were there."

"Not all of them," he noted with one finger held up. "There was one missing."

"Okay, well tell me what happened."

Ren related him the events of lunch and what was said before gathering himself and grinning. "I touched her knee under the table."

Winston lifted a brow. "She let you? She seemed like a nice girl to me."

"She *is* a nice girl. That's why it was so mean."

The detective leaned forward in the arm chair. "Ren. At this wedding you have to be my eyes and ears. You can't be going off to a separate room and having your way with the sweet little virgin cousin. The reception is going to be held at Holden Manor. It's part of the family's estate. If our killer is part of the family then they'll know the territory much better than you or I." He leaned back and thought for a few moments. "I'm going to sneak onto the property and observe the goings on. You can't be in there by yourself."

Ren appeared peeved. "I'm not a child."

"Wrong. You're exactly like a child."

"You're just angry because your skills of manipulation aren't as well-honed as mine." He put his nose up in the air and turned on the couch so he was facing the back cushions. "Besides, while we're debriefing, you should tell me how your visit to the other family went. You went with that *other* detective."

Winston was surprised by the animosity that came from Ren in discussing Rayne. But only a little. The acidic tone was normal, he supposed, since Rayne was the one who theoretically knew just about everything about Ren. From the motive of his killings to the way his handwriting leaned. The profiler was good. But not good enough for this task. It had taken him years to study Ren and Ren's movements and motives. It had taken them all years. Ren was their pet project. Now Ren was his pet.

"It went well for the most part. In that case I'm fairly certain we're barking up the wrong tree." He didn't bother to elaborate. "They were more than cooperative. All of them. Rayne wasn't suspicious of any of them. He seemed bored, honestly." He scratched his neck.

"The poor baby. Bored at an interrogation."

"It was an interview, not an interrogation. Big difference."

"Whatever." Ren rolled his eyes and picked at his teeth with his fingernail.

"I have to go."

"It's seven-thirty, where do *you* have to be? Visiting hours at the hospital end at six."

"Go to Hell."

When he stepped out onto the cement stoop of his apartment building, he took in the night air and wondered what exactly Ren would do while he was gone. Did he rifle carefully through all his things? Was he looking for porn? There was plenty. Was he looking for weakness? There was Prozac in the medicine cabinet. Was he looking for black mail? Winston tried hard to remember if there was anything embarrassing that Ren could find in his apartment. He came up with nothing. He strolled down the sidewalk as the sunset cast strange shadows around him. He put his hands in his pockets.

When he reached the small Chinese food restaurant he ordered some

Chow Mein and sat down at one of the tables. The white florescence made his reflection easy to see in the wide front windows. He could be seen well from the outside. He knew Ren wasn't following him. Nobody was. He'd been very careful and observant.

The bell above the door rang and he looked up from his food. Ben Withers made his way over to the table. "Detective."

"Mr. Withers. I heard you didn't attend your luncheon with your friends."

His lips were tight together. "I had a prior engagement. In any case, I wanted to give you some information."

Winston motioned at the seat across from him. "Sit down." He did. Winston got out his pad of paper and a pen and clicked it to signify that he was ready.

"There was a night. When we said that we were together. The night of Mr. Kingsley's death. We weren't together."

Winston raised his eyes from his pad of paper and stared at him. "You're telling me this because you want to get your name cleared first?"

"Yes. I don't want to be dragged through the mud. The tabloid papers are already hounding us enough. I'm surprised you haven't had your whole place bugged yet. There's no doubt that they're watching you. They'll try anything to get a good story out of this. They'll undermine your whole investigation if they can."

"Why are you telling me this?"

He appeared nervous and he looked around himself, out the wide front windows at the cars passing by. His cheeks had turned pink. "Because...I'm not the killer. But I think one of us is."

"Which one?"

"That's the problem," he stated, "I'm not sure. It could be any of them. When I said we weren't together I meant that every single one of us was not with the others. None of us have a viable alibi for that night. And as for the other two murders, only one of the alibis I gave to you was truthful. I was with my parents at Vero Beach in Florida the day that it happened and there was indisputable picture evidence to say that I was. But that was just the second one. We've all been each other's alibis but we can't go on like that. It'll get out and of course we'll be prosecuted for fucking around with an investigation."

"I would say," he sighed, jotting notes down on his pad, "that it is 'getting out' right now. Which is better than later. Why do you think it was one of your friends?"

"Well nothing else makes any sense. They're completely unconnected victims unless you count their friends and family. All the victims are family friends. They go to all the same events and family to-dos. Everyone knows them." He played with a stray napkin at the side of the table. "I was laying in bed the other night and it just hit me. Like a brick had fallen from the ceiling. Why did we have to make up alibis for ourselves? Why did we do that? Whose idea had it been? I can't remember for the life of me."

"Don't beat yourself up over it too much. It's not uncommon for people to forget whose idea something was. It might have been such a mutual agreement that it wasn't anybody's idea."

Ben took in a deep breath and then let it out. He was still distraught. His teeth chattered a little in his nervousness. "I just have this bad feeling. We tell each other pretty much everything. But not everything. You know what I mean?"

Winston had a thought. "Ben...can I call you Ben?" He nodded. "Good. Ben. Let me ask you something. Do you consider these guys your best friends?" At Ben's next nod he continued, "I think it's a well-known fact that we don't tell our friends everything. Or even anything really important. What I mean is this," he leaned forward on the table, "we're trapped by our friendship. We can't say things that we want to say because we're trapped by propriety. The only true honesty you'll ever get is from someone who doesn't give a shit about you. We all hide things from our friends. You believe that one of your best friends could be a cold blooded serial murderer who tortures victims and then brutally terminates them. You believe this because it's *possible*."

Ben looked down at the table.

Winston leaned back in his chair again. "It's possible because your friends are just that. Friends. You don't have many enemies do you, Ben? Not in that world you live in. This is the fun part of this investigation. There are no enemies. Only friends. At least one would know someone was after them if they had enemies. This killer hides in the ambiguity of the title 'friend.' It makes it a challenge. The motive would be insane. I'm betting that it is."

Ben shifted in his chair. "What are you going to do?"

Winston lifted a shoulder. "What a detective does best."

A week later, he was smoking his Marlboro while leaning against the railing of the fire escape. The window was open and soft guitar strumming was floating past his ears from Ren, who was sitting on the carpet with his head tilted thoughtlessly. He'd done his interviews. He wasn't half as good as Avery was at the pauses and the long silences that left them to think. He wasn't as good with the timing. He was pretty decent at the manipulation though. The subtle hint that they'd been ratted out.

But they'd stayed strong. Even the weak one, Steve, had stuck to the original alibis. He'd been lying. It had been easy for Winston to tell. The way he fidgeted and the way his eyes moved. He was trying to remember the original story they'd told. They were all fairly close to the original. Close enough that Winston couldn't bother with them. He'd have to stick with the plan. But now they knew. The pressure was a little more intense. The wedding was in a week and the killer knew that Winston was digging a little deeper into his alibi. That was if he was even on the right track. With any luck this wedding business would clinch it. It would prove once and for all whether or not he was running down the right path or if he'd missed the curve at the last fork in the road.

He closed his eyes and took a long drag of his cigarette. He held it in for a while and then let it out, allowing the calm to wash through him. He could smell the city. Dirt. People. Concrete. The music Ren was making on that old guitar he'd had in his closet—his father's—was soothing and made the world seem just a little less tangible. As if the sound itself had altered Winston's perception of reality and made it less touchable. He focused on the touch of the railing on his forearms and found himself grounded again.

There was something profoundly interesting about losing one's mind.

He puffed a little more before throwing his butt off the side of the fire escape and ducking back into the apartment through the window. He watched Ren strum for a little while before going into the kitchen and making himself a snack.

Having the killer sleep on his couch hadn't actually turned out very badly at all. He was almost the perfect roommate. He did all the dishes, cleaned the apartment daily, didn't leave anything strewn about. He was compact, neat, quiet, and the most important part about him was that he was *there*. He was company. He was someone to vent to, to joke with, and to listen to. Without Avery, Winston thought he'd be lost. With Ren, there was relief from those quiet nights with nothing but his guilt and grief to lull him to sleep.

The longer he spent with the killer the more he started thinking Ren wasn't just that frosty, bristled dog. He was human after all. A sobering thought.

He laid down on the floor next to Ren and the killer stopped playing. Winston frowned and closed his eyes. "Tell me a story," he told him.

Ren put the guitar down beside him with a hollow thump. "What kind of story?"

"A true story."

He thought for a moment, his cold blue eyes unfocused and narrowed toward the wall. Then he began.

CHAPTER 10

It was around six thirty on a cold January day. The sun had already set and darkness had overtaken the fields. He'd entered the woods with no path to guide him, tripping over downed trees and branches and cutting his hands on thorns and bark. They didn't hurt. He couldn't feel them. He stumbled aimlessly through the trees, the cold seeping in and sucking the very life out of his bones. He was shuddering hard with every step.

He would die tonight.

Blood was seeping from between his lips, dripping in strands to his throat and down his front. It was warm at first and then cold overtook it, creating a deep red web of discomfort. As cold as he was, his stomach burned.

He groaned and doubled over, dropping to his knees at the edge of the woods, his bare hand sinking into such cold snow. He could feel that. It was a white fluffy cloud of razorblades. But the pain in his hand was nothing compared to the burn in his belly. He heaved blood, splattering the white with a hard crimson. The world spun so he closed his eyes to control it. The darkness that surrounded him was full. There was nothing but the light of a half moon to show him the red of his blood and the blue of the world.

Through his fuzzy vision, he thought he could see a structure. A large one. He wasn't sure. It would be just thirty feet. Just thirty more feet and he could make it. But his legs refused to function. He hadn't the strength to get up. He bent his head so that his chin touched his chest and he closed his eyes. There was no wind. He felt small pin pricks over his neck and head. It had started snowing.

C'mon. Get up.

"I can't," he answered. "I can't—" More blood interrupted him and his body spasmed with the force of his heaving. When he was done, he was spent. "I can't," he whispered.

Get up.

"I..."

Get up.

He didn't answer. With shuddering muscles, he tried. It was thirty feet across a clearing covered in snow. It would be slippery. It would be cold. But if his blurry sight could be trusted, there was a rather large lodge-type structure at the end of that thirty feet. And he was going to make it. His knees almost buckled when he took his first step. He stumbled many times but his momentum was enough to keep him going.

He smashed his face into the door. It wouldn't matter. Blood from his nose was from the same body as the blood from his mouth. He pushed himself up against the thick wooden door. "Please," he whispered through his blood. "Please..." His numbed fingers found the doorknob and he turned it.

It gave.

He was too weak to build a fire in the fireplace so he curled up in front of it on a worn, ragged carpet that once may have had a color. In that place. Curled next to a desolate fireplace, Ren died.

"Don't worry," he said while Winston stared up at the ceiling. "I came back. It was just a little trip."

He sighed. He remembered that night. It was cold, dark, and he'd known Ren was in this old man's barn. Helinsky? Hellsky? He couldn't remember. It didn't matter now. Winston had gone in to find him, gun drawn, and he'd somehow escaped, as usual. The ever-observant Avery had noted a strange pattern to his footsteps and small bits of blood in the snow. The prints had been jumbled and mashed, dragging as if he had been in considerable pain. Winston remembered the sting of the cold on his cheeks and the way he had tucked his arms against his sides and shoved his gloved hands in his pockets. Avery had mumbled that it was as cold as a witch's tit. It had been comical at the time. Of course a heavy snow had fallen and it had been hard for Avery to follow the tracks he'd left. By the time they'd made it to the old tavern of which Ren spoke, he'd managed to elude them again.

"Who hurt you?" he asked the killer. He hadn't understood the feelings that floated around in his head at the time. Indignant fury at any who would dare harm his quarry. Hunting an injured deer was no sport at all. He felt the same rush of emotion, the same old hate welling up.

Ren strummed two more chords before setting the guitar aside and giving Winston a contemplative gaze. "There are people in this world who will lure little girls toward their cars and then snatch them up like some trapper spider. That's the kind of world we live in. Planet fucking Earth. Beautiful, isn't it?"

Winston frowned at the ceiling.

"What if I told you I was a little less than good after you let me go?"

He couldn't control the upward motion of the side of his mouth. It was a twisted little grin and he hated it. He tried to stop it but Ren had already seen it. "Other than Kent Newman, whore kicker extraordinaire?"

"Other than..." Ren's answering grin was terrifying. "If you want to hear this story, it will cost you."

"Why?" He pulled himself up from the floor into a sitting position and rubbed the back of his head. The sun had lowered in the sky. They had all night for stories and tales. He heard Ren's stomach grumble.

"Because your friends could use this information. I'm not of a mind to give something good away for free."

"What do you want?"

Ren paused while he thought. "A fake I.D. Adrian Woods. A social security card for Adrian, and the password to your personal laptop."

"Done," Winston waved his hand in the air.

Ren balked. "Do you realize the possibilities?" His expression was laughable, his jaw almost to the floor.

Their exchanges rarely left Winston in a favorable stance in terms of the element of surprise. Here he'd had it all to begin with. "Ren, those things aren't going to make you less easy to capture. At least not for me. In fact, they'll make you easier to capture or they won't change the score at all. I would know the name on the I.D. and the social security number. I would also know exactly what you were doing on my laptop because of keystroke software which would help me see exactly where you were going online and who you might be contacting. Nothing you've asked me for is anything that I couldn't track."

Ren pouted. "I'd taken *you* out of the equation."

He chuckled. "That'll be the day..."

Ren leaned forward and the action reminded the detective of a small boy. "When will we go back to being like cats and dogs?"

"When I realize again that I'm a cat and you're a dog," Winston smiled. He wasn't sure when that could ever again occur but he was hopeful it would. "Don't change the subject. Tell me who hurt you."

"I was in a mall parking lot." His eyes grew dark as if a cloud had swung in over the early evening sun. "I watched it happen. I was leaning against this very nice new Fusion. Reminded me of you, you know. It was black." He scratched his face. "What's for dinner?"

"Little girls apparently. Get back to the story."

"She was about nine. Her mother didn't even really notice. She was distracted. Isn't that the problem of our time? Distractedness. Everyone pays their dues to the digital lords above them; praise be to the God of cellphones. Bend your heads everyone, bend your heads and text your life away." His breathing was getting shallower as he continued, his eyes flitting over Winston's apartment, unfocused, "I followed him. I *followed* the spider. I thought that maybe I was doing you a favor. I thought that you might be following *me*. But you weren't." He paused for a small time, his lip twitching. He continued in a whisper, "You weren't, Winnie. You weren't with me." He came back to a nor5mal level of speaking but it was faster and with a harder edge. "He lived in this stupid little house that had garbage all over the front lawn. It was ridiculous that someone hadn't seen this dump and considered him a killer just based on his poor hygiene. But it was down this gravel road. More dirt than gravel. She was screaming in the back seat. I think he liked it. He was in a station wagon. I thought. I thought that maybe you would follow me there, Winnie."

Ren tapped his temple. "I was so sneaky. I thought I'd save her. I thought I'd deliver her to you like some celestial gift. Like I was some angel. I'd just wrap her up like a little present and give her to you like I was a boy spider and you were a girl spider and I needed to woo you. But it didn't work that way."

Winston nodded to show him that he was listening.

"He didn't know that I was there. He didn't. He wasn't that smart. He wasn't that observant. He wasn't a spider like me. I'm one of those spindly ones that can hide in a corner. He's fat and big and hairy and he comes out of nowhere and grabs. He's a *grabber*, detective. And I was almost to her. I was almost the hero.

"And he grabbed *me*. He thought I was her at first. But I was much bigger. I fought. Hard. You know how hard I can fight. I bit him." Ren's expression betrayed something like dismay as he looked out the window toward the sun. "He was...upset. That I swallowed. And he forced me to swallow more."

Winston stomach churned. "What'd he make you eat, Ren?"

Ren shuddered. "Toluene. And...and something else. God knows. I couldn't move for a long time. I couldn't see. I thought I was blind. He left me to die in his basement. I was dizzy, I couldn't feel. My numbness. My blindness. It couldn't stop my fight.

"I didn't save her." He took a breath and met Winston's gaze. "I saved myself."

Winston leaned forward and Ren flinched. He paused before moving slower and putting a warm palm on Ren's knee. "It's all you could do."

"Do you think I'm hurt? Do you think I'm hurt over her? Do you think I lose sleep over the thought of her broken and bleeding and dead? Do you think *for one single fucking moment* that I cared whether she lived or died?" He was glaring, his voice filled with a shuddering anger.

"I wanted to show you up, Winnie. I wanted to make you know that I had control over something. I wanted to make you realize how much I could do before you could stop me. I'm not sorry that she's probably at the bottom of some pit rolling in lime with all the other prepubescent fucks he had. The only thing I regret is not fighting hard enough. Not getting what I wanted.

"She's dead, Winston. It's not my fault. But if she had lived and it was because of me...I wouldn't be the hero of that story. Just like I'm not the hero of this one." With that, he stood suddenly and his footsteps pounded across the floor. The front door slammed shut and Winston could hear him until he faded down the apartment's stairwell.

CHAPTER 11

"You know," Avery said in a soft voice. "He's right." His mouth was healing nicely and his dark eyes had regained some of their sparkle. "I think he's got something more against you than just the fact that you're a good guy and he's a criminal. I think he's angry that you're the hero and he's the villain." Avery shrugged. "Sounds that way anyway. I mean who wouldn't be upset? Especially when you two *aren't* cats and dogs?"

Winston narrowed his eyes at his partner and frowned, "What do you mean?"

Avery smiled that knowing smile. "Please, Trent. Stop fooling yourself. You're deluded if you think you're any better than him. He can see right through you. You're both dogs. You might even be the same *breed*. The fact that you ended up the hero and he ended up the villain irks him." Avery sighed. "Besides, he's telling more in that story than you actually heard. This is why I'm sorry I can't be with you. He's giving you crucial information about his feelings. He's been under the thumb of someone who had complete control over his very life and very future. He's telling you in his own kind of sick way that he knows how *I* have felt. He's trying to relate to you via *me.*"

Winston nodded. "Do you think that story is true?"

Avery put his palms up in his lap. "It doesn't matter. Even if he's trying to manipulate you, you have to go along with it. Because he's your in. He's the one who's going to get you this killer no matter what.

But he's got to have a piece of you with him. He has to know that he's got you where he wants you. Even if you don't trust him—which you shouldn't—you have to make him feel that you do. And if it makes you more comfortable in doing that, I'll tell you how I feel on the subject." He took a sip from a plastic cup of water. The action was slow and deliberate and he didn't spill a single drop of it. Winston was impressed. He continued as he put the cup down. "I would bet you a thousand dollars that if your life were in immediate danger, he would save you even if it meant risking his own."

Winston was quiet for a time while Avery watched him. Avery was the patient one. He would wait with that little silence and that warm knowing stare until Winston was done thinking. Avery was the perfect complement to him. He was his better half. He was more a friend than Winston deserved. Ren, on the other hand, was the exact opposite. He was Winston's shadow. His dark side. Not a part of him but another him. One that had rotted inside. He chewed his lip and tried to focus out the window of the hospital room. He couldn't. Ren would be there for him. There was no doubt in his mind that Ren would risk his neck to protect his investments. Personal and business. He made a promise to himself to do the same.

"You've started to think about him as human." Avery's mouth curled further, distorting the wounds on his face into a horrifying display of scar tissue and clotted blood. "That's good."

Winston fixed his eyes to the blankets over his partner's knees. "I'm starting to think that it's less that I'm thinking of him as human and more that I'm accepting that I *might not be*."

"Which is good."

"Good?" Winston's eyebrows lifted as high as they could go but he still couldn't look at his partner.

"Yes." Avery chuckled. "Yes it's good. The closer you come to accepting this, the closer you come to being better at your job...at your personal relationships..."

"You mean he's teaching me about myself."

"More or less."

"I don't like thinking of myself that way."

"So dislike it. That won't make it any less true."

"I could make it untrue. I could..."

"Turn a new leaf?" Avery pushed his assistance button once. It would take forever for a nurse to come. Winston knew that from his own stints in hospital beds. Avery didn't seem to mind. His jaw was twitching a little. He was in pain. But he kept a stoic expression and a calm demeanor. He was ever the patient one. Even while suffering. "Don't make this harder than it has to be, Winston, but don't make it easy either."

"Enough about this." Winston's chest swelled with frustration. "Ren's going to be a guest at a wedding. We're going to be connected via Bluetooth the whole time. He's not going to acknowledge me. I'm just going to listen to his conversations and log them into my personal laptop. We're looking at four suspects right now. The boys, you remember them."

"Is that so?" Avery's brow twitched.

"Yes. Ben Withers came forward the other day and confessed that their alibis were bull. They're sticking to them . I'm trying to get Ren to collect data for me. Just a few tidbits. Talk to some people, schmooze while he can. But..."

"But?"

"I told you about that letter."

"Yes."

"Ren's alias...Mr. Woods. He's my only friend. The only available friend who could be harmed."

Avery shrugged one shoulder, "From what you told me, I would say that you're not meddling so the killer wouldn't have any reason to harm him. I mean unless somehow the killer was tipped off that Adrian is somehow meddling on your behalf."

"The father. The father asked him to meddle. It was during dinner. Shannon and her mother were there. It could have gotten out. Around. There's no telling what the killer might know. I'm putting his life at risk."

"And he knows that. He's willing to move forward. Calm down, Trent."

He took a few breaths and watched Avery's eyes flit to the "Call" button again. He was patient but pain wore on him. Winston wondered how patient his friend really was when it came down to the wire. "Calm down, Trent, he says," Winston murmured, "I've been responsible for death before but..."

"This one would somehow make a difference."

Winston didn't know how to respond.

"Because you're *empathetic*." Avery pressed the "Call" button again. "You're feeling empathy for him. Which makes you different from him on a very basic level. You're different from him because of those feelings for him."

"You make it sound like I'm in love with him." He put his palm against his forehead.

Avery might have chuckled but it came out as a sniff. "Empathy and love are very different. You can feel emotion past want and need. You don't want him to die not because you want anything from him or you need anything from him. You don't want him to die because you would feel responsible, you would feel sad. You would *feel* as if you had *failed*. And not just failed me by not getting what you wanted through this mission but failed *him* by putting him in this position. Because you *forced* him."

"If he dies..."

"Are you having a problem with this because you would still be the hero even if he died?"

A lump was suddenly caught in his throat and he found himself forced to look into his partner's dark brown eyes. He knew that his face would betray him. That Avery was right. That he'd hit the nail right on the head. The tail was on the donkey. Ren's life was meaningless.

And somehow, it meant the world to Winston.

She was looking at her shoes when he approached her. They were a soft velvet powder pink with a tiny bow on tops of her toes. They were three-inch heels and Sean had suggested once that they went with her off-the-shoulder thin black three-quarter sleeve sweater that she was currently wearing. She had chosen a cute pair of white capris which Sean said went with nearly anything. Her earrings were powder pink feathers that poofed at her shoulders. She had been very proud of her outfit. It was a shame that she and Adrian weren't set to go on a date.

"Excuse me, Miss Shannon Kingsley?"

She looked up. He had a kind face. It was plump with a little fuzz on his chin as if he had wanted to grow a beard but simply couldn't. He was wearing a gray blazer with a clean shirt underneath but no tie. "Hello?" She hoped she hadn't sounded too confused. She had a tendency to do that.

He grinned a little and nodded to her with a golfer's hat in his hands. "My name's Jim Valechy. I wanted to ask you a couple questions. Very professional, nothing serious."

She narrowed her eyes and looked around herself at all the people wandering down the sidewalk of the city. He had found her randomly? He had followed her? He appeared apologetic so she decided that a question wouldn't be necessary. A statement was in order. "You're a reporter."

"I...am." He nodded shyly and he put up his hand, "I don't mean to be a bother. I know that a lot of reporters have been very pushy on your family as of late. One specific reporter comes to mind." He laughed nervously. "Eddie Nero."

"I've heard of Nero," she noted in a meek voice. "Never heard of you though. Nobody asks me questions. I'm the littlest Kingsley. I don't know much of anything."

"Well my questions weren't much for the papers really. Just kind of something else I've been working on. Do you know much about the private detective on the case?"

"Detective Winston? I know a little. He's a very nice man."

"Um...if it doesn't seem too forward, could I ask you to coffee?"

"Of course." She smiled. She was a little worried that her brother might not take to kindly to her being so polite to the likes of a reporter but he seemed so genuine. She would be sure to screen her answers carefully.

He was gracious when he paid for her mocha latte. He took his own coffee black. She crossed her legs under the table and watched him scan the sparse people around them and the people outside on the sidewalk. He was looking for someone. Eddie Nero, she thought. They were professional rivals. Of course. She sipped her mocha latte. He licked his lips before beginning.

"How long have you known Detective Winston?"

She shrugged one shoulder. "I guess since the investigation started into my family. But neither he nor his partner bothered to interview me. I'm not very interesting anyway, I don't blame them."

He appeared dejected. "Oh." He fidgeted, touching his lips with his thumb before chewing the nail slightly. "I thought..."

"That I was closer to him. Just because I'm dating his friend doesn't mean I know anything about him, believe me. He's a secretive guy. If you wanted to know more about him you'd have to talk to Adrian."

The reporter was staring at her. Hard. "Adrian?"

"Of course, Adrian."

"You mean...Avery?"

She closed her mouth. This reporter was working on a project about Winston. Shouldn't he know who all of his friends are?

His eyes were narrowed and searching her face. "Detective Trent Winston is a mysterious man, Miss Kingsley. He's not a very friendly person. Other than work associates, he doesn't have much going for him. You wouldn't consider yourself his friend. Nobody really would. Except maybe his partner, Avery. And that's a maybe. Now you're...dating his friend?" He placed his coffee cup down on the table and then leaned forward over it. "Trent Winston doesn't *have* friends, Miss Kingsley. So the question remains...*who are you dating?*"

Her mind was blank. A waterfall of blank actually. A crashing, tumbling, churning, waterfall of blankness. She was still staring at him. She was still in the world of the living, she thought. His round face was still full of an inspiring kindness but with an overpowering mask of curiosity. She opened her mouth but stuttered. "Have...Have you sp-spoken to Winston?"

"Once. As I said, he's not a very friendly guy. Of course nobody's really friendly with the media."

"Well...if Winston is hiding anything from the media on purpose, I will *not* be the one to oust it. I don't know anything about the man and it's pointless to ask me."

"Can you tell me anything about the man you're currently seeing?"

She put up her nose like Sean taught her. It was a gesture that most people found to be rude. It appeared the reporter was indifferent to it. "I will not be sharing my personal details or those of anyone else. I thought we were going to talk about professional things." She stood. He looked as if he wished to ask her something else but she didn't give him the chance before she walked out the door.

She felt tired. Much too tired for all of this. It was time for a little catnap. Her car would do just fine.

Nobody bothered to look at her when she walked in other than the secretary who told her exactly where she was to go. There weren't many people there anyhow, just a rather haggard-looking man in a shirt and tie clicking away at something on his computer in the corner. The office was bland and gray and smelled like gunpowder, stationary, and printer ink. It was a cozy little office space on the third floor of a brick building about two blocks from Sean's favorite burrito hotspot. There were pictures pinned up on corkboards and on the walls and nonsense words scrawled on whiteboards that stood by a long table that was cluttered with maps.

She peeked inside Office 19 which was at the back of the main room and was somehow relieved to find Detective Winston with his finger against the side of his eyebrow, wrinkling it while he read some kind of document. Around the walls of his office were photos of grisly crime scenes and mugshots of offenders. They weren't decoration.

"Detective?" she asked in a meek voice. He looked up at her with wide eyes and beckoned her into the room.

"Close the door." He rolled his chair over to the other desk in the room and brought out the matching swivel chair she presumed belonged to Avery. Avery's desk was neat and tidy—almost dusty from disuse. Winston's was a veritable war zone. When he'd gotten her seated in the chair and straightened his papers a little, he asked in a soft tone, "What brings you here, Miss Kingsley?"

She took a deep breath. "I think I may have made a mistake." He nodded and waited for her to continue. "This might sound a little strange. But I don't know what you're up to. I don't really care. But I really like Adrian. I do. I wouldn't bother with him if I didn't." Winston didn't flinch. "Adrian's real name isn't Adrian...is it?"

The detective's gaze never left hers. "That's an interesting thought. What would bring you to that conclusion?"

"Well that stems from the mistake I made."

The side of Winston's mouth curved upward, "You mean the mistake wasn't in dating him, it was something else. You're an interesting woman, Miss Kingsley. What happened?"

She straightened her skirt. "Detective, are you aware that there is a reporter who's working on a project about you? A Jim Valechy?"

"I've heard some talk here and there."

"Well, he caught up with me. And if I'd known that Adrian was a secret I never would have mentioned him."

Winston's expression never changed but she thought she could see the color seep out of his face. It took him just a few seconds to ask the inevitable question. "What did you say?" After she had relayed the course of their clipped conversation, Winston's shoulders seemed a little more tense and he ran a hand through his short mostly gray hair. "I can't thank you enough for telling me this."

"I just didn't want something I did to ruin your plan. I know there's a plan, I'm just not in on it. And I don't want anything bad to happen to Adrian."

Winston was quiet. He looked down at the floor for a small time and then looked back up at her. In a very quiet tone he said, "He's not the marrying type, you know."

"I don't think I'm interested in that right now, detective. Right now I don't even know who he is. Where he came from. How he fits into the whole scheme. I mean...did you hire him to help you? Is that what he means when he says he's a consultant?" She smiled at herself. It was a little funny at least. "He's not your friend. Where did you find him?"

She watched as Winston's eyes flitted over to one corner of the office, staying there for just a few moments before they went back to the floor again and then to her. He hadn't meant to look over there. An involuntary movement associated with the thought of him. Her head turned. That corner was covered in maps, photographs, and little notes along with push pins scrawled in blue pen. She got up from the swivel chair.

"Miss Kingsley," he said, "You shouldn't. He's...he's more than that."

She was already to the corner. She had already seen the dark shades of blood in the photographs. She studied them. In the back of her mind a voice reminded her that these people had names. They had once had thoughts and feelings and even people who loved them very much. *I like to...paint. But. Mostly splatter paint.* These torn up people. "He did this?" It was a rhetorical question. "How did he...?"

"It doesn't matter," Winston insisted. "He's more than just his impulses. He's helping me find the killer. The person who killed your uncle. It's a deal we have. He's hardly dangerous. Especially not to you or your family."

Hardly dangerous? He's a monster. Her mind was reeling with this information. Her knees felt weak but she remained standing in front of those photographs. She couldn't possibly soak this all in. She couldn't possibly contain this information without losing her mind from it. The thing about being financially well-off was that it was easy for one to ignore anything that put a strain on the conscience. Anything that was stressful could simply be swept under the rug and forgotten. Poverty. Politics. Anything. But she couldn't ignore something that was so blatantly staring her in the face. She couldn't ignore something that put chills through her spine and a squirm in her gut. This was Adrian. The real Adrian. Winston couldn't even go to the trouble of denying it. Only explaining that he was *hardly dangerous.* Was *this* what he meant by *hardly dangerous?* The deep reds in the photographs. The splattering and pooling and smearing of sanguine color made it much too real.

She couldn't bear to imagine this. The way Adrian would have moved in order to do this. Her fingers touched one of the photos. It was of a crime scene in a basement. There was no face. A close-up of a wound was all it was. A wound that was so obviously made by something she didn't want to think about.

Teeth.

Not a knife or a gun or even something unplanned like a lamp or a sharpened stick or a fireplace poker or...or anything else in the whole damn world.

Fucking TEETH.

She couldn't pretend to be okay anymore. She was shaking. Trembling with such vigor that she had to turn around. The way Winston was looking at her made her fear even more tangible. Because the expression in his hazel eyes was enough for her to know that this really wasn't an elaborate joke. This was the real and true story about Adrian and this was how Winston knew him. A consultant. A consultant on murder and how to get away with it. Her hand unconsciously went to her mouth and her fingertips curled against her lips.

A vague thought that this may have been the strangest day of her life was nagging at her. The day where she found out that the man who she'd been spending her time with was actually the Boogeyman. The Wolf. The true Darkness in this world.

The detective implored her. "This is how it has to be, Miss Kingsley. He's going to help you. You and your family. You have to believe me."

She felt the tears in her eyes, hot and frustrating. "He's...not dangerous? How can you...how can you *say* that?"

"He hasn't lied to you. I'm the only one who's done that. If anyone is dangerous, it's me. He wouldn't be involved with you or your family if I hadn't brought him to you. I'm the one who's dangerous." Winston put a hand to his head. "This is a very delicate situation, Miss Kingsley and I ask, no I *beg* for your discretion."

She ignored him. "All this time I thought he maybe could..."

"He's a serial killer, Miss Kingsley. He can't love you. And since you know now, I won't feel so awkward in telling you to not fall in love with him. That would be a very stupid thing to do." He was staring at her. Waiting for her response. Waiting for her to tell him to fuck off and die and to never speak to her again. That really *was* what she thought of doing. It would have been very right of her to do so. But it wasn't Winston's fault even if he said that it was.

It was Adrian's. And hers. Winston had been entirely averse to their first date. She hadn't forgotten the anger in his tone when Adrian had first asked her out on a date. He'd been trying to protect her from this—from the truth and from being hurt. Not physically. She really believed the man wouldn't harm her. But emotionally. A broken heart?

She wondered how many broken families and broken hearts Adrian had produced. He was a factory for the things. Murder. Mayhem. Disorder. Romance?

She took in a shuddering breath and sat down again in the swivel chair. She was still staring directly at the private detective. She could barely breathe past the lump in her throat. She couldn't speak properly. There was too much worry in her mind. Too much that was wrong with her life at this point.

Her nearly-boyfriend was a serial murderer. The very thing she feared most. That was what he was when she'd thought that he was a little bit more *something*. Brutal. She shook her head, wide-eyed and terrified.

Winston sighed. "Miss Kingsley. You liked him. I know you did. He can't love you. But he *can* help you. He's a human being. You have to understand that right now. He's only a human being. He can't grow a second head, he can't unhinge his jaw to swallow you whole, and he can't transform into a werewolf. He's only a man. He's vulnerable, he's weak, and he's into you. You hold all the power in your relationship with him. It only goes as far as you want it to." He put his thumb and forefinger on the bridge of his nose and closed his eyes. "Please take him to this wedding with you. If for nothing else, to help find this killer. You can even tell him that you know and just keep up appearances. He'll understand. I promise you. Just play along with us and understand that he's more than just his impulses. He's more than just a murderer. He's very much more."

She brought her hand down from her mouth.

"No."

Winston opened his eyes and moved his hand. "No?"

"I don't want him to know that I know. I'll take him to the wedding but he can't know that I know. I don't...I don't want him to act different. I want him to be Adrian. I don't want to think about any of this. I want to pretend..." She tried to breathe normally and found herself failing. "I want...to pretend I never saw any of this."

Winston's lips were thin and tight shut for a small time while she looked at him. He was considering this. When he spoke, it was in a low tone. "I think I made him slightly angry yesterday. He hasn't been back at my place. If you'd like to look for him, he's probably at the park. Thank you, Miss Kingsley. Give us a chance. We won't let you down."

CHAPTER 12

A dense fog was rolling down the Potomac and soon it would be covering the park. The late afternoon sun would bounce off of its foggy particles in droplets of light, creating little tiny rainbows and an ethereal appearance to the environment. She walked along the fence that separated the river from the green space and looked around at the sparse number of people who were walking. Most people were at work contemplating going home. She was here. Contemplating him.

She had called their driver for a ride and while she was in the back seat, she had pulled up her mobile network and had looked up the term "serial killer" on Wikipedia. The results were less than satisfactory. She had more questions about him than she had answers. Had he been sexually abused? She knew already that his family was rather unstable, which she learned was typical of serial killers. But the other things mentioned...necrophilia, sadism. She wondered about the other killers she had read about. Those who had blended in with society until chance encounters had suddenly exposed them to the outside world. Could Adrian...blend? Winston had told her that there was no reason to be scared of him—that he was harmless to her and her family. Was that true? Could there ever be a time when she wouldn't feel as though she were threatened by his very existence? The cold reality was stifling her. This whole time, there had been no face for the fear and the dread that she felt and there it was, in front of her. Adrian. The man who'd touched her thigh under the patio table and made her feel such wondrous and forbidden things. The man who made her feel wanted and warm in her stomach.

She tried to remember the way he had looked at her family. Did he plan to murder her brother, her father? No. Of course not. Shannon, she thought, calm down. Adrian wouldn't kill anybody.

That was wrong. Adrian *had* killed. Innocent people. People who had families and children and jobs and read books just like she did. Tears started to pool in her eyes while she looked at the river and touched the fence with her fingertips. Was *Adrian* just a mask? A mask that he'd placed on himself for her? Some kind of "mask of sanity" that was some psychologist's idea of his playing pretend with her and the rest of society? Or was Winston right?

Was he more than his impulses? Was *Adrian* the dominant part of him and the demon inside a rarity?

She let two tears go and then wiped her eyes with the back of her hand. She walked a little bit further and then saw him. It was too far away to know for sure that it was him, but she knew it was. It was in the way he sat, with his forearms on the tops of his thighs and his back bent forward in an arch, his attention focused on the waters of the river. She wondered for a moment, as she approached, what *he* was contemplating. Something deeper than what she could see on the surface of his being? Something more than what Adrian—the lie—would think? Maybe how he could hold himself in. Hold himself back.

She breathed deep to gather her courage. She could smell the tang of the river and the moisture in the air from the oncoming fog. It would surround them. It would make the world into a distorted image. A too-white photograph. A scene from a horror film. And she would be face-to-face with its antagonist.

No.

That was wrong too.

"Hey stranger," she heard herself say with stunning earnest. He turned his head with wide unassuming eyes, still lost in his thoughts. He had been completely unaware of his surroundings. Simply in tune with the environment and with his own mind. "Is this seat taken?" She gestured limply toward the bench he sat on and he looked at it for a few moments, still stunned by her very presence. He looked back up at her and almost appeared as if he were about to cry.

His voice was small. "No."

She sat delicately so as not to move the bench at all. He seemed a little fragile. He was dirty. His face smeared with clay-like soil and his bleached hair lack-luster as if it were covered in a fine coating of dust. His hands were in his lap and his fingers had dried mud on them as if he'd been digging with them. His clothes, a tight navy blue T-shirt, and jeans, had speckles of dried mud and dark spots of something that looked like ink in small sprays. One across the collarbone on his shirt and the other a smattering on his jeans around his right hip. She swiped her hands across the tops of her thighs to smooth any wrinkles out of her skirt before she addressed him again. "I'm glad I found you. I missed you."

He didn't answer right away but he did look at her still. "You. You missed me?" His voice was soft. He sounded confused. He sounded like he didn't know what to do or say. He hadn't thought this encounter through. He hadn't planned what he would say to her. How she would respond. This wasn't part of some kind of scheme. She'd caught him out in the cold.

"Well you know. Us women folk. We're so delicate." She reached into her purse and found her chapstick, applying it easily. "I really love this park. It's such a nice place to think."

He suddenly became self-aware and looked at his hands, becoming fidgety and sitting up straight. "I um. I need to...take a shower. I'm not. I'm not exactly..."

"No worries. You look like you did some gardening. Mother was always good at that kind of thing. Not me though. It'd be nice to have a garden that one could look at and be proud of but I've got what mother calls a 'black thumb'. I think that means I'm a blight on the gardening community. Some of them even act like it might be contagious." She smiled despite the rapid beating of her heart. "I hope it is."

She was trying not to panic. She was trying to make it sound natural, the way she was speaking and the way she was interacting with him. *Hardly dangerous*, her mind echoed. He certainly didn't seem dangerous. Not with the way he was right now. Winston's words of his weakness and his vulnerability were apparent here in the softness of his voice and the way he held his body. He was unassuming and small.

He turned his attention out toward the fog that was steadily rolling down the river toward them. It would be upon them any minute. A type of Armageddon that Shannon was willingly looking forward to. An erasure of the present and the moment and the setting that could, perhaps, calm the errant thoughts that weighed down on her mind. The way he was acting was also a sort of comfort to her—and yet that worried her as well.

"What's got you down, Adrian?" she asked, leaning forward and then toward him. She wanted to reach out and touch him. Feel the warmth of his vitality through his shirt. Convince herself that he was human again. He seemed it. So very lost. So very defenseless. So very distinctly human that she could almost cry with it. But she couldn't feel his warmth. Couldn't feel the blood that pulsed inside him. Couldn't visualize his body as a functioning organism. She had to touch him for that. Touch the softness of his skin and the lean hard muscle underneath.

He's more than just his impulses.

"It's nothing."

"It's never nothing." She felt herself grin. He glanced at her and his eyes lingered on her mouth, curved upward at one side.

He sighed, a long exhale. "I'm just reliving things. Things I thought were gone. You know. That videotape that rewinds while you're doing your shit during the day but right at the end of the day, sometimes when you're laying down to sleep, it replays. All the things that you've done wrong. Everything that's escaped you and you can never get back."

It was a baring of his soul in vague terms that could be construed to mean anything. She applied it to what she knew of him. The bodies. The murders. Things he'd done wrong. So very, very wrong. But in a way, he hadn't revealed anything about himself in that statement. He hadn't really told her anything useful at all. "I think I know what you mean. Sometimes in the middle of the night I'll go down to the drawing room and I'll stare into the fireplace. It's easy for me to regret doing nothing at all. I suppose normal people regret things that they've done. I tend to regret a lack of doing. I think that's normal."

"Is anything about you abnormal?" He asked the question with satire in his tone. Hidden within it. As if he didn't really mean to tease.

"I sleepwalk. I have terrifying dreams where I'm being chased in the woods by something. Or someone. I think someone. They mean me harm."

He lifted his hand with the clear intent to touch hers but faltered. Probably because of the dirt. She grasped it firmly and held it beside her on the bench, the gritty feeling of the dirt on her fingers a texture that reminded her of his reality. He was warm and she could feel the blood and tendons and muscle under the flesh of his hand. She watched his cheeks under streaks of mud take on a pinker hue. He spoke. "Where do you go when you walk?"

"One time I made it all the way to the front door when Sean stopped me."

He squeezed her fingers and her heart raced with both fear and an alarming sense of affection. The kind she used to feel with him. "You really love your brother."

"I don't know what I'd do without him."

There was a small pause and the fog finally overtook them, giving the world around them the predictable sleepy, muffled quality that she had been eagerly anticipating. It brought with it a small chill but not bad enough for a decent shiver. It was still a warm day. The slight breeze rustled the leaves on a nearby dogwood tree and she shifted a little.

His next words were careful and slow. "I'm not who you think I am."

"I know."

They sat in silence together with their hands linked in a firm grip. They watched the mist undulate over the waters of the river and swirl around them with tiny rainbows and wispy edges.

His voice was almost nothing but a whisper.

"I'm sorry."

She felt tears.

"Don't be."

A quiet jingle interrupted them and he reached into his pocket with his free hand, flipping the little pre-paid phone open and answering it with a drawling "Yell-oh?" There was a long time where Adrian didn't say anything at all. He just listened. She could sort-of hear the voice on the other end of the phone line. Cordial, demanding, it had to be Detective Winston. Who else could it be? When Adrian spoke, it was with a calm that filled her with dread. "Okay. Do you want me to take her home?" Another pause. She could feel her face drain and she suddenly felt cold. "Your place then. You gonna come home? I need to know things." He looked at their hands and licked his lips. "Tell them she's at yours. Safest place in D.C." It was the end of the conversation. He didn't even say good-bye. He flipped the phone shut and gave another sigh. This one rattled her to her core.

"Winston? What did he say?" Fear churned in her stomach. Adrian's expression was almost doll-like. Void of all emotion. Her lower jaw started shuddering in fear.

"I need to take you back to his place. There's been another murder."

"Winston. I forgot you were on this case. Oh wait. That's right. Nobody can forget it." The words spilled from the lips of the 46-year-old balding chief like acid out of a waterspout. There was no doubt a little animosity had cropped up between the police department and Winston's private detective agency. Considering the crime solving of the rich and famous was now generally done by their own personal detectives, the police had every right to be peeved.

"Just let me know when you're done, Blaze, I won't get in your way." He lit up a Marlboro and puffed on it while he watched the older man snort and hobble on his sore ankles back toward the crime scene. It was on the second floor of a rather large house with a winding staircase and cherry hard wood flooring. The accents on the banister were silver-looking but Winston was almost certain that they were in fact white gold. It would reduce the risk of tarnishing and betray the worth of the family. They were extremely wealthy. Of course, Winston hadn't missed that the victim had only a short time ago had contact with him. He dragged on the cigarette deep and let it out through his nose, relishing the burn.

Ben had been just about to take a shower after having worked out in the family's personal gym. He was covered in his own sweat and his own blood. Winston had already had a peek at the crime scene but for now he was banished outside to the front yard like a bad pup. He watched police come and go. He nodded at the medical examiner, Hayden Myers, when she walked up the front walk.

"Trent," she bubbled, "why aren't you bulling in there? Aren't you getting the big bucks for this?"

"I got a peek at it. No worries. I'll be talking to you later about it too."

If he wasn't mistaken he could have sworn the M.E. actually blushed when he said it. He watched her walk into the house with her bag slung over her shoulder and took another drag on his Marlboro. The air was warm but a dense fog had descended over this part of the city. The murder had not been too long ago. Just an hour maybe. He took a few steps back from the house and examined the window to the room with the crime scene. It was open. The roof was above it, the shingles pitch black. Winston squinted through the fog. There was an imperfection on the roof next to where the large brick chimney came jutting out of the top of the mansion. A lightness. He couldn't see it properly through the fog. He filed it away in his mind for later reference as Blaze once again emerged from the house, panting as if he'd gone on some two mile run.

"What you got, Blaze?" he asked with his cigarette bobbing on his bottom lip.

"I don't like you, Winston."

"Don't care. Out with it."

The older police chief sighed and put his hands behind him, two fingers from each tucking themselves under his belt. It was his classic stance that allowed his blazer to pull back and reveal his gun. Winston wondered if they were supposed to be comparing sizes. "Twenty-four year old Benjamin Withers, multiple stab wounds to the chest and abdomen, three of them possibly fatal. He was cut with five or six parallel lines across the forehead, antemortem. There's a lot of blood up there."

"Anything weird?"

"Other than five or six parallel lines on his forehead?" Blaze lifted his ample eyebrows. "There were some markings on the window sill. Mud. But it doesn't seem to go anywhere into the room. Just on the outside sill. It seemed a little out of place with the way the room was spotless." He shrugged as if he wasn't sure if Winston would follow his train of thought. "Got any ideas for motive?"

"I do, actually," he surprised himself. "He came to me the other day and talked to me in a Chinese restaurant. Wanted to tell me that one or two of his alibis were bullshit before it got out some other way."

"And you didn't tell me because?" Blaze was growling.

"I didn't know he was going to keep it from you. He expressed a fear of the police department. I hope he didn't think that *I'm* one of *your* dogs. He could have. Would have made for an interesting investigation." Winston chuckled.

"You know full well that he hadn't told us anything. Ya fucker."

Winston offered him a cigarette and after a slight pause the Chief accepted it and allowed Winston to light it for him. "Blaze, there's one thing I don't understand."

"What's that, kid?"

"If he was out for revenge. For Ben giving away his alibis as false. Then wouldn't the killer have to have had his own alibi with Ben? He would be giving himself away if he killed Ben. It would narrow the list of suspects considerably. It would give a lead that's too huge to ignore." He licked his lips. "I'm starting to think that this killer is a little dumber or a little smarter than previously thought. Are we looking at the smaller range of people, or the larger?"

Blaze slowly let out a little bit of smoke and grunted. "Kid. You always make these things harder than they have to be."

"And yet I'm the one with more serial killers under my belt." He raised one brow toward the Detective before turning around. "Can I look at the scene now?"

"Knock yourself out."

It smelled heavily of blood inside the large room. There was a four poster bed and a few large overstuffed chairs. A desk in the corner, a table by the bed, clothes laid out on the bedspread, his shoes kicked off near the door. He was lying on the floor face down, his feet toward the door, his arms cocked at strange angles from his body. His head pointed toward the open window. Hayden was just packing up her bag and the crime scene guys were taking all their evidence.

"Trent," Hayden smiled. "Poor guy tried to fight but it looks like the killer snuck up on him. Probably wrapped an arm around him and stabbed him from behind. He wasn't dead before the cuts were made. Must have been just awful. What a way to go." She tsked a little and shook her head back and forth. The girl was positively unfazed by death and gloom.

He observed the body and the surroundings. Blaze was right. No mud anywhere in the room, but a clump of it on the outside window sill. As if someone had scraped the bottom of their shoe on the sill to remove it. He turned abruptly.

Hayden called out. "Trent, where are you going?"

"To the attic if I can find it. There has to be a roof access."

"The roof?" She was befuddled. "Why would you want to get on the roof?"

He smiled at her and simply shook his head, leaving her baffled. He then preceded to open doors, closing them when he realized that they were merely closets and swinging open more. He finally got to the one heavy door that held behind it a winding staircase that wasn't anything if it wasn't ominous. He climbed the steps carefully and drew his gun, holding it down toward the stairs with his finger on the safety. Just in case. The attic was filled with boxes of things and smelled of dust and age. Papers, books, music sheets, and old cardboard littered the corners as little strands of dirty sunlight fell through sky lights high in the ceiling. There was a ladder built into one of the wooden walls, the splintered wood old and worn. Winston made his way over to it, keeping his eyes on the rest of the attic as he went. There were plenty of crannies.

He inspected the wood and determined that he didn't think anyone had come this way. Up or down. He put one hand out and gripped and found himself climbing. The roof access was a slanted trap door that opened outward and he pushed it easily out, finding himself on the back end of the house. The fog swirled around him, thicker now than it was before. The shingles were gritty and traction was plenty. He didn't have a hard time walking the roof at all. Nobody noticed him. None of the uniforms down on the ground even bothered to look up. He watched his footing carefully and investigated the roof for the imperfections he'd noticed earlier. It wasn't hard to find them. Foot prints. Made in mud. He knelt by one and scraped some up into a bag which he slipped into his pocket.

Then he looked harder. Not full footprints. Only half prints. As if they walked on their toes and the balls of their feet. A thought flashed into Winston's mind and suddenly rage filled him. He had to breathe deeply in order to quench it.

Worn treads. Almost none at all. About a size thirteen, he would guess.

CHAPTER 13

He slammed into his apartment with heavy steps and paused when he saw her at his kitchen table. The snarl that had disfigured his lips and bared his teeth abated when she looked up with those big green eyes and she smiled at him with a faint sort of warmth. He had forgotten how it felt to have a woman in his apartment that greeted him. Of course Shannon Kingsley wasn't there for him. And what she said next was hardly "Welcome home, darling, I made you tea and your favorite pot roast."

Instead, she was much more brutal. "Why do they always put the redheaded girls with the African American men? I mean. Is it the contrast they want? I don't understand."

His mouth opened slightly when he saw the *Penthouse Letters* open on the table in front of her. She was perusing it with a careful attitude and a curious expression. He wasn't sure what to say to her. In fact, he thought he might be dreaming. Perhaps if he simply walked out of the apartment and walked back in again, it would all be different. He turned around and left. He waited about five seconds in the stale hallway air and then walked back in. Shannon was staring at him blankly, still sitting at his table, still with her fingers on a page of *Penthouse*. A blonde was eating out a brunette. They were both naked save diamond necklaces and four or five inch heels. Why wasn't Shannon's face as red as a beet?

"I was hoping," he started, "that you were a dream. That I would wake up. But no. You're here. You're...doing what I thought you were doing." He sighed. "I don't know why they put gingerbait with the black guys. It's just...a known rule. I won't even bother to ask where you found that. I know where it was. Where's Ren?"

"Ren?"

"Adrian."

"Oh." This time her cheeks turned pink and her tone was doleful. "He's in the shower."

"Where are his shoes?"

"By the door."

With that, he said no more. He simply spotted the busted up Toms and picked them up, examining the dried mud on them carefully before renewing his rage. He thought about bursting into the bathroom with a good kick to the door and punching the bastard square in the nose but thought better of it when he heard another shiff of paper on paper and realized that Shannon was still in the apartment. Still looking at a porno 'zine with wide eyes.

He looked out his window at the fog which had grown a strange deep grayish orange color with the fading light of sunset. He rubbed his eyes with his fingers and groaned. "Tell me about Ben Withers."

"Ben?" she smiled. "He's a rather nice fellow. Kind of low-key I would say. That's the right word. Of all my brother's friends he's most definitely the strongest. He's the most athletic you see. He won trophies in polo before. Very good with a mallet." She nodded to herself. "He's also very cautious I should think. And he's never really been much of a team player I have to admit. Has to be the star."

Winston bubbled his cheeks out and then let out the air that was trapped in them in a burst.

Shannon frowned. "Why would you ask me about Ben? Is..." she stopped. So did the shower. Her little delicate hand started to tremble on the page of the magazine. "Is...he...?" her voice wavered and Winston could see the moisture start to gather in her eyes. Color started to fill her cheeks.

Winston pulled out one of the kitchen chairs and sat next to her, putting his hand on her elbow when she turned to face him more. "Miss Kingsley, I'm sorry."

"Oh my god." It came out like a whisper and she covered her mouth with her hands. It was like someone had turned her personal waterworks on. Tears streamed from her eyes and sobs racked her bird-boned shoulders. She rattled so hard he thought she might come apart.

Ren sauntered into the kitchen with wet spiked hair, wearing a clean Georgetown University T-shirt and Scooby Doo boxer shorts. He immediately went to her, scraping another chair across the linoleum as he sat on her other side and gathered her into his arms. Winston had never seen such a tender expression from him and watched them with a kind of dumb awe while Ren petted her hair and shushed her very quietly. It tugged at his chest. That Ren could even be capable of something like a tender touch. He watched the killer smooth Shannon's hair and his thumb brush the soft flesh under her eye to rid it of her tears. He kissed the side of her head while her face was buried in the nook between his shoulder and his chest. Her hands had balled in the fabric of the clean T-shirt that had actually belonged to a younger Winston what seemed like a long time ago.

Grace had wept into that same T-shirt. He could feel the weight of her again on his shoulder. The way her blonde hair had tumbled over his back while she cried. The warmth of her tears as they soaked into the fabric and then the coolness when he'd gotten her calmed and laid down and settled. The way her watery eyes had looked at him without a single negative thought when he'd brought her chamomile and put it on the coffee table in front of her. He'd leaned on the edge of the couch while she sipped it, reading to her from *The Great Gatsby*. What a strange relationship. He frowned to himself as his eyes unfocused. What an odd sort of love. If that's what it was in the first place.

Ren murmured something to her that Winston didn't quite catch, but Shannon had and she nodded. Ren, in one fluid movement, stood and picked her up in his arms as if she weighed no more than a feather. He walked her over to the couch and laid her down upon it and pulled Winston's afghan over her and petted her hair, speaking softly to her. "We'll deal with it in the mornin', sweets. Can't solve anything now."

He could hear her little sniffle and the faintest sound when Ren kissed her head and returned to the table, shuffling in his bare feet. He was glaring at Winston.

"Bedroom. Now," the detective mumbled.

As soon as the door had clicked shut Ren spoke. "Could you *be* more callous?"

"Standard questions. I needed to know."

"You could have asked *anybody else* and yet you chose her. Why? Because you're a fucking dick, that's why." His voice was kept low. He was mindful of her. Careful. "I know why you live alone. I know why you only have Avery. I know why you're friendless, *Trent*." It was the first time Ren had ever used his true first name. "Because you're a fucking asshole."

Winston was unmoved and he lifted a brow. "Tell me what you were doing on Ben Withers's roof today."

Ren wasn't looking at him. He was staring at the drawers in Winston's nightstand. He swallowed once and then a dark smirk spread across his face. "I should have known you'd know it was me."

"You didn't kill him."

"Didn't I?"

"Don't lie to me, Ren. You were never in the house."

The smirk died. "Fine. Since you know me so well, what do you think I was doing there?"

"Don't play with me." The words came out of his mouth like a hiss. "You might think that there's nothing wrong with pushing little Winnie's boundaries but I'm about five seconds away from breaking your goddamn nose again."

Ren gave him an appraising stare, all humor gone from his face. "I was out and about, you know. Things I normally do. Saw the group of guys leaving a bar downtown. It was such a small place. Nothing fancy. They were dressed well and I realized that it was Shannon's gaggle of men. There was only one I didn't know so I followed him when he split from the group. I thought he was rather interesting. So I followed him to his house."

"And you were on the roof because?"

"Well, I had to go around his house to not be spotted by him or anybody else. That's how I got so muddy. They'd had sprinklers on in the garden and I managed to get myself covered in mud. And I just climbed onto the roof. It seemed like the best way to get a peek into the house. It turned out that it was, by the way. He's got a sister you know."

Winston's lip curled. "She's fifteen."

Ren's face contorted into disgust. "It doesn't count if I didn't know, right?"

He rolled his eyes and sighed, "Just tell me what you saw when you got to Ben's room."

"It took a little while. He was doing his little gym thing, the guy spent *forever* in that stupid gym. Of course, his sister was doing pilates in her room." Ren winked at him conspiratorially. "When I found his room, there wasn't much to report. It was a typical room. From the window, I couldn't see if anyone was hiding in there, if that's what you're going for."

"You were on the roof or next to the window when the murder occurred."

"How do you know I wasn't staring at some fifteen year old's fine ass? She did have a fine ass. I'm sorry I don't have a picture phone since Mr. Stingy wouldn't spring for one."

Winston paced the room, fingering open the blinds to peer outside but couldn't see anything through the dense fog. "I know you weren't because that's not how you are."

"I didn't see anything."

"I think you're lying."

"I think you're a faggot. So I guess we're even." Ren moved toward Winston's bed which he casually rolled onto, lying on his stomach with his face in the pillow. His voice was muffled until he turned his head to the side. "Your smell is all over this bed."

"I sleep there." He took the pack of Marlboros out of his pocket and inspected the last three before taking one out and rolling it in between his fingers. Ren knew something. He just simply wasn't telling. There was a reason for it. He wouldn't keep it from Winston unless he had a true reason for doing so. So what was his motive? To make him beg? He wouldn't do it. They would stick with the original plan. Whatever Ren knew could wait. Even if he knew who the killer was. Winston was trying to be patient. Trying to bide his time. Yet with a reporter breathing down his neck and now curious as to whom exactly Adrian Woods was...this patience thing was already wearing out. "Tell me more about the story today. The one that ends when you're at the park."

"There's nothing left to tell."

"You're not the hero, huh?"

Ren was quiet.

"Why don't you tell me more about when you died?"

"That's going to take a cigarette break."

They were tucked against the side of the apartment building, Ren sitting on an old railing with his feet up under him, settled against the bottom rail easily like he'd balanced this way a thousand times before. He nursed his Camel with a contemplative stare at the night's heavy fog. It had brought with it an odd chill that reminded Winston of the cold winter days that lay ahead.

"You died," Winston reminded him.

"I died." He let out his drag, the smoke curling and getting lost in the fog. "Just for maybe a minute. But I did die. I know I did. Because nothing hurt anymore. There was no pain. No fear. Nothing. There was just brightness. Like when you faint and those crazy lights start to cloud out your vision. Well it was like that. And white. Very, very white."

"But you came back."

"It was so unfortunate. And I didn't even gain any superpowers. I can't even hear the voice of God."

Winston grinned. "Would you like to hear the voice of God?"

"No." Ren scraped the bottom of his shoe on the rusted metal of the rail. "I already know what he'd say in any case."

"What's that?"

"Nothing," he mumbled, looking down at the dirt. "He wouldn't say a goddamn thing. Even if I could hear him."

He stared at the killer intently. "Why do you think that?"

Ren grinned, "Because people like me are why God doesn't talk to us anymore."

"What'd you do after you came back?"

"Built a fire. Found blankets and pillows. They were kinda moldy and rotten but they were good enough for me. I holed up in that place in front of the fireplace for a while before I felt good enough to explore. Found some canned foods still left in the kitchen that weren't infested with botulism and ate those. The basement had books in it. Started reading."

"Do you like to be alone, Ren?" he asked. He didn't know where the question came from.

"Yes. No. I don't know." He scratched the side of his head.

Winston's lips thinned. "You know who the killer is."

Ren didn't respond. "You're not going to tell me." He sucked in air through his nose as if that could quell the deep rage that burned in his belly and constricted his chest. He could kill him. The anger that roiled inside his chest was almost numbing. He couldn't feel his hands. For a few panicked seconds before he took another breath, he was sure that he could lose control. That he could simply fight Ren. To the death. On cold pavement in a dense fog. The air made a whistling sound through his gritted teeth and he pressed his palm over his heart in an attempt to calm it. He could *kill* him. His voice was strained when he spoke again. "You're...not going to tell me. You're...not..."

Ren blinked at him lazily. "Gonna have a heart attack, Winnie?"

Winston coughed and gripped the upper rail to steady himself. "I'm...going to kill you."

"You can't kill me. You're too angry for that. You're better as a cold, calculating bastard. You couldn't kill out of pure rage." His lips spread back to reveal what seemed like a thousand teeth. "You're not allowed to do that."

"I'll do whatever I want." He made a jerky motion toward the killer.

Ren leaped from his perch and onto the pavement, shuffling backward and popping his cigarette into his mouth before lifting up his hands in preparation for a physical altercation. His speech was impaired by his Camel. "Come at me, brah."

Yet Winston couldn't. He simply stared at him. The anger in his chest made it too hard to breathe. The potential for harm made his body thrum with energy but he couldn't seem to take a single step forward. "Fuck you." He flicked the rest of his Marlboro at him, sparks dancing from the tip when it hit the wet ground at Ren's feet. "Don't tell me."

Ren backed away a few more steps.

Winston mumbled as he turned around toward the street. "You're still going to that wedding."

When he made it back to his apartment, he was mindful to shut the door quietly and lock it behind him. Ren would come in through the window. He thought about locking that too but when his gaze found the delicate sleeping beauty on his couch he decided against it. She would look for him. She would look for her protector. Her dog. Even if she knew what he really was, she did still need him. She still needed his strength and his presence. Even if she was afraid, Ren would show her that her fear was for nothing. Her hair was splayed out over the couch cushion, her cheeks still shiny from her tears. God knew what kind of pain they would put her through. If she If that reporter put his nose where it didn't belong.

He pushed his way into his bedroom and fell face-forward on his bed. It smelled very faintly of Ren. He fell asleep that way and left the door open. When he woke there was light falling in through the window, the white of it reflecting in contemplative dark blue eyes. He stared into them for a while, trying to make some kind of connection with the soul that lay beneath them. There was nothing. They were blank.

Ren murmured without breaking eye contact. "You left your door unlocked."

Winston didn't respond.

"Are you still going to kill me? If you choke me now, I won't fight."

He didn't respond to that either.

Ren continued to hold Winston's gaze and they silently laid there for longer than Winston would ever care to admit. At least five minutes.

Maybe more. It was broken by Ren, whose eyes suddenly flitted to one side and his head tilted up. "My girl's awake. What's for breakfast?"

Winston closed his eyes again and mumbled, "Whatever you want to make me."

CHAPTER 14

"Where were you last night?" her mother whispered with a conspiratorial wink above her large bug-like Gucci shades. "You never came home. Sean was worried."

Shannon gave a weary smile. "Sean should be worried. Of course, I see how worried he is today since I'm back and he's just fawning all over me asking me what bad man made me stay out all night." She rolled her eyes a little. Sean was off with his friends mourning the loss of Ben by attempting to formulate a fundraiser to help pay Winston's detective bill. Nobody was truly worried that the youngest Kingsley had stayed out all night without calling to let them know where she was. In fact, her mother was just tittering on about how she didn't know that Shannon even had it in her to be adventurous or, did she dare think it—scandalous?

"Nothing interesting happened." She shivered, a sudden chill sweeping over her. She looked over her shoulder at the garden behind her and thought perhaps she could have seen a sliver of movement in the shadow of a small maple. She blinked and it was gone. "What a terrifying thing. To happen so close to Sean. He must be distraught." It wasn't what she was talking about. The terrifying thing was more than just Ben's death. It was Adrian as well. But nobody could know.

Mother nodded and her expression turned serious. "He's almost as upset as your father is about this whole murder business. Of course, now he's off trying to fund that detective's efforts. They're all so intense about the whole thing now." She managed to get her little grin back. "Did he comfort you when you cried?"

"Mother, Ben is dead." She wasn't mad at her. Not really. She was more mortified at herself at feeling the way she did about the way Adrian had picked her up and carried her to the couch. The whisperings of comfort and affection that he'd sprinkled over her after she'd found out about the death of her friend. He was more than just his impulses. He was human. He had the capacity to comfort.

Her mother fanned herself with her napkin and leaned back in her chair. "That doesn't mean that your sex life also has to die. Not that you really have one. I can't wait until you finally lose your virginity so we can talk about more interesting things." She pouted a little and then smiled, "Speaking of your virginity, how is Adrian these days?"

"Mother," she warned. The very idea of Adrian as a sexual being had flown from her brain after she'd found him to be a monster. Now, her own mother was throwing it back in her face. They couldn't know what had happened to her or what Adrian really was. It was only normal for her mother to be interested in setting the two of them up to give Shannon a chance to bloom. But the man wasn't what they thought.

"He's cute you know. Very cute. Very sexy. Do you realize how depressed I was when you came back and you were still some fresh-faced girl?"

"I haven't known him for that long." And now that I do...

"And yet he was the person who held you when you needed someone. Weren't you with Detective Winston too? What'd he do?"

Shannon tapped her finger on the patio table. A breeze ruffled her hair and she breathed in the crisp summer air. Winston was something else entirely. She didn't want to talk about him. All she could think about was Adrian. His bleached hair, his shining and yet blank blue eyes, and his gorgeous little smirk. Her face felt warm when she thought of his palm on her knee and the way his strong arms surrounded her when she cried. The smell of his neck and chest when she inhaled. The taste of her salty tears and the soft, sweet things he'd told her. It was enough for a romance novel. If only he weren't what he was.

"Oh, that look in your eyes is answer enough. Just give him what he wants, girl. He's not going to leave you as soon as you do. He's not the type."

"Mother, you don't know anything about him." The irony of that statement was killing her. She almost started to laugh but suppressed it. How could she say that when she didn't know anything about him either? Not even his real name. Winston had called him "Ren" but even that sounded like some kind of nickname. He was a killer. A serial murderer who killed people (presumably innocent people) in a brutal and heartless way. A messy way. Like an animal. She shivered again but it was so slight her mother didn't notice. Adrian...or Ren, or whoever he was, had held her gently and had smelled of soap and new things. He had created feelings inside her. But to give him her virginity? The thought made her blood cold.

He was a bad guy. A villain. Detached and devoid of morals and a human code that made people possess that little thing called humanity. That's how serial killers were. That's what she'd read. That's what everybody thought. They were sociopaths or psychopaths. They lied. They could mimic true emotions with ease. She tried to not frown in front of her mother. She tried to keep her face straight but she could feel her brows twitch. Adrian was a masquerader.

Her mother took a sip of her iced tea with mint and crossed her legs under the table. "Sometimes it just feels good to be bad." She'd said it so nonchalantly but it fit too well with the thoughts that were running through Shannon's head.

The photos came back to her. Swimming through her mind with perfect clarity. A picture of a man perhaps a few years older than she. On a dark gray concrete floor. His eyes were white. White. Gone. Lifeless. His mouth slack. His throat simply gone. Where he should have had a neck there was just a mass of red and brown. A jumbled mess of reds and pinks and she'd turned around before she'd had time to process that there was a tiny pinch of white peeking out from the shredded mess that had been this man's neck. That was his spine. She blinked and swallowed and then took a sip of her tea. It still didn't calm the butterflies in her belly. She was dating a man who could kill. She was also dating a killer who was working alongside a detective to find Ben's murderer. Because a killer could find a killer. Wasn't that right? Wasn't that the way things worked? But the question wouldn't stop coming up. Wouldn't stop floating through her mind like a bad smell. Why? Wasn't there always something behind it? Why did he do it? What was in his past that would make him need to kill? Why did he even want to?

A stronger breeze swept over the garden, fluttering the tablecloth and forcing the trees to whisper amongst themselves.

Sometimes it just feels good to be bad.

She was in her room crocheting when there was a soft rapping at the door. When she looked up, Sean had already eased his head through, the bells that he had attached to her doorknob jingling at his entry. His trademark smile had a little tilt at the sides. "Hey sugarpop," he said in a soft tone. "Can I come in?"

"What a question," she smiled, "Of course you can come in." She put down her work and patted the spot beside her on her bed. He slowly came in and sat down, his hands together on his lap.

He bit his bottom lip while she looked to him to start a conversation. It was obvious that he wasn't quite sure how to start so she took his hand. "I'm sorry," he said, "I've just been a little off since yesterday."

"That's completely understandable, Sean. I'm so sorry about what happened. How are the others taking it?"

"Oh, just like me, I guess. It's been pretty hard on all of us. There's not much we can do now that he's gone. We're going to have to try to put our faith in some detective Father hired and who knows anything about his credibility."

"Oh Sean," she sighed, "he's got a reputation. He'll find this guy." Or Adrian would. She gripped her brother's hand harder. "He's got a stake in it too, remember? His partner is still in the hospital because of this killer."

Sean suddenly frowned. "Mother said you were with him last night. That's why I didn't make such a fuss over it. I was terribly worried." He lifted a brow. "It's good you were with him though. I don't like some of these characters who've been hanging around. I'm alright with the detective and Adrian but just watch out. Today the five...I mean the four of us ran into a reporter who was asking funny questions about Detective Winston. We told him to fuck off but he doesn't seem like the type to stop just because we told him to. I don't want you to talk to him. I don't want you to be quoted in some kind of fucked up publication he's got for personal gain." The edges of Sean's voice had taken on a distinct tension. His eyebrow was twitching. "For some reason he's different from the rest."

Shannon laid her head on his shoulder and closed her eyes, breathing in the scent of his aftershave and the flowery soapy smell of detergent. They silently sat together for a few minutes, just breathing together. She loved him. His company. His presence near her. He was her protector. But he couldn't be forever. "I won't talk to him. I promise. He approached me the other day. I thought he was going to ask about the murder, but when he didn't I blew him off."

"He's a shady character and I don't like him. I already talked to the police about him and they said they'd look into it. I hope they give him hell." He gritted his teeth and suddenly burst with his anger, hitting his thigh with a hard fist. "Why can't this all just stop? This is madness. This is insanity. This is destroying our lives. Ben is gone." He squeezed her hand in return and put his other palm on his forehead. "How can anything normal happen ever again?"

She let go of his hand and wrapped her arms around him, squeezing him tight against her. She held him that way. She felt like a five year old trying to comfort an adult but she did it anyway. She couldn't not do it. She couldn't leave him in his grief. The sallow look of his face had shocked her. Ben's death had greatly pained him. The death of any of his friends would have done it. He was hurt and there was nothing she could do about it.

"Time," she whispered. "Time is what turns kittens into cats."

His hand cupped her shoulder and he turned his head far enough to kiss the top of her head. "What would I do without you, peach?" She could hear the crushing weight of grief and tears in his voice.

She squeezed him tighter. "Time heals all things. And I'll be with you the whole way."

He was quiet.

"Normal things will happen again. You'll see."

"What if..." he breathed in, "time just hurts?"

CHAPTER 15

He showed up at her door in a sleek suit, black with a black tie and shiny black shoes. She wondered if it was actually Winston's but it had a tailored appearance, every hem in the correct place and the fit of it absolutely perfect for his body. He had a pair of sunglasses perched on top of his head, a stark contrast against the artificial white of his hair.

"Come in, come in, come in." She pulled him by the sleeve of his suit into the foyer. "Everyone is getting ready. We're almost done. You've arrived just in time." She fretted a little over her hair in the hall mirror. There was always that one stray.

Sean tapped his way down the hall looking debonair in his tailor-made suit and his hair gelled into a style that was cute but subdued. That was the one contrast between her brother and Adrian: Their hair. While Sean's hair held the glossy tamed appearance of its true color and a trained shape, Adrian's was classically bad-boy with a blank white and tufts popping out this way and that almost as to make it look purposeful. Of course, that was only in outward appearance to the untrained eye.

Adrian held himself differently. While her brother and the other boys held themselves with their backs straight and their chins high—to indicate that they were the royal highnesses of any occasion—Adrian's back was just slightly slouched, his body language loose and informal, approachable she should think. Even his smile was devilish and lopsided. She considered them both for a few moments longer, Adrian studying her shoes while Sean was fiddling with his cufflinks.

"Well." She clapped her hands and they both looked at her. "You two just look so cute."

Adrian's crooked smile widened and Sean's brow popped up. Her brother was the first to comment. "Cute? I would hope to think that I could at least look better than 'cute.' I've heard that three out of the five bridesmaids are single and I for one am hoping to make use of one of those upstairs rooms at Harmsfield."

"Oh, don't be so crude," she snipped. "Adrian, you look simply adorable." She took a step toward him and straightened his tie while he lifted up his chin for her. When she took her hand away she couldn't help but touch her fingertips to his small goatee and smile at his chuckle. Her cheeks grew hot, so she took two steps backward to keep herself from his mouth. His teeth. And those damnable lips that she couldn't help but wonder about. Maybe the way they would have felt in a kiss? "Um," she tried, but her eyes flashed to her brother. He was smirking at her and his covert little wink did not escape her. "Father is driving us all in the Mercedes." It was a stupid thing to say. But it had to be said and Adrian just nodded to her and put his hands in his pockets.

She sat in the middle of the leather seat with Sean to her left, looking out the window and daydreaming she thought, and Adrian to her right. His hands were in his lap and he leaned over toward her and breathed into her ear very softly.

"You're beautiful."

She tightened her thighs. Two words. Two words and she had to tighten her thighs. The embarrassment was evident on her cheeks. Would she spend all of this time blushing and getting chills? Someone might think she had an illness if the man kept this up. She tried to will him to stop being both frightening and arousing at the same time, but she couldn't stop herself from stealing glances at him. She wondered if he felt the same kind of tension. The heaviness in the air between them as her mother and father chatted among themselves in the front of the car. Could he feel it? Could he feel anything at all?

She bit her bottom lip and held back a sudden rushing urge to cry. What if... What if he didn't feel anything at all? What if he didn't know he did these things to her? These horrible, wonderful disturbingly amazing things?

Before she could brood on it any longer, the car stopped and Sean opened his door. Adrian helped her out of the Benz and held her hand while they walked through the warm summer sun down the stone path to the stately manor her Aunt had affectionately dubbed Harmsfield. It was mostly constructed of old bricks salvaged from a defunct factory somewhere down south that had been dismantled systematically to retain the value of the materials. It had taken them three years to build and boasted over thirty bedrooms, close to twenty bathrooms, a ballroom, a billiard room, and countless other miscellaneous rooms. The kitchen was nearly as large as a small house in and of itself.

Mother turned around and walked backward, a feat in the three inch heels she was wearing. "The ceremony is going to be out back. We're going to cut through the house. Afterwards, I guess they're going to have the reception in the ballroom. Should be quite fun. I do like summer weddings. How about you, Adrian?"

He grinned at her, his eyes hidden under his shades. "I've got to admit, Mrs. Kingsley, I've never been to a wedding before."

Her mouth must have formed a perfect 'O' shape at this announcement and her hands went to the sides of her face. "You're kidding."

He shook his head. "I'm not much for formal affairs."

"But you look so dashing." She waved her hand at him. "You'll be fine. Besides, this will give you something to expect for your own wedding someday." She giggled while she turned back forward and Father opened the door to the house. To Shannon it sounded more than a little evil. Adrian cocked his sunglasses up on his head again and his eyes conveyed just a hint of anxiety. It shocked her just slightly. That he could be worried. Anxious. Stressed. Was it from what Mother had said about his own wedding? She squeezed his hand and he looked toward her. The worry in his eyes melted and again they were blank slates. He smiled at her and squeezed back.

They sat together on wooden fold-out chairs that were sitting in two sections of ten rows, the aisle between them marked by a long white carpet leading to a latticed archway. The classic ideal for the outdoor wedding, of course, she thought with a roll of her eyes. Adrian was still holding her hand. The lattice had vines all over it, dark purple and lavender flowers sprouting over it in a haphazard sort of way that could only have been the natural formation they had made while growing. They'd obviously planned this wedding for long enough to grow their own vines. Light piano music accompanied the bridesmaids as they made their way up the aisle. Everyone turned when the last one was in place. Everyone but Adrian. He wasn't interested in the bride. Shannon noticed that he hadn't turned and tried to see what he was looking at.

The faces of everyone. Expectant. The piano was a little more intense as the bride and her father slowly came down the aisle. She was smiling and had little tears of anxiety in the corners of her eyes. But Adrian's face was stoic. He was examining everyone. He was reading their faces as if they could tell him something. Perhaps he was curious about them. She frowned. Or maybe it was something else that had captured his attention. It was the first time she'd noticed the small black Bluetooth that was in his ear. Was there someone talking to him?

She squeezed his hand again and his eyes met hers. She tilted her head toward the bride and he finally looked at her with disinterest then came back to Shannon. It was hard to read his expression so she just settled for turning forward and resting her head against his shoulder. It would be enough for now.

There was an hour break between the vows and the reception in order for the photographer to get some good photos of the bridal party and, of course, the happy couple. The guests were corralled inside to the ballroom where they were given their seat assignments and let loose upon the open bar. Adrian sipped a Coke while she was nursing a gin and tonic. They stood together in the crowds of people. She was nervous for him to meet everyone. She wondered if her father had given him that list of people to talk to. To schmooze. He was already so charming.

Goosebumps rose on her arms and she looked up at him. He was most definitely human. Most definitely attractive. Like one of those vampires in those shows. It was a ruse to attract prey. Her stomach squirmed and she wondered if she might just want to become the next target. To have such an adventure.

"Shannon," her mother's sister, Aunt Beth, chirped after emerging from one set of people as if she'd parted the Red Sea. "Introduce me to this mystery man the family keeps talking about."

"Aunt Beth, this is Adrian. Adrian, Aunt Beth." She was trying to keep a legitimate smile but found it hard in front of the portly woman who'd slapped her wrist one too many times as a child. She had no problem smacking the hands of her niece and nephew but couldn't possibly touch her own children. Predictably, they'd turned out as complete assholes and they were probably around here somewhere. *Thank God for Adrian.* If he weren't here: she would have been subjected to these people without him. At least he could protect her. But who would protect her from *him*?

Her aunt gave him an odd look, as if she were thinking of purchasing him. As though he were a slab of meat at the butchers and she was going to take him home and roast him. "You're a little bit of a scamp, aren't you? Trust Shannon to know how to pick them." Her brow was nearly to her hairline.

Shannon pursed her lips and felt her eyelid twitch once or twice. The woman had nerve.

Adrian was not down for the count as he opened his mouth readily. "I must say I have a way about myself. I often like to tell myself that she got bored with the stiffs and decided a little *risky venture* was for the best." He winked at her and she could feel color in her face. "Girls tend to like a man with a few rough edges. Shannon just likes a challenge." The devilish way he'd told her aunt off had given her courage.

She grinned. "That's right," she agreed. "Gotta smooth a man out. You know what they say. Men are like good linoleum. You lay them right the first time and you can walk all over them for the rest of your life." Had she really just said that? From the way Adrian was laughing and the alarmed look on her aunt's face, she really had. She couldn't help it. She had to laugh along with her man. Tears were gathering in her eyes and for the first time in her life, she didn't care what her family said about her. Just like that. She put her arm around his and her laughter bubbled over and subsided while she had her head against him.

Aunt Beth had disappeared. More than likely about to tell the rest of the family what a tramp her niece was. She didn't mind in the least.

"I think you just made my stomach hurt," Adrian chuckled.

Sean appeared before them, a whiskey on the rocks in his hand. "Saw that." He grinned and winked.

"Oh god." Shannon started laughing. "Please tell me that's somehow on video. I just completely destroyed my reputation."

Sean scoffed. "That blow-hard aunt of ours should keep her mouth shut about you if she knows what's good for her." He took a sip from his glass. "I've got dirt on that woman and if she dares say a word, I'll have it around so fast the divorce lawyer will be digging around for that pre-nup she and Uncle Sid signed."

"You *what?*"

Sean nodded and tweaked her nose. "I've got dirt on that woman. Why do you think she hates me so badly? I'm the one who figured her out. We're at a stand-off right now. She doesn't talk about you or I and I don't dish about her and her uh...other." He wiggled his eyebrows and he and Adrian high-fived. "You see I'm not as squeaky-clean or smooth as I look. Adrian and I have more in common than you might think."

Adrian smirked and Shannon couldn't help but snort. *You have no idea*, was the thought that was going through her mind. *You couldn't be more different if you tried.* "I think," she said, "as long as that means that you two will be friends, I'm cool with that."

"Speaking of friends," Adrian stated, "how is that fund raising going? I'm sure though that Winston's not charging enough to require such efforts..."

Sean shrugged one shoulder. "We're trying to get together plenty of cash so that we can give him a reward. I mean. That's if he's the one that cracks the case of course. If someone else were to do it then the reward would go to them. Although I highly doubt that anyone else should. Winston's got the tools and the mindset. I'm sure he'll do fine. And so far we're very close to our goal. It helps when Uncle Al's friends were all rich."

"What's your goal?"

"Fifty grand."

Shannon smirked when Adrian's mouth opened inadvertently. She took a sip of her gin and tonic while the rest of the entourage, sans Ben of course, swooped in, their faces smug and charming. They had left their women somewhere else. She felt suddenly glad to be a part of them. They had never dumped her somewhere else. Sean had never allowed it.

Kyle nodded toward her and she nodded back before he said, "So we've got the perfect idea."

Sean grinned mischievously, "Yes?"

Preston started, "We're all sitting at the same table. So all those pesky little wedding traditions like clinking glasses to get them to kiss are going to be the obligation of the most troublesome table." Their grins were so large they looked almost like they might burst from their faces. "And of course we'll cause extra trouble."

Steven chirped, "For Ben."

There was a resounding solemn chorus of "For Ben" from the group and they all took a sip of their drinks.

Sean nodded. "That's the way it has to be fellas. We must cause as much raucous humor as a formal affair allows. Perhaps pushing the boundaries of convention and acceptability." He drew his eyes to Shannon. "Shannon?"

She looked to Adrian, who just gave her a big smile before she turned her attention back to her brother. "We're in."

Winston had the seat all the way back and his legs stretched out in front of him. The Fusion was just roomy enough for him to do things like that. The paper was getting boring and he couldn't bring himself to read the opinion section. It was like allowing chimps to send letters into the paper and printing the most controversial of them. He wished the editors would keep the original spelling errors. Then people could see how disturbingly obtuse those people who wrote in really were. He was experiencing the wedding from the front of Harmsfield while parked on the side of the road closest to the large mansion. The sounds and voices from the Bluetooth were echoed and sometimes jumbled but when Ren stood close enough to the guests, it was easy to make out their conversations.

It'd been about an hour into the reception and he'd made his way around rather well, discussing things easily with the guests with Shannon as his guide. As troublesome as he'd thought she would be, Shannon Kingsley had turned out to be one of his best tools. As the charming young criminal made his rounds, Winston was busily checking off the names in his notebook and reading articles of the paper between. He kept a close ear on the conversations between Ren and the four young men who'd sat at the table.

What an odd case though. I mean what a sicko. Steven.

We shouldn't talk about such morbid things at such an event. What an awful thing to think about. Poor Ben. Kyle.

Come on, guys, there's just something about all of this. I mean why would anyone want to kill Ben? That's the question, isn't it? What did he do? What did he say? Is there something going on that we should be concerned about? What happens if one of us is next? Preston's comment had caused a deep lasting silence around that table that had gone on for at least a minute.

Sean was the one to clinch it. *I think this involves us. Whether we like it or not this involves each and every one of us. I don't know what the killer wants. I'm not sure what we're supposed to do. Perhaps nothing. Maybe it's a warning.*

Shannon's meek voice was hard to hear but Winston just barely caught it. *Just be careful. Everyone. Please?*

The discussion around the table had ground to a halt and she could tell they were all lost in their own minds. Sean was the first to break the silence, his voice wavering a little. "There's one thing that I can't seem to get out of my head." Everyone looked at him, their attention rapt. "That it is possible. Here tonight. That the killer is in this room. In fact it's not just possible. It's *probable*."

Shannon shivered. "You *would* think of something so morbid."

"Adrian," Sean murmured. "You were invited by my father to snoop around this place, see if there were any suspicious characters. Did you see anyone you could consider suspicious?"

Adrian shrugged one shoulder. "I have one or two ideas but it would hardly help you now. The killer isn't going to attack someone in broad daylight in a room filled with a hundred people."

"Sure," Sean nodded, "But what happens if one of us wants to have a little fun upstairs with a bridesmaid or two? I mean, let's be honest, I'm sure there are people up there now with their affairs and their hook-ups. Any of them could be in danger. Are all your suspicious people still in this room?"

Adrian sat up and looked around himself, scanning the ballroom area before his eyes came back to the group around the table, each leaning forward, straining to hear his next words.

"Yes."

A sigh of relief was heard around the table and they all seemed to relax but Shannon knew the reality. They were all as tense as ever. She perhaps more than the rest. Adrian was Winston's only friend. And there had been that threatening note. Perhaps Adrian was the one who was in real danger here—or was he? She eyed him, strong and slender and so very much animalistic. Perhaps Adrian was goading the killer in some fashion. She tried to remember all their conversations from that night. Had they spoken to their killer? Had they been face-to-face with him?

What would happen if the two killers actually met? She had been trying very hard to erase Adrian's crimes from her memory but she couldn't help thinking back on them. To know was to have a little bit more power over her situation. She tried to remember both of their M.O.s. A comparison of sorts. A weapon of a knife and the weapon of teeth. Surely teeth were more fearsome but a knife was easier to wield. She was biting her bottom lip. She wished she had her crocheting here with her. It would have taken her mind away from the horror of this strange scene she was trapped within.

It was nearly two hours later and everyone had taken to dancing after dinner and coffee. She was sitting this one out, watching Adrian moving awkwardly about the dance floor with a six year old girl standing on the tops of his shoes and a smile across her little face. Watching him dance with a small child was both heart-warming and chilling at the same time. On one hand was a sweet guy who could hold tiny hands and humor a child's heart. On the other, he was a predator who could blend into crowds and act the perfect human being. If the man on the dance floor who was dancing with little Stacey Mattela was a cold-blooded animal then who couldn't be the other killer in the room? Shannon felt her arms erupt with goosebumps and she found her eyes wandering over the wedding guests. It could be anyone. *Anyone at all.*

She suddenly felt like a spy in an old movie where all the colors were dimmed due to poorly-remastered film with color by Technicolor. She was watching her brother and his friends dance with their respective quarries while the song changed. Adrian had sent the little one on her way and was making his way over, his gorgeous little smirk firmly in place and a terrifically evil look in his eyes. That odd mixture of arousal and terror started to well up in her gut.

"Hey," he mumbled, sitting next to her. "I heard that this place has this really great garden."

"It's nearly famous." She nodded.

He leaned toward her and whispered into her ear, his warm breath playing over its soft ridges and forcing her to tighten her thighs again. "I'd like to see it."

She took him by the hand down the great hall where there were several people standing about drinking and carrying on. They didn't notice the two of them. There were two other couples on the back patio but they were so engrossed in each other they also didn't notice Shannon and Adrian as they passed. It was dark outside in the garden, which was around three acres of land that was lit by electric lamps set to a timer. The stone path wound its way about the flowers and trees and was marked every so often by benches so that even the elderly could appreciate the beauty of its depths. Her heels tapped against the masonry as she led him deeper into the garden, the murmurs of the other couples on the patio gone in the rustle of the small trees and bushes. They were suddenly under the yellow light of a lamp. To her right were a few birds of paradise. To her left, bunches of hibiscus in every shade. Before her stood her very own human Jimson weed.

She suddenly felt out of breath. His eyes were intense and somehow warm. It was a first for her—to see him so warm. It surprised her when he burst forward and took her lips in their first kiss, a subtle and yet demanding push that sent shocks through her body. She twined her arms around his neck and clung to him, his hands holding her and caressing her back, pulling her forward and against him. When he pulled away from her, he pulled her down to one of the benches and let go of a little nervous laugh.

"What?" she asked.

"I'm sorry. That was completely uncalled for. I'm sorry."

She slid as far as she could on the bench as to be as close to him as possible and squeezed his hands. "Don't be sorry, I liked it." As if to prove it, she pushed forward and claimed his lips. He kissed her earnestly and released a small groan that she found completely and utterly arousing. The terror she had felt had melted away and more warmth took its place. There were more kisses, each more spine-tingling than the last and soon she found herself nearly boneless in his arms, her lips swollen from his kisses and her cheeks as hot as the sun. "I like it," she mumbled against his lips when he kissed her again. She was snapped out of her stupor when she felt his ultra-warm hand slide over her thigh, hiking up her skirt until her knee was bared to the cool garden air. She took in a gasp and gripped his shoulders.

He paused. "Do you want more?" he whispered carelessly.

Her mind was so muddled that she wasn't sure to what he referred. How much more? Her mouth moved before she could control it. "Yes. Please."

His fingers slipped underneath the fabric of her skirt and lifted the dress's hem nearly to her hip, his soft pattering touches skimming over her cotton underwear and suddenly, unintentionally, her body shifted and her thighs opened. It floated past her tipsy brain that no man had ever touched her this way. She wasn't sure what to expect from a fully-experienced "scamp" as her aunt had called him. Was she supposed to be playing hard to get? Was this the gray area between innocent and whore? Her mother would be ecstatic. He was gripping her under the strap of her panties, where her thigh met her hip. His mouth was giving feather kisses over her jawline and then her throat where he nibbled her sweetly.

She still had his shoulders in her grip and she pulled him closer, her breaths coming in deep quick pants. "I've never..." she panted, "I've never...d-duh...nnn..."

"I got you, sweets," he whispered, "We can stop." He pulled back and there was a searing heat in his formerly cold eyes. Her Jimson weed had bloomed under the cool light of the moon as it shined down on them from above.

As quickly as everything had started, it ended. Adrian's sudden, jerky movement startled her and all she could do was sit there with her dress comically hiked while she watched Adrian rise from his position and whirl around like some panther. He lunged—it was the only word for it—at a black form in the walkway and a noise erupted that sounded to Shannon as though it had come from the throat of a dog. There was a flash of something silvery in the moonlight and the dim yellow electric lamp and a harsh yelp—again the voice of a canine—before deep satanic growls and both dark figures disappeared, one chasing the other.

She blinked. Her hands were still propped in the pose they had been when she had been gripping his shoulders. Now they were simply floating in the air as though she were holding an invisible version of her nearly-lover. What exactly had just happened to her? She slowly brought her arms down and, though trembling, she managed to fix her dress. She looked about herself but without Adrian with her, the garden had taken on an unearthly atmosphere so she quickly toddled off toward the house. On her way, she tried to recall what had just occurred. Most definitely a struggle. With someone who had been watching them. Adrian was a natural born predator, she thought easily; he could probably sniff out danger. But to attack? Was that an urge he had? Or was it something having to do with the murders? Her breath caught in her throat as she reached the patio. Nobody was outside. Had the murderer been watching them kiss? She checked her reflection in the glass doors to the inside before sliding one back and entering. The warm air from the

126

house cleared her body of the chill from her encounter but couldn't rid her of the adrenaline still coursing through her veins.

"Shannon." Father beamed. "Where's that man of yours? We're ready to go home if you are."

"Let me find my purse, I'll text him." Her voice might have contained a bit of a waver but if it did her father did not mention it. She made her way back to her seat in the ballroom. The whole scene had quieted down for the evening but seemed gray and old to her, something so far away from her life now despite her living within it. Her purse was slung over the back of the chair. Only Steven was present, sitting alone with his coffee, and his chin in his hand. He had most likely been the only one to miss out on scoring a girl. She pitied him while she opened her purse and rooted about for the borrowed cell phone her brother had given her. He'd said it was for when she was alone. After all this murder business, she couldn't blame him for worrying.

Call Winnie. From a number that she assumed was Adrian's. She searched her contacts for the detective and dialed it.

It rang.

Rang.

Rang.

Goddamn you strange bird detective poo-poo head, pick up your gosh-darn phone.

"Miss Kingsley," was his breathless response to her plea. "Hang on."

She waited. On the other side of the phone were muffled voices and a constant hum she thought might have come from Winston's car.

"Hey, still with me?"

"Of course." She knew that the ballroom wasn't silent. There was still music playing. There were still people talking all around her. But she couldn't hear any of it. All she could hear was Winston's voice.

"Just go home with your family, I'm taking Adrian home. We'll explain it all. I promise. Just tell your parents Adrian got picked up."

She gave a short affirmative and clicked the "End" button, effectively bringing her back into the muted but real world of the wedding long past. She picked up her purse and dropped the phone into it before finding her father and telling him the news. If there was something off about the way she was saying it or acting, he didn't mention it and eventually everyone sans Adrian was piled back into the Mercedes. Sean yawned and gave her a lazy smile.

"Did you have a good time, Shan?" he asked in a low tone, taking her hand as it rested on the leather seat.

It suddenly dawned on her that her entire family thought she'd been ditched by her man. "Yes, I had a wonderful time. It was kind of destroyed when my little garden tryst was interrupted."

Her father was silent but her mother more than made up for it with her girlish gasp and a cascade of giggles as she turned almost completely around in the passenger's seat to look at her. "A garden tryst? Why was this perfect, wonderful, amazing thing interrupted? What an awful thing to happen. I'll just have to know who interrupted it so I can fully admonish them later."

Her father finally made a sound. It was a low chuckle. When he spoke, his voice was filled with humor. "I just love our family." He shook his head. "It seems like every one of us is some kind of black sheep. I'm glad we've succeeded in the attempt to instill some kind of rebelliousness into you two."

Sean was grinning. "Thank you, Father. We appreciate that."

Mother was still frowning. "Who interrupted you?"

"I think it was the killer."

The car went silent but Father kept driving.

She continued, "I expressed a nervousness so Adrian stopped. Very admirable of him, I would say, since up until that point I had been very...acquiescent. Then there was a shadow in the path and Adrian must have sensed them coming because he very quickly tussled with them and then chased them away. I don't quite know what happened."

Her mother was chewing her bottom lip. "And Winston came and picked him up. How curious. How curious indeed. I wonder what happened."

Sean nodded as he looked out the window. He had said it earlier in the night. That it was not only possible but likely that the killer was in their midst. He had been proven right. Her brother seemed to always know those kinds of things. She had the notion in this moment that he wished he hadn't. That he wished he could have been surprised by such news. But he wasn't. He wouldn't ever be.

She couldn't possibly tell them all that it had happened so quickly that she hadn't even truly seen much of anything. And that the way Adrian moved was so animalistic that she shuddered to think about it. Or perhaps the way the two of them fighting had created sounds that were drawn from the depths of hell itself. She chewed her thumbnail while they drove the rest of the way home, the outside world a place suddenly ominous and chilling. There was a killer about. Or perhaps worse: Two of them.

CHAPTER 16

Winston's brow was peaked when he opened the door but he was not surprised to see her standing there. Her brown hair was pulled up into a messy bun and her young eyes were wide and filled with anxious curiosity. He ushered her inside his apartment and peeked one way and then the other down the outside hall before shutting the door and locking it.

"Where is he?" she asked carefully.

"Bathroom. Door's open. Go ahead." He watched her rush to the bathroom door and her eyes become even wider.

"Adrian," she whispered. Winston walked up behind her and pushed her gently into the room.

"I'm fine," Ren assured her. It was true, he was fine, but to Shannon Kingsley the bathroom must have looked closer to a bloodbath. He was sitting on the toilet in a tattered pair of jeans Winston had once worn to paint his grandmother's house. They were streaked with the color of the paint—a sickly shade of yellow—and dark swatches of discoloration from his blood. "It's just one or two more scars to go along with the rest of them." He smiled at her, close-mouthed and adorable. Winston supposed that was the smile that had originally won her over. It did almost nothing now as her jaw was nearly on the floor and the girl was nothing short of horrified. Ren was shirtless. Open boxes of .99 cent bandages from CVS were scattered around his bare feet and the contents of them were wrapped around his stomach—for a deep but nearly harmless slash on his side—and around his upper left arm for a superficial flesh wound that had managed to bleed enough to make a head wound proud.

Winston provided in an uninterested monotone, "It's nothing he isn't used to."

There was blood, in streaks, spatters, and droplets, all over the bathroom. Especially in the tub where Winston had forced him to take off the ruined formal clothes. There was even a perfect handprint on the ceramic lip of it where he'd gripped it to get out.

Shannon's face was pale. "You're hurt."

"Well the killer's hurt too. Bastard got away from me."

"Surprised you with that knife," Winston snickered. "Heard that." He motioned toward the Bluetooth that was sitting on the counter next to the sink and Shannon glanced at it.

"That's what you were doing?" she asked. "You were on the phone with him?" Her cheeks gained a pink hue and she whirled around on him. "You were on the phone with him *the whole time*?"

"Well..." Winston tried to give her a reassuring smile, but all that he was sure he gave was a crooked wolf's grin. She punched him hard in the shoulder.

"Pervert." She crossed her arms and turned back to Ren. "You could have told me."

Ren sighed and stood up, touching the bandages on his side a little with his fingertips, his face contorted in pain. "Sweets, there's a lot of things I could have told you."

Winston's mind reeled with them. *Like who the killer is. Since you know. Or maybe the fact that you're a serial murderer. That might have been relevant to the fact that she's falling in love with you.* He shook his head. There were some things that Ren, in his mind, could never tell her. The first and foremost was that he was a felon on multiple counts of brutal horrifying murder.

Shannon went to him and wrapped her arms around him, careful not to disturb his wound. He held her as well, his cheek against the top of her head and his eyes on the detective. Winston was distinctly unmoved by this event. He watched it unfold before him as though it were just a scene in some unrealistic Lifetime movie. The antihero embracing the internally tortured damsel in some twisted and horrific plot. The plot that just so happened to be this Private Eye's life at the moment. She backed away a little and studied him, her fingers tracing over scars long healed. One on his collarbone. Another on his chest. One on his shoulder and...

"Adrian," she whispered when she touched his forearm just below his elbow. He shied from her and cleared his throat. "Are those what I think they are?"

He crossed his arms to cover the insides of his elbows with his hands. "I'm not...exactly a model citizen, sweets." His face was turning pink under those boyish freckles. "That part of my life is over. The...drugs. That's finished. It wasn't even a very long time to begin with."

Winston blurted, "Oh. Reminds me. Your test results were mailed here."

Shannon turned a little, shocked as though she had forgotten that Winston was standing there. Of course she could have been shocked by any number of things. Her boyfriend was almost killed by a maniac, she just found out he was a former heroin addict (something that was curiously unsurprising to Winston), and somehow she had to wrap her mind around the fact that he was really, actually, in all terms, "not a model citizen." Ren's choice of words made Winston want to laugh. Shannon blinked, "Test results?"

Ren's eyebrows lifted. "You read them?"

"Of course I read them, you idiot, why else would I have been practically bathing in your blood? The sick homo in me couldn't help it." He quickly clamped his mouth shut when Shannon stared at him. Being polite to Ren wasn't something he thought he could do. "Anyways. You're clean. Despite all the shit you did to ensure that you wouldn't be." He mumbled the rest as he walked back toward the kitchen. "Fuckin' junkie-ass faggot." The brand new package of Oreos was practically calling his name. He could hear their low conversation as he left them and searched for his cookies.

"You thought you might have an STD?"

"I didn't. Winston thought..."

"But you shot heroin. You didn't think that maybe you could have gotten something from a drug habit?" She was getting more and more agitated.

"Sweets, sit down. Less than a year. Maybe six months. It wasn't all that long of a time and furthermore I did not share anything." He was getting exasperated. "Besides, I don't even have to worry about it, which I wasn't anyway, because Winston just told me they were negative. So it doesn't even *matter*."

"But, but, *drugs*?" Winston could hear the tears in her voice.

"For the love of Christ," Ren sighed, "Sit *down* sweets. You *can't* tell me those snotty guys your brother hangs out with don't snort cocaine at every fucking party."

"*What?*"

Winston chuckled while he poured himself a glass of milk.

There was a deep silence that came out of the bathroom. It was that moment where Ren realized he'd said something that may or may not have deeply offended her and he'd decided to pause the moment. He tried to imagine them. Shannon would still be standing. She had a little fire in her. Much like Tomi had, he thought. She would get a rise just out of defying him. They would be staring at each other. It was Ren's turn but he had clammed up for the moment.

Shannon took it for him. "What do you think of me then?"

"Does it matter?"

Winston stopped munching his cookies and perked his head up. Ren's voice had taken that signature turn toward a deeper, more menacing tone. A dog who'd been backed into a corner. He stood up and meandered toward the bathroom to save him. He swung himself in with one hand on the door jam and gave them an award-winning smile. Neither of them was particularly impressed. "Hey, you two. How about we stop talking about how Ren's a dirty cocksucker and how you're a sheltered snob and we all just sit down and have ourselves some fuckin' cookies?"

Ren was the first to take him up on the offer, stomping out of the bathroom past him toward the kitchen. Winston congratulated himself and internally gave himself the "Wingman of the Year" prize. Shannon was still standing in the bathroom with unshed tears in her eyes.

"Miss Kingsley," he said in a softer tone, "remember what I told you?"

She finally sat down hard on the toilet seat with her hands in her lap, looking up at him pathetically. "I remember," was her meek response. "But I'm having a really hard time."

Winston knelt down in front of her until he had to look up into her eyes. "It doesn't matter what he thinks of you. Because there are things you are that are simple givens and things you could be that are just speculations. He might think you're a spoiled rotten little brat but does that matter? Not really. Since he also thinks you're fantastically beautiful, interesting, and corruptible. He's always been attracted to rich girls."

She sniffled and one side of her mouth turned up. "Really?"

"Yeah. But only if they had a little spark in 'em. One of them brained me so hard from behind that she thought she might have killed me." He chuckled. "Be gentle with him, Miss Kingsley. He's not a good guy but he's what you got right now."

She nodded.

"You have to understand that he's not like you. He's probably the exact opposite of you. He's been beaten, abused, raped, starved, tortured, and nearly killed. And I have to admit I'm one of the worst perpetrators of those things. He's a survivor. That's what he knows how to do. Don't make him have to survive you."

She almost fell forward, her arms coming around his neck and her face buried in his shoulder. He held her while she sobbed into him, her body convulsing with the force of her weeping. When they emerged from the bathroom, her eyes were red and puffy, her face splotchy and her hair a little bit of a mess. He brought her out to the kitchen table where Ren was sulking with about three whole cookies stuffed in his mouth. She sat down next to him and sheepishly took a cookie out of the package. She took small, etiquette-laden bites out of it as though she were at a tea party instead of Winston's kitchen.

Ren mumbled something that was completely incomprehensible through the cookies that had been stuffed into his mouth.

Winston tsked him and said bluntly, "Don't speak with your mouth full."

He swallowed obediently and his head dipped even further down but he did not repeat what he mumbled.

Shannon, done with her first cookie, cleared her throat. Ren didn't look at her. "I apologize for blowing your past out of proportion. Nothing of who you were before we met should be any of my concern." She picked another cookie up and began to slowly and politely eat it. Ren still wasn't looking at her.

Winston wanted to wap him upside the head with a rolled up newspaper but he recognized that Ren was more than a little butthurt about the whole situation. It was funny how easily he could be hurt by her. He wondered if he could be hurt by Tomi in the same way. If she had ever said something to him to incite this kind of cold, withdrawn mood.

When Ren stood up suddenly, the chair scraping against the linoleum, Winston knew exactly what was going to happen and exactly where Ren would go. The two of them watched as the killer calmly put on a shirt that was over the back of the couch and walked toward the window, opened it, and disappeared down the fire escape.

Shannon still had tears in her eyes.

Winston ate a cookie. "No worries. That's normal. He'll be back later."

She stood gingerly. "I should go home."

He nodded. "Get some rest. I've gotta go through my notes from tonight anyway. And if he shows up at your window, be sure to let him in."

She looked confused but nodded anyhow and he winked at her before she stepped out the door.

Sure enough, it was two hours later that she heard it. A soft rapping on her window pane while she sat crocheting. For a moment she was reminded of Poe and whispered to herself, "Tis some visitor tapping at my chamber door. Only this and nothing more." She set down her crocheting and moved to her window, drawing back the curtains and opening it to find nothing. The eerie stillness of the night suddenly sent chills through her spine and she hugged herself in her bedtime T-shirt and touched her naked toes together, peering into the midnight darkness. She murmured, "'Tis the wind and nothing more."

As soon as the words had gone from her lips and she had been resigned to closing the window, she gave a tiny 'eep' as Adrian suddenly appeared from the side of it. A strange feat indeed for him to come in that way, as it would have been terribly hard to climb the side of the house. She moved back and he crawled his way in, his muscles moving so much like an animal that she couldn't even stand to watch him until he was standing before her. He was still wearing those bloody jeans and his feet were bare and a little dirty. His arm was cut and bleeding.

She hurried to her vanity and opened the drawer that would have her Band-Aids. She chose a Bugs Bunny one and opened it, applying it to his scrape with an expert hand. When she looked at him again, his eyes were filled with that same searing heat that she'd seen before in the garden.

He muttered to her. "Continue?"

For a moment she wasn't quite sure what he meant, but her mouth moved easily. "Though thy crest be shorn and shaven, thou art sure no craven. Ghastly grim and ancient raven wandering from the nightly shore—Tell me what thy lordly name is on the Night's Plutonian shore!" She trembled before him as he took her upper arms in his hands and gently pushed her to sit on her bed. He took her lips in a firm but careful kiss.

He backed away from her but was still close enough that she could feel the tickle of his breath on her face when he whispered, "Nevermore."

She kissed him again and twined her arms around the back of his neck like she had earlier in the evening. His hands were on her back and she pressed her body against him, deepening their kiss until she thought she might faint from the sheer intensity of the tremors in her body. She felt like she was a teenager, hiding in her room with the baddest boy in school. She felt as though she was doing something terribly wrong. Terribly bad.

But then hadn't her mother put it best? *Sometimes it just feels good to be bad.* She gasped when he moved his mouth to her chin, then her throat, nibbling her ever so gently before sliding his lips to her ear and nipping it which caused a rippling of arousal through her body straight between her thighs. His hands were gripping her waist and his thumbs found their way under the hem, pushing up the thin fabric until the whole of her stomach was bare and the material was bunched under her breasts. The stray thought that she wasn't wearing a bra made her arch her back and yearn for him to push it up and over. She wanted him to see her.

He pushed her so she was lying on her back, her head nestled in her soft pillow, her hair splayed around her head haphazardly. He examined her and she squirmed under his searing gaze. She bit her lip when he kissed her belly and moved upward, pushing up her shirt so he could kiss her sternum. She sighed when she felt the cool breeze from the still-open window on her bare breasts and almost shrieked when his hot mouth covered one of her taught pink nipples. She had to clap her hand over her mouth as he suckled her and lapped at her. Her legs were tight together but his hand had other ideas as it slipped under the band of her pajama bottoms and skimmed over the strip of panty that hid her most sensitive area.

He removed himself from her breast and moved toward the other. Between them, he murmured in a husky lust-laden voice, "Don't be afraid of me."

Her thighs loosened but she still gave her breathless response— "Should I be?"

He didn't bother to answer or even pause to consider the question. Perhaps he thought the answer should have been obvious. He sucked her and his fingers rubbed her lightly through the cotton of her underwear. She wondered if he could feel it getting damp and a part of her was aroused even more by her innate sense of mortification.

His movement was sudden and she harkened back to his jerky motions in the garden. His head was up and turned toward the door. He very quickly sat her up and pulled down her shirt, disappearing so quickly that she almost didn't know where he'd gone.

"Shannon?" came the muffled tone of her brother's voice.

Her throat wouldn't work but she managed a squeaky "Yes?" when Adrian poked her ankle from under the bed.

He opened the door slowly and then closed it behind him, his movements like that of a fragile doll. He didn't seem to notice her odd appearance. Her mussed up hair or the deep color in her cheeks.

She felt like she could just die from embarrassment but there was no way for her brother to tell that she was about to talk to him with such wetness between her legs. Not to mention that she had hidden a rogue libertine under her bed.

"Shan," he sighed, sitting next to her with his eyes on his hands. "I hope you had a good time at the wedding. Despite what happened with Adrian." He was toying with the ends of his sweater sleeves. "I'm sure he's alright."

She nodded. "He's fine. I went to visit him. He's a little shaken up, I suppose." She shrugged one shoulder and allowed her hair to curtain on the side facing her brother. He wasn't looking at her anyway. "He's just what our aunt describes, a scamp. He can handle it." There was a small silence in which she knew her brother was thinking of the way to put his next words. They were most likely the words he'd come to say in the first place. She'd jostled him somehow.

"Love." He started with his favorite pet name for her. The word was filled with ownership, as if the name of "Love" could make her his forever. "You're my only sister. You're my only reason for being at this moment. Nobody could hold a match to you in my heart." He gave a great sigh. "I like Adrian. I do. I think he's great. But..." She could see his mouth twist unpleasantly through her curtain of hair. "I just don't want to see you hurt."

She squeezed his hand.

"Consider me the opposite of Mother," he told her. "I'm wary of your venturing into a world where he has the upper hand. Mother would argue that you have to gain experience and have adventure and I'm sure Adrian is a good guy but he's also rather..." Sean was searching for another word. She knew he already had one but he'd chosen at the last moment to reject it. She could only speculate on what her word would be. An internal game of MadLibs where she ran through a list of words to describe him.

Malevolent. Vicious. Depraved. Evil. Destructive.

"...peculiar." It was a decent word. A careful one. Sean was known for being careful.

"He is a might bit odd," she agreed softly, "but I'm sure it's nothing to be worried about."

Sean frowned and nodded his head a little. "I'm certain you're right. Perhaps I should worry less about you. You are, after all, an adult. But if he ever hurts you. I want you to know that I'll kill him."

"Sean," she stated louder than she'd intended, pulling her hair back so she could examine his expression.

"Don't say that's unnecessary because it is quite necessary. Nobody else will tell you right up front. If he ever hurts you. I'll do what I must." He looked quite determined.

She took his hand in both of hers. "What in the world would make you think that he would ever hurt me?"

His jaw clenched and he stood up, walking to her vanity and staring at himself in the mirror before going to her still-open window and peering out down toward the sprawling front yard bathed in the silver light of the moon. She simply watched him while he put his hands behind his back, the sweater he wore obviously a little too big for him. He was wearing a dark set of pajama bottoms and bare feet.

When he didn't answer her, she spoke instead. She could tell when her brother was bottling something up. When he wouldn't tell her exactly what was wrong. "Dearest, why don't you have a cup of tea before bed? You look tired and obviously something has you upset. Sleep on it and tell me in the morning."

He turned toward her with his eyelids drooping and an expression that she wasn't sure if she'd ever seen from him before. It was colder and harder and reminded her more of Adrian than it did her brother. "You're right, Love. I'll see you in the morning." With that he was gone, whisking out of her room almost as quick as Adrian had whisked himself under her bed.

She put her head between her knees to look under, finding Adrian in the shadows, his eyes shining from the dim yellow light of her lamp reflected in them. "I'm almost positive he didn't actually mean it," she supplied.

"I could take 'im." He gave her a rakish smile before he started to crawl out from under her bed. He didn't say anything but when he stood, he gingerly placed a hand on his side.

"Oh goodness," she fretted, "I don't have any Bugs Bunny Band-Aids big enough to help that." She sat him down on the bed with her and brazenly lifted his shirt, tutting while inspecting how he was bleeding through his bandages. "It's not *too* bad but you shouldn't have jostled yourself about so much."

"You shouldn't have such a nosy brother," he chided but quit when he saw the pout on her face and changed the subject. "I suppose I should go then." He scratched the back of his head awkwardly. "But...for the record: I'm sorry."

She put her head on his shoulder. "I'm sorry too. I guess I just didn't think much about what might be in your past."

He smiled, "I shouldn't have insulted your brother. It was wrong of me."

She giggled. "You're not used to apologizing."

"I'm not used to the need to be humble."

"Do you really need to be?"

He turned his head and kissed her hair, his warm hand settling on her thigh. "I want to be." He breathed her in and then out and then murmured, "I told you before that I'm not who you thought I was. I'm still not. There's more I just can't tell you."

"Is there anything you can?" Her fingers traced over the faded scars on his arms and wondered how many faded scars he had that were invisible.

"I'm going to die young."

She backed away from him and frowned. "What in the world would make you say that?"

He put a hand on her shoulder to steady her. "Don't get all up in a tizzy. You live by the gun, you die by the gun—that's all I'm trying to get at. I've probably got more people in this world who'd like to see me hanged, drawn, and quartered than I do people who've legitimately liked me. Or even were ambivalent to me."

She was still frowning.

"Sweets, I've got a sordid past you've probably never even dreamed about."

"Despite the past, maybe there is a way to change the future."

To that he looked stumped. His mouth was hanging a little open and his brows were just slightly together. It was as if he had never thought of something so simple as to remove himself from his past.

"What's stopping you from being someone else? From changing your future? Is it about not being able to change? I suppose that would be considered a legitimate excuse at least." She sucked in her bottom lip. There was a deep coldness in his gaze and he removed it from her slowly, looking out toward the moonlit sky.

"Salman Rushdie once said '*At sixteen, you still think you can escape from your father. You aren't listening to his voice speaking through your mouth, you don't see how your gestures already mirror his; you don't see him in the way you hold your body, the way you sign your name. You don't hear his whisper in your blood.*'"

She put her hand on his cheek. "You're predispositioned to...what?" She knew the answer, of course, but was he willing to tell her?

His gaze came back to her and he looked pained, sorrow evident in his expression. It was something she'd never seen before from him. "Violence." He hung his head. "That's why your brother thinks what he does. He can see it in me. It's written on me plain as day. As if it were a mark I can't rid myself of. I became what I am at sixteen and I'll never be rid of it. Shannon, you shouldn't even consider me worth your time. I have too much blood on my hands."

Or in your mouth, she thought darkly. "I don't think my brother should know anything about you. How could he? Why should he? To assume something of you so easily is preposterous. Especially when I know he very much likes you."

Adrian's mouth was still turned down at the corners. He didn't seem convinced. He seemed forlorn almost, as if he was facing some kind of existential crisis where he was unsure of just about everything on Earth. His very own existence. The existence of everything. Of course she knew his real predicament. He knew what he was. He thought he was less than she. Less than the rest of the human race even. Even with such a thing that he was—a killer—he could perhaps feel something. Something like a self-loathing. If only for a small while.

It was in this rare moment—or a moment that she thought was rare, at least—that he seemed more human than ever. That he seemed something less of a demon and something more like the Adrian she wished he were.

If only he could be that way forever.

One precious thought stuck in the back of her mind. Something she could hold onto. Something she could hope for.

What if he could be?

CHAPTER 17

She sat at the dining room table and ate what Leslie had brought out to her. Toast and marmalade first, then over-easy eggs and some divine home-made sausages on the side along with a bowl of fresh strawberries. She was munching a strawberry and doing a little reading in one of Mother's old books—a saucy little historical romance—when Sean appeared in the doorway looking as dapper as ever in a silk vest with a short-sleeved white shirt and dress pants. A matching flat cap was perched on top of his head and pushed his hair forward which gave him a young, handsome look.

"Sean," she grinned. "Sit down. Leslie's made the most incredible eggs."

He took off his hat and laid it on the table while he sat across from her. She sipped her milk and watched him take a nibble from a strawberry.

"I have a question for you, Sean. Out of pure curiosity. I don't mean to offend. You seem to be quite blunt with most things I talk to you about so I hope you'll be blunt with me here."

His brows raised in surprise. "I wouldn't lie to you, Shan. And since you've asked me to forego the sugar I'll do so, but I warn you that I do tend to coat things with you."

She waved her hand at him. "Please. Goodness gracious. Just don't beat around the bush."

"Then shoot."

"Have you ever done cocaine?"

He was clearly surprised as he sat back in his chair, the strawberry between his fingers forgotten for the moment. "Well. Wow. What would make you ask that, Shan?"

"Don't divert me." She narrowed her eyes at him.

"Yes. I've dabbled."

A sharp, unpleasant feeling stabbed her in the gut. Winston was right. She was a sheltered girl in some kind of gilded cage and Adrian, being a dirty...what had he called him? A cocksucker? She blinked. Adrian knew of these things. Knew everything. "Why?" she blurted.

Sean gave her a one-shoulder shrug. "Why not? It makes you feel like you're the best and the brightest. And even if you *were* the best and the brightest you couldn't feel as good as it makes you. Quite possibly the best drug I've ever done. In terms of how it makes me feel anyway."

Her jaw had loosened. "You've done *others*?"

He was grinning now, his eyes lazy. "Shannon, you are so cute. I would have thought you would have asked Adrian of all those dastardly things he's more than likely done. I assure you his knowledge of any kind of *underworld* would be far more extensive than mine." He remembered the strawberry between his fingers and finished it off, licking the pink juice off his lips and fingers while still giving her that strange lazy look. As if he were bored.

"This is crazy."

"It's a good thing you don't get out much, Shan. You'd be blown away by most of the world. In fact, I would warn you that one day you might turn around and see a very different Adrian staring back at you."

Her eyebrows twitched downward. She already knew the darkness that lay in Adrian's heart. Not Adrian. That wasn't even his name. Ren. Ren was what Winston had called him. Was it time for him to know that she knew? Or was that just something she should forever keep inside her? For his sake? Or for hers?

She would still be thinking about it later when she went for a walk down the front steps and past their front gate. There was a sidewalk that led into the city. It was a rather long walk, but she didn't mind. She'd worn her favorite set of sneakers and felt rather good about her skinny jeans and tight T-shirt. Her sunglasses were over her eyes, giving the world a blue tint.

"Miss Kingsley," came a voice to her left. She rolled her eyes when she turned and saw a car pacing her. A small Geo Metro hatchback with the rather young reporter Valechy in the driver's seat. He was pulling the car over as close to the sidewalk as he could so he could talk to her over the passenger side seat. The car was small enough that this was no problem. "Miss Kingsley. If we could have a word?"

She ignored him and continued walking.

"I think you'd find it rather enlightening what I've discovered about your Mr. Woods."

She stopped and so did he. She looked around for other cars or people but saw none. The car smelled like cigarette smoke and baby powder when she got in. He started off at the correct speed and waited for just a few moments under her cold stare before he began.

"I was curious, you see. To see what the good Detective was up to in terms of the murders. Well, thanks to the good graces of some kind of deity, I've managed to uncover something rather interesting and should probably just go into private detection myself. I fancy I've probably just gotten rich right here just from the amount of publicity a book with something like this in it would get. Unfortunately for me, I make a shitty sadist and I didn't set out with the intent to ruin Winston's life by recording it in a project."

She was silent through this strange monologue.

"But I'll have you know that your Mr. Woods is most certainly not who you think he is and I'm more than one hundred percent certain that Winston's done everything on purpose. You, like some little damsel cast under the shadows of these murders, and *him,* acting as your rock, this character that is so terrifyingly unlike him. As soon as I saw him I knew I'd seen him before. Younger. With black hair. Without that scruff about him you must think is so adorable. I knew I'd seen him on someone's mantlepiece. And it hit me. I was doing some snooping down in the Outer Banks trying to see about Winston's early career. I interviewed this kooky woman who'd never looked me in the eyes when she talked about anything. Her little boy. Her little boy had *made a mess* before he'd left. Well, that was an understatement. He'd completely destroyed his father's head with a crowbar before he left and had bathed her in his blood while she lay beside him in bed. Now that is some kind of mess." Valechy was getting more and more excited, speaking faster. "Now imagine this. Six years later the same kid's killed probably over twenty people. Maybe thirty. Most of them spur of the moment with his *teeth* which, in itself, is horrifying but sometimes he'd kill them and *pose* them. Most of the time with their guts all strewn about in spiderwebs. You've got about 22 feet of bowel Miss Kingsley and lemme tell you, none of it went to waste."

He swallowed and continued, "He was Winston's first serial killer. He was Winston's breaking out point into this strange field that he made a name for himself in. He's got a way with them, Miss Kingsley. Serial killers, I mean. He's got this way of thinking like them. And I've gotta be honest, he's quite a strange bird when it comes right down to it. Maybe he's found a way to control him. Maybe he's found a way to just come to terms with him. I don't know what his secret is but he's using him in some way. As some plan. To capture your uncle's killer. It seems like a movie. Fantasy. A long-shot for Winston even. Not that he doesn't almost completely baffle me usually with how illogical his hunts are..."

Shannon put up a hand to stop him. "Wait." She took in a breath and let it out. "What's his real name?"

"Renatus Ringo Rockey."

She couldn't help it. After all the things Valechy had just told her, she couldn't help but let out a harsh laugh. Adrian had told her the truth. His middle name really was *Ringo*. "And you're convinced that Adrian is him?"

"Yes. Completely sure."

"And you plan to do what with this information? Blackmail?"

"I'm not sure it would be quite wise to blackmail anyone associated with the Rottweiler of Roanoke. In fact, Winston might be considered untouchable considering what he's done to several police investigators who attempted to harm his investigations in the past." He shrugged while he drove. "I mean it might just be me but I'm rather averse to having my torso hung from a tree by my own intestines. Pardon the imagery, but I've got to hammer it down. He's not exactly..."

"The marrying type," she finished and he gave her a small surprised glance. "Believe me. I've already been warned about his inclinations toward womanizing by the detective."

"I wasn't exactly talking about his womanizing, Miss Kingsley."

She nodded. "I know what you were talking about, but I've been very good at trying to pretend I'd never seen any of the photographs. At least, I think I've been very good. He's just like what Winston said. He's only human. He's just a man. Nothing more. Nothing less."

"You already knew?"

"Since before my cousin's wedding."

"And you're not shocked at all?"

She sniffed. "I was. In fact, I still am rather worried about it. But I refuse to allow that to guide me somewhere else. He's been very kind to me and I think everyone deserves a second chance. He just doesn't know the possibilities. I'm surprised you didn't go to the police."

He frowned and pulled into a parking spot next to a cafe. "I have more respect for Winston than that. He's got a reason for doing everything he does. He's got a plan. And the capture of your uncle's killer is more important than the capture of a dormant dog who seems like he's been doing nothing but making a fine attempt at getting thicker around the middle and trying like hell to get up your skirt."

She felt her cheeks getting pink while she got out of the car and slammed the tiny door that clicked into place as though it were a toy. "He is *not* getting thicker around the middle." She followed the writer through the doors of the cafe and into the cruel air conditioning that chilled her suddenly and left goosebumps over her arms and shoulders. "Why are you telling me this?"

It was his turn to blush while they stood in line for coffee. "I...I didn't want you to...compromise yourself if you were thinking of doing so. Young women in your position. The family's wealth and all. I didn't want you to be in danger of ruining your reputation or a chance to marry someone worth your status."

She giggled and gave him a light pat on the arm. "Don't you worry your head about little ol' me. My mother is constantly telling me to go be a little promiscuous and adventurous. Nevertheless, you wouldn't just go around telling girls that their boyfriends were serial killers for just that reason, there has to be something else."

His little eyes flitted about. "Well," he started as if he were reluctant to finish. "I didn't want you to be surprised when he left. I didn't want it to come after you'd thought you could be with him. You know. *With* him. And of course I didn't want to completely come out of left field when I asked Winston for half of his reward." He scratched the back of his neck.

"I'm sure Winston will have no problem giving you half of his reward if it means you'll keep his secrets, but I warn you Mr. Valechy, I wouldn't become greedy if I were you. I would place your request as exactly what it is—a request. Else that might be seen as what you have professed to be avoiding." She cocked a brow. "I'm sure that would be another way to find yourself on the wrong side of some blood-gargling psychopath."

He snorted and coughed before laughing and wheezing a little bit.

"It would be more of a request," the reporter assured her and at her nod he said to himself, "Yes. A request. Not…not blackmail. I'm sure he would see it that way. He's a very interesting character. Once donated a reward that was given to him by a girl's father for finding her. Donated it to her even." He kept nodding to himself as if that would make it better.

"I'm sure it'll turn out fine," she stated. She wasn't sure how Adrian would react to something quite like a subtle attempt at blackmail. As Valechy had said before, blackmail wasn't exactly something one would wish to try with someone associated with a serial killer. "Did he really hang someone from a tree by their entrails?" She gave him a sideways stare while he ordered his coffee from the barista and she stepped up to do the same.

"Yes. A rather unfortunate police detective named Maldeen. He was content to allow Winston to have his way until he started actually getting somewhere and Maldeen thought he could swoop in and take the

leads Winston was giving him and boot the poor private eye out." They stood together waiting for their coffees and Valechy cleared his throat.
"After Winston was all but thrown out of the investigation, Maldeen was found with his innards all over the place, strung up like a web about ten or twelve feet above the ground and his torso hung with a length of gut. Just his head and torso. That Rott's serious when he wants to be."

"Oh, I can believe that," she smiled but inwardly her guts were squirming about. She was doing one hell of a job at remaining straight-faced while she thought about the amount of dedication it must have taken to create that type of scene. "I think he's got a lot of oomf when he wants it. If you know what I mean. He could...take his time." She swallowed and avoided the journalist's eyes.

Valechy nodded and when their coffees came he sat with her at one of the tables, fingering the top of his coffee cup while thinking. "He's been dormant. For a while. But he's like a volcano. He could burst at any time. It's just a matter of time. Not an 'if' but a 'when' and it's just killing me to know this and have this inside me. I thought I was going to bust. I think that's why I had to tell you. Because if I didn't tell you I was just going to explode in the middle of the street."

She patted his arm across the table. "It's a good thing I took a walk then isn't it? I wouldn't worry if I were you."

"I can't help it." He put a hand to his forehead as if to check for a fever before taking a sip of his coffee. "What if he starts killing again?"

She shook her head. "Mr. Valechy, do not worry yourself about things like that. If he starts killing again and he's still under his alias of Adrian then you can count on this—you do not have to feel responsible for telling anyone. Because I will. So consider your hands washed of this situation. I'll put a stop to it because I'll probably know before anyone else. Except maybe Winston, but God knows what he'd even do in that situation."

"But..." he started.

"But you would feel responsible for the lives lost. I understand that sentiment. You're free to torture that one out for yourself. I won't stop you. Winston might. But I won't. I'll understand." She sipped her iced coffee and shivered. It was much too cold in the air conditioned cafe.

She narrowed her eyes at the chubby journalist. "Did anyone think to ask Winston where he might have been when Maldeen died?"

To that the reporter was taken aback. "Well. I'm sure they did ask him and I'm sure I know what the answer was. That he was in his house asleep. I mean the crime was in the middle of the night. Ren is known for things like webbing entrails..."

"Which is why it would have made sense." Shannon sighed. "Winston and Adrian are so close in disposition."

Valechy was drawing up like an offended bird. "But yet they are so fundamentally different. I mean comparing their fundamental characteristics would be like...like apples and oranges or dogs and cats."

She arched a brow. "I might not know much about the world, Mr. Valechy, but I know enough to know that Winston and Adrian are very much alike." She paused and looked out the window at the sunshine. "Despite what you might say, Adrian's not all bad and Winston's not all good and they're very close to being the same shade of gray." She was sure about what she'd said so she sipped her iced coffee and crossed her ankles under her chair. "Did you know that Adrian knows how to crochet?"

Mr. Valechy didn't seem to be very impressed by that idea, his face blank.

"I'm beginning to think he's never lied to me once. He's just *not* told me things at all if he thought they were things I didn't need to hear. Which is both comforting and disturbing at the same time." She narrowed her eyes at a figure on the other side of the street. A rather snake-like man in a dark gray suit. He crossed the street at the crosswalk and seemed to be unsurprised when his almond-shaped and unsettling eyes fell upon Mr. Valechy, who hadn't noticed him yet. "Mr. Valechy..." she started.

"Just Jim."

"Well, Jim, there's an odd fellow on the sidewalk who seems to have noticed you. Er. Us."

He glanced over and gave a dramatic eye-roll and a sigh. "I'm very sorry for what's about to happen, Miss Kingsley."

"Sorry?" She was unsure about what he'd meant until she heard the bell above the door give its merry jingle and the man with the slicked back brown hair and angled shoulders strode into the cold air as though he might have always belonged.

Valechy muttered while leaning toward her, "Just let me do the talking."

She thought that there was a faint hiss before the stranger spoke his words but it could have simply been her mind playing tricks on her.

"Valechy," the stranger started, "How's your research coming along?"

"Quite well, Nero," he sniffed. "Nero, this is—"

"I'm aware of who Miss Kingsley is," he interrupted and put his hand out to her which she gave him gingerly. She had to suppress a shiver when he touched the back of her fingers to his dry lips and gave her a creepy smile. "Eddie Nero, he said. You can just call me Eddie if you'd like."

She tried not to gag. "Is there something we can help you with, Mr. Nero?"

He seemed a bit put out that she had refused to call him "Eddie," but answered her nevertheless. "I was just wondering what in the world you would be doing with little Jimmy since the bulk of his research seems to be focused around that surly gray-haired detective."

They gave each other a glance and Valechy answered, "Miss Kingsley is just giving me an outsider's take on the investigation. She has lost a friend in these past few weeks if you'll recall and she can provide an interesting personal report in an attempt to humanize the victims a little more. Make them more tangible to the reader."

Nero snorted and leaned forward, his hand on the edge of the table. "Oh, I don't know about that, *Jimmy*, since I've seen this little minx coming and going from that odd detective's apartment. Along with that ever-so-interesting *boyfriend* of hers."

She frowned. She wasn't quite used to being talked about while she sat within hearing distance.

Valechy was starting to look again like a ruffled bird, his cheeks turning a slight shade of pink. "That is simply inappropriate, Nero, and I won't have you discussing it in front of Miss Kingsley. What she does with her spare time is purely up to her own discretion and I won't hear of it from you of all people. Slinking around like some little sewer rat sniffing out a catastrophe or a scandal. You're unfit to be in Miss Kingsley's presence." By the end of his small tirade, his face had become a few shades darker and Shannon was elated.

"Did you know," Nero continued without bothering to reply, "That he comes and goes through the fire escape? What an odd fellow, I should say. And certainly he can't live in the city. Just a companion of the detective's I suppose? Perhaps his courting of Miss Kingsley is simply a ruse and he and the detective are..." he trailed off so he could watch Valechy's face become twisted with rage.

"...Out."

"What's that, Jimmy?"

"Get...out." He took a deep breath. "Get out before I throw you out."

"Hmm, an interesting threat. No worries, Valechy. I'll be leaving. But I won't be *leaving*." He turned and slithered out the door without a sound save the bells that jingles from the door frame.

She turned back to Valechy and asked, "What's he mean? That he won't be *leaving*?"

"He means that he'll be watching. All of us. He's a dangerous man, Miss Kingsley. I would stay as far away from him as you possibly could. And keep Adrian away from him. I would hate to think of what would happen if they ever met. Although, rest assured, Adrian would be ridding the world of someone I don't particularly care for."

"I'm sure Adrian and Winston's relationship would look quite strange from an outsider perspective. So it's not too surprising that he might jump to that kind of conclusion. In fact I'm surprised you were even able to look at Adrian and make the connections that you did."

He sighed. "When you've been staring at the same photos and research for as long as I have, you have difficulty *not* seeing similarities. And when things just fell into place so easily—it was a no-brainer. I was surprised that I hadn't made the connections *before*. Just goes to show you that I'm the journalist who's more focused on the past research and Nero's better suited for the present. That's why he's working for a newspaper and I'm writing a book." He shook his head. "He doesn't have the kind of background knowledge of Winston to make the types of deductions that I have. But I'd be wary of him, Miss Kingsley. He'll sniff around for weakness and as soon as he has any kind of scent, he'll stick to it better than any bloodhound. I'd start making sure you're in a secure location before you speak to Winston or Adrian about anything sensitive. Also warn Winston about taps on phones if he has a home phone."

She shook her head. "They work with cell phones only."

He nodded. "I'd just be careful. And tell your friends to do the same. Nero's not out to solve this murder or be kind to those trying to do so. He's out to get the juiciest story. The best scandal. Even if it means ruining lives."

She touched his hand gently and found it warm. "Thank you Mr. Valechy. I should say the same for you. Be careful in dealing with Winston and Adrian. They might seem like the heroes of this story...but they're just as dangerous as the villain."

The two of them were smoking on the fire escape. They were both leaning forward on the railing, their bare feet getting slowly imprinted by the grate under them. Their elbows were just inches apart and the scent of tobacco floated out from them into the night, the smoke forming ethereal dragons that lived for just a few seconds before disappearing into the slight breeze. They flicked their ash at the same time and brought up their Camel and Marlboro to their lips in a synchronized sweep of the hand. One the left hand. One the right. Faint music was coming from the apartment below them. The *Cheers* theme song, muffled but audible on their landing of the fire escape.

The night was hot and a storm was brewing in the distance. From their height they could see the black thunderhead rising against the navy blue night sky, its planes and shadows formed by the light of the full moon. Lightning sparked inside of it and they were silent together, watching the bright white lights flash through the invading force that would bring upon them a fierce storm.

They had time to smoke just one more cigarette before the storm would roil over their part of the city so they did. When they were finished, the thunder was echoing across the landscape and the rains were just a few minutes away, the darkness overtaking their sky without effort. The first of the rains fell as Ren was shutting the window.

Winston cleared his throat while he sat down on the couch and put his feet up on the coffee table in front of him. "They sent Avery home today. He's healing up well. There'll be scars, of course."

Ren didn't reply. He picked up the guitar and sat cross-legged on the floor.

"Do you really know who the killer is?" He had been doubting for days it seemed. If Ren really hadn't seen the killer's face and was simply toying with him. Like a dog with a wounded cat. "Don't lie to me, please." It was futile but he might as well try.

Ren strummed once then put his palm over the strings to silence them. "I know who the killer is."

Winston leaned his head back and closed his eyes. "What is your motivation to keep it a secret?"

Ren shook his head. He wouldn't answer that one. He strummed more and began to pick out a song over the pounding of the rain. Lightning flashed outside the window and the thunder drowned out the music for a moment before it was back and a different song. A slow, sad song that Winston couldn't exactly place. When Ren started to sing, he popped his head up and was slightly awed by the smooth deep thrum of Ren's voice. A voice that Winston had never before heard.

They stayed that way until the song was over and Ren picked the last of the notes out of the old guitar. They haunted Winston's consciousness, replaying over and over, warbled and muffled in his mind as though he were laying at the bottom of a pool.

Ren held the guitar as if he were to play more but couldn't. When the muffled melody faded from Winston's mind, all he could hear was the constant song of the rain around the apartment.

Ren spoke again with clarity and confidence.

"You wouldn't understand my reason." He tapped a finger on the guitar which made a hollow sound.

"I think you underestimate me."

Ren looked him in the eyes but didn't respond. "I don't want you to fail, Winnie. I want you to succeed."

"So help me." He leaned forward, his elbows on his knees and his hands together in front of him. "Help me succeed. Help me do the right thing. Help me and I'll help you."

"You can't help me."

"What about all that stuff about a new name? A new social security card? Internet access? A fake driver's license? I'll get you all that stuff." A tiny speck of frustration was in his gut, welling up like a spring. He suppressed it. "I'll do all that for you."

Ren closed his eyes and hung his head. "It's one of the boys."

Winston slid from the couch down on one knee, kneeling before Ren with his head tilted to one side imploringly. "Please. Which one?"

"I can't. I won't. I need time."

"Time? For what?"

He shook his head. "There are things simply beyond your ken, detective, and though I may not be one of them, *this* is." He got up and moved toward the kitchen. This was his signal for Winston to quit pestering him. For Winston to leave him alone. If he didn't then he would force Ren out into the driving rain to huddle under a tree or an overpass for blessed silence alone. He tried to imagine the poor dog, when the rain cleared and the moon shone down, howling out his pain in his sleep. The killer stood facing the cupboards with his hand resting gently on his side. His quick movements had hurt him.

"There's whiskey in the cupboard over the fridge," he supplied and Ren reached upward with his free hand, careful not to stretch too far. "Rum too. Pick your poison. The shot glasses are up there too."

Ren ambled back with two glasses and the bottle of *Maker's Mark*.

"That's good shit right there," Winston grinned. "Smooth."

"I wouldn't know. I don't drink often." Ren shrugged one shoulder.

Winston scoffed, "At least there's one thing you don't do, faggot." He smiled and Ren smiled back. "Tell me another story."

"Okay," Ren grinned while Winston poured their first set of shots on the coffee table. "The last time I got drunk. I was living in this set of woods next to this rest stop by the side of the highway. There were vending machines and I was living off of Pop-Tarts, Skittles, and pints of milk. I managed to filch money off of some of the truckers who would stop by there for a bathroom stop but I was running out. There was a point where I didn't have much money at all and I was close to starving. I was drinking rain water and I must have looked like shit." He swallowed and took the shot that was in his glass. "You're right. That's fuckin' smooth." He sighed. "I was sitting on the bench that was in front of all the photos of the missing kids. The roof was over that part and it was raining pretty hard. The place was empty. There was nobody. But this truck comes in. *Hardy's Haulin'* or some shit like that. Fuck if I know." He wiped his mouth with the back of his hand as if he'd just eaten something awful and Winston poured him another after he took his own.

"This guy comes out of it. He's not bad lookin' I s'pose. He was gray and maybe fifty or sixty but fit and looked like he could hold his own. Kinda looked like the type you'd find at a biker bar. Fuckin' mustache and sunglasses. Sunglasses on a rainy day. The fuck. I was a kid. I was just-turned-20 and I asked him if he had any spare change for the vending machine." He shook his head. "He looked around himself like he was looking for someone to be watchin' 'im. Then he turns back and tells me that sure, he has about fifty cents to give me in his pocket. Fifty cents was enough for some M&Ms so I took it and he took a piss and I was eating them when he came out. He told me he had more stuff in his truck. He was amiable enough. So I went."

"Ren," Winston chided.

"Shut up and suck a fuck, I was hungry and I could just kill 'im if I wanted and eat *him*."

"I'm sure that's exactly what you were thinking." The detective rolled his eyes and took his second shot, closing his eyes and letting the burn wash over him and the weight of Ren's words fill his mind.

"His truck was warm and the seat was cozy. There was a sleeping area behind the seats and it was fairly large and looked really comfortable. He reached back there and pulled out this bottle of clear rum and he gave it to me in soda in a plastic cup. He sipped some himself but didn't offer me any more food. He just talked a little, asked me about myself, where I came from, stuff like that. My stomach was growling and I was starting to get a little fuzzy around the corners. He gave me another cup and I obediently drank it. Then he pulls out this turkey sandwich. It had lettuce and onion and tomato and he said the mayo was like this tangy kind that was absolutely delicious. Said he got it from this deli not too far back. But if I wanted it I'd have to help him out a little." Ren licked his lips and took his second shot. "I was thinkin' he needed help hiding a body. I was a little miffed since I don't exactly *hide* bodies as that is not my *forte*. You know what I mean. Anyways. He didn't mean that. He started unzipping his pants and I was just baffled. I had no idea what was going on.

"Turns out," Ren laughed, "he wanted me to suck his cock right there in this truck in this parking lot."

Winston's lips were tight together and his eyes narrowed at the young killer across from him. He poured the both of them a third and set the bottle down with a clack on the glass table top.

"I was trying to gauge how hungry I was. You know? 'Cause I was pretty hungry but I didn't know if I was hungry enough to suck a dick for a turkey sandwich. I kinda looked down at my M&Ms and he waved this sandwich at me. And I was more than drunk. I was drugged. And I gotta say I took it like a champ. Tried my best, Winnie, tried my very best. And you know what? Killing the guy never really crossed my mind. I was half-in and half-out but there was a lot of spit involved and I fuckin' *enjoyed* that turkey sandwich." Ren nodded and swallowed his *Maker's Mark* and coughed a little after it. "He laid me down in that comfy little bed. When I woke up I was still wearing all my clothes, it was night time, warm, and his back was touching mine. He hadn't even touched me. Not that what he did wasn't wrong or anything. I'm sure it was, but. I mean I needed a turkey sandwich and he needed a blowie."

Winston tsked, "That's disgusting."

Ren shrugged. "He fondled my thighs a little in the morning but didn't bother me for anything else. Just thanked me and slapped my ass when I left the cab. No lie, I didn't eat anything for days. That's how fuckin' great this sandwich was. He was sent as a gift."

"Oh yeah?" Winston laughed. "A gift from the Lord. An angel came down to give you a turkey sandwich and face-fuck you."

"I didn't say he was a gift from *Heaven*," Ren pouted. He was starting to sway where he sat and he sighed heavily. He awkwardly changed the subject. "I wish she would magically somehow be slutty."

"Who?" Winston finished off his own third shot and put the bottle on the floor next to him.

Ren shrugged.

"Shannon? Boy, that girl is *way* above your head." He chuckled at the thought of Miss Kingsley acting slutty. "Do you want her to be slutty so you can just have her? Is that what it is? You're not a fan of deflowering virgins? Does she have less value if she's slutty so you wouldn't mind having her?"

Ren growled, "That's *not* what I *meant*." There was a fierceness in his cold dark eyes that Winston suddenly feared.

"Okay. Then why do you say that?"

"She knows what she wants. She knows how to get it. But she's just not sure if I'm the person to give it to her. And I'm not sure about that either. Women don't gain or lose value based on their sexual status. They should all have the same value. But that's the problem. I'm not the kind of man who can think of them all as takeable. They should be accessible or inaccessible. I mean. In a way they are. Inaccessible until they allow you to have access. But." He balled his fist and put it against his forehead. "This is very difficult. It's not women who have a fluctuating value." He tapped his forehead with his thumb. "It's *me*."

Winston nodded his head. He was, as Ren had put it, fuzzy around the edges. For one mad second he thought about just slapping the shit out of that scummy little fuck in front of him but he didn't. He didn't because he was right. The fluctuating value of a person wasn't based in their sexual status or their career or anything externalized. The fluctuating value of a person was based in the eyes of those who viewed them and in turn was directly influenced by that second person's idea of self-worth and the dominant media culture. This was too much for Winston's tipsy mind so he put a cork in it. There was too much in Ren's eyes that betrayed him. That Shannon could never be his equal. That perhaps nobody could be. A deep sadness. A longing. A missing puzzle piece.

Ren shook his head and continued to play the guitar, picking out the same sad song as he had before but he didn't sing. He just played continuously while Winston sat there across from him. The storm raged on through the night.

CHAPTER 18

She was sitting with Leslie on the back patio sipping tea when Mother sauntered out with a pair of designer sunglasses perched on the top of her perfect hair.

"Oh Shannon, good. I'm glad you're here. Your father and I have been talking and we've tried to come up with a little something that will help Sean out of his latest funk."

She raised her eyebrow and she and Leslie shared a glance. "You've *noticed* that Sean's in a funk? Since when do you guys actually notice when he's not acting right? He's always like this. He's a ball of change."

Her mother huffed a little, "He's just been a little more quiet than usual and he hasn't broken any of my knick-knacks in the last few days. That's very unlike him. It's almost like he's too angry to even try to break them."

"You've noticed that he breaks them?"

"Of course I have. That's why it's so odd when he's gone so long without doing it. I think he's bottling something up. That's why your father and I have decided that you and the boys, including Adrian, of course, should go down to the lake house for a little vacation. That's if Adrian can get off work, I suppose."

"He'll be fine," she dismissed. "The lake house? But Mother, that's..."

"Rather far, I know, but I think it'd be better for your safety and to get away from this whole business for a little while. Besides, you and Adrian need some serious alone time so you can stop being so uptight about everything." She chuckled heartily. "This is only for you guys to get away from everything and start actually considering your twenties as a time to be *enjoyed*. Shannon dear, please do something rash." Her brows knitted, "That sounds very unlike what a mother should say to her daughter, but I'm saying it now because I mean it. You've got to do something out of the *ordinary*."

If only you knew, she thought.

Mother beamed at Leslie with an evil little glint in her eye. "In fact I think Leslie should go too. You've earned yourself a bit of a vacation and I think they could do with a little eye on them. And of course Shannon could do with a bit of girlish company since she's such a tomboy."

Leslie smiled at Shannon and gave her a little wink. It would be easier with Leslie there. It would be *much* easier.

Shannon couldn't help but grin. She'd originally had a mischievous idea about the whole vacation. Her grin faded when she thought about Adrian. And her. At the lake house. Together. She gulped to herself.

Sean appeared out of nowhere and took the empty fourth chair between Mother and Leslie, his hands in his lap. He looked at each of them and then gave a comical frown. "What's going on in this odd little triangle? I've missed something. That or something's afoot, and I'm prepared to deal with the latter. What have you women been plotting?"

Shannon replied, "We're plotting to kidnap you."

"Oh yeah?" He lifted a brow. "You and what army?"

"Your friends is what army. I'm sure they'd love a late-summer getaway at the lake."

"The lake," he smiled. There were many old childhood memories in that smile. "I'm sure that's not a very awful place to go as a kidnap victim. I'd be delighted to accompany the perpetrators. In fact, I will even assist them in their quest." He got up. "I'll be in my room packing and awaiting the dark figure who shall swoop in through my window." He gave a pointed look to Shannon and she felt her heart drop into her bowels. "I assume Adrian will be joining us?"

"Uh." She was having a hard time controlling herself. She couldn't speak. *He knew?* "Um. Yes. I will ask him."

"Good. I look forward to seeing him."

She sat awkwardly for a few moments before Mother started blathering on about something else. "I've," she interrupted her mother, "I've got to go."

"Are you feeling alright, dear?"

"I'm fine. I just need to talk to Adrian."

She smiled that lecherous smile. "Of course dear, run along."

It was a particularly hot day and as she stood down on the sidewalk in front of the detective's office building she wasn't quite sure where she was going or why. She didn't know where Adrian might be, but she did know where she could find Winston at such a time of day. She tapped her shoe on the sidewalk and tried to ignore the people who were passing by and staring at her while her dusty-pink sundress fluttered around her in the wind. It tossed her hair around her shoulders and she tucked it back behind her ear before she finally made up her mind and wandered in.

The air conditioning was not bad inside and she promptly headed over to Office 19 where Winston was usually hidden away, tucked behind his desk as if talking to the world were the worst of his fears. When she pushed open the already ajar door she first saw Winston sitting at his desk with a pen dangling out of his mouth, caught between his teeth while he typed away on his computer. When she noticed the other man in the room, a slight breath came out of her throat with a tiny exclamation. "Oh."

He was taller than Winston. What she noticed first were the wounds on his face. Mostly-healed traumatic injuries on either of his cheeks. It appeared as though some malicious character had attempted to...her stomach churned. *Widen his smile.* The second thing she noticed about him was that he looked rather tired. The corners of his real mouth turned up just slightly when he saw her and he nodded toward her in a sheepish way as if embarrassed by his appearance. When he turned away from her toward the other desk she noted that one whole arm was covered in an odd-looking scar that was a dark brownish-pink color. He was wearing a T-shirt so it was impossible to tell how far the scar went under his shirt.

Winston looked up at her and took the pen out of his mouth. "Miss Kingsley, this is my partner Avery. He's just here to pick up some stuff and then he's going home to rest. Right Avery?" It sounded like a warning.

"It's good to meet you finally. I'm very glad you're recuperating. Awful business." Shannon made a small wave and held out here hand.

Avery turned around again and lightly shook it.

"I'm sure you've been most curious as to how the investigation has been going. But Winston's been doing such a wonderful job." She was trying not to stare at his face, her eyes flitting around the room. To Winston, to the photos on the walls, to Avery's dark pink left hand.

"I'm not curious at all really," Avery muttered. His voice was deep and rich and calming.

Her heartbeat steadied even in her confusion. "But—"

"Winston's told me all about his efforts in the investigation. And yours too."

Her wide eyes found Winston smiling at her from his desk. "You mean you know about everything?"

"Of course. Trent and I are partners. He's always had a darker side." Avery winked at his partner and it looked as though he was trying to smile but it hurt so he kept his mouth straight. It shone in his eyes anyway. "You're the one I'm curious about, Miss Kingsley. Why keep up such a charade? Because you're passionate about finding the killer? Because you have some kind of innate sense of justice?" He sat on the edge of his desk and crossed his arms over his chest. "I'm curious as to your motivation to continue playing this game that Winston's set up. He's a bastard you know. You shouldn't trust him."

Winston didn't object.

Shannon cleared her throat daintily. "If you must know why I continue to march on in such a manner then I will tell you. I think I'm quite in love with Adrian. He's the embodiment of everything adventurous I've never done in my life and I don't care if I'm hurt by it. I would rather experience it now and be ruined by it than never experience

163

it at all." She nodded her head as if trying to convince herself.

"So it has nothing to do with the case or Winston at all." She could tell that if the man could smile his grin would be huge. His eyes glittered with appreciation. "You've got your own purely selfish wants and needs and your actions are guided by something more than just logic and reason. You're human." He shrugged and put up his hands in a surrendered pose before he slapped both palms against his sides. "You're making a mistake."

She wasn't sure what to say but she blurted, "I would say I have a right to do that. He *is* a bit...odd."

There was a pause in the room before Winston and Avery started chuckling together and Shannon's cheeks turned a bright pink.

Winston was still chuckling when he stated, "Wonderful, Miss Kingsley, wonderful. Now I'm assuming you came here for a reason?"

"Yes. Yes I did." She frowned at them both. "You've got me all jumbled up now. I came here to tell you that the boys and I are going on a small vacation to our family lake house and Adrian was invited to go with us."

Avery nodded, "Perfect. A great place for Winston to sneak around and for Ren to cause panic, mayhem, and disorder. And when I say mayhem I'm not utilizing it in the colloquial way meaning havoc, although I'm sure there will be plenty of that too." He raised a brow at Winston.

"Don't put up such a fuss," Winston chided, "He'll be fine. He's got a little more self-control than that."

"You're right," Avery sighed. "It was nice meeting you, Miss Kingsley. I'm going to go home and pretend I don't know anything while Trent whips up Ren, or should I say Adrian, a nice set of fake identifications."

Winston gave a little puff of air in Avery's direction while the detective left, limping a little and moving slowly out the door past her. "Don't listen to that mopey sod," he mumbled, "he's just jealous he didn't think of it first. Using Ren that is. It's not exactly the first time."

"Not the first time?"

Winston shrugged one shoulder and went back to typing while he spoke to her. "We ran into him while working a case back where Avery and I used to live. He was my one that got away. Ruined my engagement, ruined my confidence, destroyed me. I thought I was going to get him. But turns out he was more valuable to me if he was free. He started giving me things. He tracked down a killer and he gave me a runaway. He was the stone I used to kill two birds."

"I see." She did see. At least a little bit. It was killing the man to have to see Ren as human and to see him experience emotion. "You're still angry at him. For everything. He can't make that up to you. Even though he's trying."

"Is he? What could he possibly gain from trying to make me forgive him?" Winston's typing was getting angrier and angrier. His fingers mashed down on the keys so hard she thought he might break them.

Shannon approached the detective's desk and sat on it, her body twisted so she could look him in the eyes. He finally stopped murdering his keyboard and looked up at her. There was something other than frustration and anger in his expression. Something that was more like desperation. "This is going to sound silly," she mumbled, "but bear with me. I'm under the impression that Adrian is convinced that he's trapped within his past. That he's still sixteen and he can't do anything about it. No matter what, he'll always be this angst-ridden teenager whose only skill is in murder. That's what he believes. And you're the hero of the story. You're the one who's going to lead the charge to victory. He's upset that he can't ever take the role of lead man. You know? He'll always be under someone's thumb. And usually it's yours."

"So what does he have to gain from sucking up to you?" She held up her thumb and forefinger just an inch apart. "A tiny iota of internal satisfaction and peace."

Winston's eyelids drooped down and his face lost all expression. "Brilliant," was his sarcastic response.

"Well if you don't like my theory then I've got nothing else." She stood up and crossed her arms. "You probably know something I don't know too. Which would keep me from figuring out a less-than-pure motive."

At that moment the door behind her opened and she stepped forward to allow a rather suave-looking gentleman enter. He gave her a single glance before addressing Winston in a formal tone. "It fits. It all fits. But which one of them I don't know since *they all* fit. I'd focus on the smallest one if I were you but keep your eye out for them all."

She watched Winston's face as he reacted to this news. It didn't move. But his words contradicted his expression. "The smallest one. Okay. Thanks Rayne, if you need me I'll be in here growing eyes out of the back of my skull."

Rayne muttered on his way out, "Thought you already had them..."

She balked. "Are you *all* this nutty?"

"It makes for an interesting work day," he answered, taking a sip from an apparently forgotten Starbucks cup. He wrinkled his nose at the taste—or perhaps the coldness—and looked up at her from his chair, a playful little smile just hinted at the corners of his mouth. "So you're in love with Adrian. That's an interesting development. I hope you've thought about this a little. Has he casually deflowered you yet?"

"Casually *what*? No. Goodness no." Her cheeks were turning pink again. "Nothing like that. Though I suppose that's par for the course?"

"Naturally. Although to be honest I've known about quite a few of his conquests and only one holds any similarities to you." He tapped his pen on his desk and appeared to be thinking quite hard. "Yeah. You're a lot like her."

"Who exactly?"

The detective cleared his throat and shuffled some papers on his desk. "The runaway he gave me three years ago. Her name was Tomi. Remember, I mentioned her almost braining me with a stick?"

She nodded. "Oh. But he gave her up?"

"Yep. I made him a deal and he chose himself over her. That's who he *is,* Miss Kingsley. He'll choose himself over a woman any day of the week. He's not a lover. He's a fighter. A self-centered fighter."

The lake house was secluded in a dense smattering of forest surrounding a lake that had been affectionately dubbed "Duck Pond

Lake." It was three stories high and unpainted, the stained wood giving it a rustic look despite wide open picture windows and french doors which made it more modern and spacey. Winston wasn't enjoying the house like Ren was going to. He was simply observing, carefully planted at the edge of the tree line with a pair of binoculars. He blessed the design of the house for those wide picture windows that would allow him to see most of what was going on inside.

So far he had made a list of all the rooms he had a clear view into. He could see the majority of the living room and the dining room. He could see a sliver of the kitchen through the french doors. And he could see just a bit of one of the bedrooms. He had a clear view of the back of the house, the back patio, and the dock that jutted out into the lake.

He was taking notes when he heard it. A twig snapping. The sunny day suddenly turned darker and colder as a chill came over him. He fought it hard. "What are you doing, Ren?" he asked.

There was no response. Winston's heart was suddenly in his throat and he turned around quickly, scanning the dark forest behind him for any slight movements. This was no animal. Someone knew he was there. Someone had followed him. His hand moved to his side and rested on the comforting texture of his gun.

"I'm armed," he warned the forest. "And I will not hesitate." He waited for a long while. There were no other sounds. He went back to his note-taking, uneasy and disgruntled.

They were laying on a blanket outside in the morning sun. Dew still kissed the tips of the blades of grass in the back yard and the air still held its night-time nip. They were staring up at the sky together, the sun hidden behind a stray cloud. Goosebumps rose on her arms. They had been silent for over ten minutes. She could feel his warmth next to her and she breathed in and out heavily. They would be heading out to the lake house that afternoon. For some reason she was dreading it. It was supposed to be a nice getaway but Adrian hadn't acted relieved in the slightest. In fact he had seemed more crestfallen than elated.

She turned her head and looked at his profile. There was a scar under his left eye. A thin raised white line. Almost perfectly straight, as if made by a blade. It was the only scar she could see. He was wearing a three-quarter length sleeved T-shirt that effectively hid those that had caused her so much anxiety. He still had boyish freckles over the bridge of his nose and some faded on his cheeks.

He shifted so he could look at her out of the corners of his eyes. "Yes?"

"You were right."

His brows raised.

"My brother did cocaine."

He turned back and faced the sky again. "Sorry."

"You don't have to be sorry. I'm sure he enjoyed himself immensely." She paused before her curiosity got the best of her. "What does it feel like?"

"Cocaine?"

"The other one."

"Heroin." He nodded. "Depends on the stuff you get. Sometimes I'd just get really warm and then throw up. Other times I'd be sitting under trash bags in some back alley and it would feel like I was floating in some ethereal place with the most intense feeling of happiness and comfort I've ever felt in my life. It was like nothing I'd ever felt before. Or ever will again." He shrugged. "Depends."

"How many kinds of drugs have you tried?"

He chuckled, "Just about all of them, I suppose."

"Have you hallucinated?"

He frowned. "Not to the point of absurdity, no. But on 'shrooms every sound had a color and on acid every inanimate thing seemed like it was breathing or had a heartbeat. And on acid I seem to remember having this urge to just walk in a straight line forever. The idea of *forever* was pretty amazing. But then again *everything* was pretty amazing."

"Where did you get these things?"

He shifted again to look at her. "Around. Some are easy to find. Some are hard. Depends on where you are, who you know, and what

168

kind of things are circling around in the trade. For example it's pretty damn easy to find some good weed but many times, it's hard as shit to find good acid. There's just not a huge market for it."

"You sound really experienced." The wind rustled the trees above them and the sun came out from behind the errant cloud, shining down on them sweetly.

"You could say that." He rolled onto his side and propped his head up, his cheek in his palm. "You know what else I'm experienced in?"

Murder? Mayhem? Torture? "What?" Her eyes narrowed up at him.

He leaned down and softly touched his lips to hers. He whispered against her cheek, "Kissing."

She allowed him to kiss her more deeply and responded well when he expertly probed her mouth with his tongue. She was on the verge of moaning when she remembered where they were and pushed gently on his shoulders. She murmured, "They could see us from the house."

"They could. If they were looking."

"I don't want them to."

His deep blue eyes were intense but she stared him down and he retreated. "Sorry."

She shook her head, "Don't apologize. We can kiss later. I'm just...shy."

"Worried Winston's watching? He's not. He's busy staking out your parents' lake house."

"Why would he do that?"

Adrian shrugged one shoulder.

"He thinks that the killer is one of the boys? That's...that's awful." She blinked. "Well if I had to guess which one...oh, I couldn't do that. I would guess that it's *not* Preston. Wait...maybe...no..." The weight of it fell on her. The killer was one of Sean's friends? "He has to be mistaken. There's no way."

"He's pretty set on it."

It would mean that they had falsified their alibis. It would mean that she had sat with the murderer at a wedding. It would mean that she'd known him for her entire life. It would mean that she had gone to his golf tournaments, polo games, or graduation ceremonies. It would mean that Sean's friend, *her* friend, was capable of being a cold-blooded killer. Worse, he was capable of *lying* to her about it. She looked at Adrian, his face blank as he watched her thinking. Would Adrian lie if faced with the truth? If she asked him, could he tell her a bold-faced lie? She licked her lips and for one mad second she thought about blurting it out. *I know you're a killer.* It was stuck in her throat and her jaws seemed glued together.

"I wouldn't worry about it."

Her mouth became unstuck suddenly. "But they're *raising money* to pay him."

"I won't argue this with you," he warned with a stern glance. "It's upsetting you."

"Well of course it's upsetting me. These are my friends. I've known them forever. I just can't see them doing something like this. I mean it's just wrong." Her inner voice kept repeating the same word. *Hypocrite.* She was close to loving Adrian despite his murderous past. Why was it so horrible for her other friends to have been killers? Were they "too good" for something like psychopathy? The beautiful summer morning had turned a few shades grayer to her eyes. "He has to be mistaken. They're not bad people."

Adrian's brow twitched. "Nobody said they were. Shannon, remember, they're innocent until proven guilty. Besides, nothing's going to happen. It'll be fine. Just a few days out at your parents' lake house. Who is there to murder?"

She found his eyes and her voice was forced into a whisper by her realization. "You." Tears welled in her eyes at the thought of his injury. Hadn't Winston gotten that threatening note? Hadn't Adrian been threatened? And if they were all sleeping in the same house, then wasn't he in rather serious danger?

"Come on now, sweets," he laughed. "I'll be fine." He picked at the blanket between them and smiled at her. "Like I said, nothing's going to happen. Everyone will be just fine. If you're still unsure then I'll just make sure that you're always with me. So someone will have witnessed my fate and you can hold me as I lay dying."

She choked and her tears overflowed suddenly.

"Shannon?" He sat up and his grin disappeared. "Hey, that wasn't meant to make you cry. It was supposed to make you laugh."

She sat up and wiped her eyes on her forearm and hid her face in her hands, trying to quell her sobbing. When she couldn't stop she just leaned over toward him and he held her tight against his chest and calmly shushed her as quietly as he could, petting her hair slowly until her crying turned into hiccups.

"I'm sorry," he whispered, "I shouldn't have said that. I'm not going to die. I promise."

"Yuh-you c-can't promise that." She buried her face in his chest and held his shirt in tight fists.

"Come on, sweets. Come on. Let's go inside and get you a glass of tea. It'll make you feel better. You know, one girl I met used to think that nobody could kill me. That I was the devil."

She sniffled and hiccuped and turned her face away from him. She wasn't sure if she wanted to know anything about whether or not he was the devil. She wasn't sure what she wanted to believe.

"If I can convince you that I'm the devil then you'll never have to worry about me again." When she looked up at him with her red-rimmed puffy eyes, he was giving her an award-winning smile. A smile that would have convinced anyone that Adrian—or rather *Ren*—was in fact Satan himself as it contained that single identifying factor that had hit her before. His mouth looked like a shark's mouth. As if he had rows upon rows of shiny white blades lurking in there just waiting for their next taste of human blood and suffering. It was nothing short of terrifying. A chill passed through her body as if it were in her very blood and bones and her hiccups left her suddenly. When he spoke again it was in a grittier, low-toned voice that betrayed how long he had smoked and how much darkness was inside him. He was still smiling when he said clearly, "There's something about perception that makes all the difference in the world. You know it's all in your head, right?"

She shut her eyes hard, willing Adrian to be Adrian again and not this demon called "Ren" any longer. She put her hands over her eyes again and did not open them until he had gently pulled her hands away.

His eyes were kind and the smile gone.

"I'm not going to swallow you whole," he murmured. "Though that doesn't mean I don't bite," he laughed, and started to tickle her and despite some protests from her end he got her to laugh, her tears forgotten, cold things at the corners of her eyes. When he stopped, he was hugging her tight, her head nestled in the warm nook of his shoulder. "I know you're afraid. Not just because there's a killer out there but because he quite possibly has been lurking under someone's skin. Someone normal. Someone you know."

CHAPTER 19

She and Adrian arrived at the house first in her little Jetta. They parked in the garage and walked around to the front door so Adrian could get the best possible first impression of the lake house in all its grandeur. Leslie would be arriving later, but before she did, Shannon wanted to get out some of the Swiffer dusters and dust of some of the antique furniture so Leslie wouldn't feel obligated to do so when she came. She opened the double front doors and took in the scent of old books, furniture, and memories. It was the smell of any good antique store.

She watched Adrian's face as he inspected the interior of the house, his glassy ice eyes moving over the expensive décor and the luxurious rugs, tapestries, and portraits. It was open and filled with natural light thanks to the very generous amount of large windows which gave it a good summer house appeal. She very quickly went about and opened many of these windows to allow for a good cross breeze to air out the stale parts of the living areas and sitting rooms.

When she turned around again, he was nowhere to be found and she had to search him out, finding him in the kitchen inspecting the food stores in the pantry. "Enough food for you?"

"Plenty," he mumbled.

She wondered if he was in a darker mood because it was hot. "Why don't you take off that long sleeve and put on a T-shirt?"

He cocked a brow. "You're not the only person in the world who can recognize a track mark when they see one. You don't even watch TV often."

She crinkled her nose and handed him a duster from under the kitchen sink and instructed him to move about the house and dust things. She watched him moving, reaching behind things and around things. Delicate and lithe and much like a careful little creature who easily moved around silently. The thought that he moved like a snake passed through her mind but then left when she shook her head. Not a snake. He had too many angles for a snake. He carefully reached around a lamp to dust the little table beyond it, concentrated fully on his work. Finally, she couldn't watch him anymore. He wasn't human enough. He didn't make enough mistakes at such a task. She busied herself with taking a few steaks from the basement freezer and putting them in the kitchen refrigerator for them to thaw so the boys could have something to grill later.

When Adrian walked into the kitchen with a rather gray-looking duster, she didn't look at him but stated, "Steven."

"What?"

"Steven. That's my guess. Because it's only human to guess wrong and he's the one I feel the least amount of affection towards. He also seems to be the most likely candidate seeming as he is always the nay-sayer, the pessimist, and the bullied one. He seems like he would be smart enough even though he doesn't quite show it very well, but he's always being pushed around by the others. It only makes sense. I mean they *all* could make sense but I just don't think Kyle has the brains for it." She shrugged at him while he looked at her with blank cold eyes.

He jerked his head to the side to show her that he was considering her statements to be valid and then he turned around and plopped the dusting pad into the trash can. Without request, he opened the cupboard under the sink and got out the wood polish and a rag and wandered about the house polishing the wooden surfaces as if it were only normal to do so. She nodded to herself and took out the vacuum, sucking up all the dust bunnies that had collected throughout the empty times. She focused on the chandeliers as they seemed to have become a rather good place for the spiders and were inundated with cobwebs.

The thought hit her then. He was much like a spider. Despite the warmth in the house, she suddenly got the chills and goosebumps rose on her arms. "Adrian?" she asked. He didn't respond. She moved about the ground floor and he was nowhere in sight. The can of polish and the rag were sitting alone on the shining dining room table, the rest of the furniture already polished. "Adrian?" she asked again.

"Yes?"

She turned around, "Oh, there you are. You scared me for a second."

"I was just curious about the basement is all." He smiled at her.

Curious about the basement. He's examining his web. She swallowed hard. "Oh. The house is rather new so there's nothing interesting about it. I wish there could have been something neat about it like a coal chute. But there isn't." She laughed nervously. "We used to play hide and go seek and we'd try to hide down there but we were always paranoid that it was haunted. I suppose it's not since nobody has died here." *Yet.* A creeping fear started to coil in her gut. The returning knowledge that she would be trapped for the next few days in a house with a killer.

"Interesting." His eyes were still cold and his mind was turning. "Would you show me the upstairs?"

"Sure." She smiled, but it was forced. She watched him as he examined each room, the windows, the beds, the closets that were filled with clean white linens and extra towels. Almost every room had its own small bathroom with a stand-up shower and a toilet and sink. Only one room, the master suite, had its own jacuzzi tub, double sink, and king-sized bed. There was another sitting room with huge skylights on the second floor and Adrian smiled up at them, watching the birds fly over them from the massive oak tree that stood on the east side of the house. "Did you wish to see the attic as well? It's finished."

He nodded without looking at her. He was busily thinking, and such a thing worried her. He was planning. Calculating. *Preparing.*

When she led him up the stairs to the attic, she heard him take in a deep breath. The attic was one large single room with many futons and comfy chairs scattered about. A persian rug lay on the floor in front of a massive flat-screen television that had a sleek black Xbox 360 *Elite* hooked up to it. Five black wireless controllers were in five different seats. *Just enough since Ben is gone.* Light flooded the room from all the different windows that were scattered around the attic, the shadows from the branches of the oak playing across the wooden floor as the leaves fluttered in the breeze.

"They really like to play *Gears of War*. Ben got it for Kyle's birthday. I just watch."

He nodded. "How long before you think they'll get here?"

She shrugged. "Oh, one never really knows. They lollygag all over the place before they actually make it somewhere they want to go."

"Good." A handsome grin spread across his face and he turned toward her and took her hand, leading her across the attic floor to the futon in front of the TV. When he sat her down, she was shocked when he was suddenly on his knees in front of her. His hands spread open her thighs so his body could move between them and he pulled her forward, claiming her mouth easily in a soul-deep kiss that went on for an unknown amount of time and could only be described as earth-shattering. His tongue moved in and out of her mouth in a slow motion and she ached for him in her most secretive of places. Unwittingly, she gave a soft moan through her nose and he leaned her back against the back of the futon, his hand grazing the soft skin of her side under her shirt.

When he broke the kiss, he gave feather-light ones down her jaw to her neck and nipped at her skin there while his hands were busily touching her and pulling up her T-shirt. It wasn't long before he'd gotten the shirt completely off of her and he was kissing her again while his hands reached behind her and she arched her back. The click of the hooks of her bra coming loose was enough to send more ripples of apprehension through her body. The soft light of the sun coming in through the windows illuminated her pale breasts and she turned her head away and closed her eyes. She didn't want to see him looking at her but she could feel him doing so. Her whole body prickled with anticipation and he did not let her down. His mouth came over one nipple and his palm rasped over the other.

When he had spent enough time lavishing her breasts with affection, one hand slid down her belly and with one harsh motion unfastened her shorts. His head rested against her chest, his ear to her breast as if he was listening carefully to the pounding of her heart. She gripped his bleached white hair and pulled tight, gasping lightly when his hand delved boldly under the thin fabric of her panties and cupped her.

"Adrian," she whispered.

"Shannon," was his response. She was relieved to find that her name from his lips had sounded shaky and unsure. As if casually deflowering her may *not* actually have been his intent. "We can stop any time." It was a genuine offer and she was surely going to take him up on it.

"Not yet, please." She shook her head, but she couldn't open her eyes.

His fingers parted her and one slid inside her. Her other hand gripped his shoulder hard and the one in his hair pulled. He took a harsh breath through his teeth—perhaps a reaction to her pulling his hair—and he pushed a second finger into her. He moved them in and out of her while his other hand played with her breast and he raised up his head to claim her mouth again in a kiss that mimicked his hand.

When he pulled away from her, she thought perhaps they had been interrupted again but he was simply moving backwards to look at her. She finally opened her eyes and gazed at his intense expression. He was watching her breathe—her breasts moving up and down with the soft force of every inhale and exhale. He leaned forward and his fingers tucked into the sides of her shorts and the straps of her panties and pulled until he had taken them off of her so that she wore nothing but her boating shoes. If he took those she would be completely naked in front of him, her thighs spread, her cheeks pink, and her body aching for whatever he could give her.

Is this what it feels like to want someone? Does it always hurt? She blinked while she watched him lick his lips. A hungry animal hovering over its prey. She thought that if he didn't touch her soon she might scream with her wanting. Her *needing*.

Turns out, she didn't have to wait long. She cried out when he dove down and she felt his mouth on her. Hot, deep, searing, pure, the most amazing thing she'd ever felt. His thumbs spread her open and his lips and tongue moved over her and she couldn't stop the desperate sounds that poured out from her throat as shock after shock moved through her body. He had to hold her thighs apart, as her instinct was to curl away from such an intense feeling. She wasn't sure if she wanted him to stop or continue, she wasn't quite sure of *anything* really and there was an odd ringing in her ears. She could barely focus on her own voice, the moaning cries that were peppered over "Oh god" and "Adriannnnnnnnnahhh." Her hands were still buried in his hair, clawing at his short punk style and her head was thrown back on the futon, her vocalizations thrown toward the ceiling of the attic recklessly and with abandon.

Something was caught in her chest. Something she didn't recognize. A ball of pure frustration that was about to explode if he didn't stop. She had to make him stop. She couldn't even see anymore. Her vision was white, her breaths nothing but gasps, her muscles twitching uncontrollably, her thighs pushing so hard together that his fingers were digging into them to stop her from crushing his head between them. She didn't even scream out loud. It was nothing but a soft whine and hiss from her throat and finally he stopped, putting his palm over her throbbing womanhood and his other hand on her chest, pushing her into the back of the futon, holding her steady while she breathed hard and heavy and tried to regain her bearings on this reality.

The world was coming back from the foggy white of her release and she vaguely recognized that there were tear tracks running from the corners of her eyes back into her hair. She wiped them with the heels of her palms and stared at the man in front of her, his white hair jutting out at odd angles and his dark ocean blue eyes clouded over by lust. He still had his palm over her and she could feel herself pulsing from the aftermath of her orgasm, her legs trembling around him.

"Shannon," he breathed. "You're beautiful."

She hid her face behind her hands until he took his own from her body and gripped her wrists, pulling them away from her eyes. "Don't look at me," she whispered.

"Why not? You're amazing."

She shook her head and closed her eyes against him. "You've said that before."

"And they've all needed to hear it. Just like you. Women are beautiful. They just don't know it all the time." He kissed just below her ear. "We should get you dressed before the boys show up. I don't suppose your brother would take kindly to such a predicament."

He helped her in putting her clothes on and she finger-combed her hair before getting up on her wobbly feet. There was a wetness still between her legs. "I...I have to go to the bathroom," she managed to mumble.

"Okay," was his response. She could hear the humor in it. His smug little man-smile.

They descended the stairs to the first floor and she went to the bathroom while he waited in the kitchen. Just as she was finished making sure she looked at least somewhat presentable, the front door opened. It was Leslie. She emerged from the bathroom just in time to see him helping her with her heavy baggage, asking her which room she'd like him to take it to. Shannon popped back into the bathroom for a few seconds to make sure her cheeks weren't too pink before she stepped out again and walked into the kitchen.

Soon the boys would show up. Soon everything would come together. *And then fall apart.* She closed her eyes against her own thoughts and turned around to look out the large windows toward the back yard and the dock. It was picturesque. It was as though nothing bad could ever happen. It was as if she were transported back in time to her childhood when the worst thing that could happen was Sean's teasing or losing her teddy. The sunlight glittered off the surface of the lake and pattered down onto the grass through the leaves of the trees surrounding it. There was nothing that could go wrong here. Right? Winston had to be mistaken about one of the boys being the killer. It had to be some kind of misunderstanding that had led him to believe something like that. But in the end, didn't it just make sense that way?

The door opened again and she heard the ruckus that was Sean, Kyle, Preston, and Steven crashing through the door, their loud voices echoing down the hallways.

Winston was in his jeans and a thin hooded sweatshirt, his camera sitting heavily against his chest. He usually wasn't the type of P.I. to require such tools, but the zoom feature on this camera was easier to focus than normal binoculars and one could never tell when photographs might tell a story a little better. He grinned to himself and took a sip of his Coke from the bottle at his side. It may or may not have had a few shots of Jack poured in recklessly from the bottle in the trunk of the Fusion. Tipped in without the aid of a shot glass or a funnel. Just the steady hands of a man who knew what the hell was going on. Or maybe he just wasn't sure at all.

The boys had just arrived at the house. Their loud banter was enough to alert him. Their tomfoolery would be enough entertainment to keep him interested at least until night fell. He had set it up so that Ren would have him connected via Bluetooth, but that was only if Ren was willing. His hesitancy to actually go through with the plan was starting to weigh heavily on Winston's mind. He wondered just what exactly was going through Ren's head when he stated that he needed more time. More time *to do what*?

His ears perked but he didn't turn around. There was something or someone behind him. It wasn't Ren. The killer hadn't left the house. None of the boys were behind him either. They were all in the house. Goosebumps rose on his arms and the back of his neck prickled. He spoke evenly and plainly. "I have a gun."

"As I'm fully aware," came the response.

Winston finally turned his head to see a husky-built young man he recognized as Jim Valechy. A nosy little journalist who was trying to write a book. Since the book he was writing was all about Winston, he didn't bother to introduce himself. He merely gave the journalist a rude once-over and then turned around again.

"I know what your plan is and I urge you to reconsider."

"Is that so," Winston mumbled as he peered through the camera's viewfinder. "Have any bright ideas then, kid?"

"Well, um..." So he'd stumped him. Already. The journalist was certainly no engineer, that was for certain. His plan for confronting Winston was merely just that. A confrontation. No solutions. No suggestions. Just a simple "stop." "I guess you could...I mean."

"Is it important for you to stop this?" Winston asked him suddenly, breaking his concentration.

There was a pause. The journalist had to think. Was it important? Was it really important for him to stop this whole scheme from playing out? "If Rockey gets away, I would be indirectly responsible for all the lives he took afterward. Did you think about that, Winston? At all?"

Winston stared hard at him. "I don't concern myself with trifles."

"*Trifles*? You consider these people as *trifles*? Winston, please. You're not really saying this, are you? You're in this job to protect people, to help people, to find some answers for them."

"I will not feed into your romanticized version of me. Tell me why you're here or stop wasting my time."

Valechy started to puff up like he was trying to make himself look bigger out of some instinctual ritual, like a cat arching its back. "I'm here to try to protect you. To get you to stop this stupid scheme and turn Ren in to the police before the whole thing starts ending up with bodies everywhere. You should get out of this while you still can. You should give him up."

"I should just give him up? Really? Is that your solution to everything? Just throw it away if it's a little dangerous?" Winston's voice was low into a hiss and his eyes even harder on the young man in front of him. There was a pressure in his stomach. A familiar feeling of rage within him. "Do you have any idea how complicated this whole thing is? How in-depth this entire plan is? Do you have any idea how I even got him to *listen* to me? This shit isn't *easy* you paunchy little asshole."

Valechy took one step back at the odd insult.

"If I gave Ren to Blaze now it would ruin the whole investigation. Not to mention Ren and I would probably end up sharing a cell since I know for damn sure the fucker would sing as long and loud as he could like the jailbird he is." Winston kicked at a branch beside him, his glare boring into Valechy so hard he wished he could actually make a hole with it. Right in the bastard's forehead. "I'm almost done with this shitty little party and when I am, I'm letting him go one way and I'm going the other. You got that, you clotpole?"

Valechy was nearly speechless.

"And *stop* writing a goddamn book about me. I don't need more people thinking I actually *care*." He turned around again and looked through the viewfinder. Sean Kingsley and the boys were already in swim trunks, towels on their arms, marching toward the dock in bare feet. They were smiling. Ren was lingering on the patio still wearing his khaki cargo shorts and his dark gray long-sleeve. Shannon was next to him, watching her brother's friends with her arms crossed, shaking her head a little at their antics. "Why don't you write about things people actually want to read?"

Valechy was silent for a few moments but Winston knew he was still standing there. When the journalist spoke again, it was with finality. "Fine. I will. Forget you. You're not who I thought you were anyway."

"Join the fucking club," Winston spat over his shoulder while the disheartened Valechy ambled away. A few seconds later the camera drooped from Winston's eye and the world shifted into shades of gray. He wondered for a moment and then looked again over his shoulder.

CHAPTER 20

"C'mon Adrian." Preston jerked his head toward the lake, his hair plastered to his forehead, wet from his initial dive off the end of the dock. "Take a swim with us. You've gotta be hot. It's a good exercise and Shannon should come too. I know she's got this hot little string bikini. She only wore it once last year because Kyle couldn't stop staring at her, the boob." He laughed.

Adrian tapped his finger on the patio table's surface and stared at his iced tea. "I'm not a very strong swimmer."

She could tell he was lying. She piped up. "We can go swimming later. I don't wanna wear that bikini in front of you guys, it's embarrassing. Why don't we swim at night?"

"Spoil sports," Preston joked before running back off toward the dock and doing a flip into the water.

"Thanks," he sighed.

"I have an idea." She caught his arm and rolled up his sleeve, surprised that he allowed her to do so. "Why don't you get a tattoo here?" Her fingers ran lightly down his forearm and the scars there. "Then you wouldn't have to worry about someone recognizing them. Just get something to hide them."

He shook his head.

She grabbed his hand and held it on the table's surface, squeezing hard. "Why?" *Are you afraid it'll make you too identifiable? Are you afraid it'll get you caught?* She almost said it. She almost blurted it out. *Stop running. Don't run from me. Stay here. Forever.* She thought that last word that had floated through her mind would have scared the living daylights out of him and it might have already done so in her. *Forever?* She bit her bottom lip.

"I don't know," was his response. He was still looking at his iced tea despite her hands holding his. "I'm just not huge into getting all tatted up. I might just be a pussy. Can't handle the feeling of being stung by forty-thousand bees or something." He gave her a nervous laugh.

She shrugged. "Up to you." She flipped her hair over her shoulder so she could look out across the expanse of the lake and across the yard to the edge of the wooded area. Something glinting from the trees caught her eye. "Is Winston watching us?"

"Yep." He took a sip of his tea.

"Hmm. He should hide better."

He raised a brow and leaned over to get a better vantage point to where she was looking. "That's not Winnie."

"What?"

"That's not Winnie. Winnie's over that way," he jerked his head in another direction so as not to make Winston's position obvious.

"Then who is that?"

"Fuck if I know," Adrian leaned back in his chair and breathed outward as though he had no care in the world. His cold eyes watched the boys as they swam and fucked around with Steven, nearly drowning him with their rough-housing.

There were clouds gathering in the southwest: a hint of a storm later in the evening. They wouldn't swim tonight, she thought. That was fine. There were other things they could find themselves doing. Her cheeks turned pink when she thought of their secretive actions earlier in the day. The way he had made her feel. Her thighs pushed together and she felt that now-familiar wetness between them. She watched him watching her brother's friends, possibly deciding which one could be the killer. His poise was incredible. The way his body was shaped. Like some kind of animal, tense even in relaxation, every string of muscle perfectly shaped and sculpted as if honed through thousands of years of evolution and dozens of months of wild running through harsh terrain—mere survival the only goal. He was more than just a man, she thought, he was fierce and frightening and something closer to a monster.

He was the man she had always been afraid of. The man she feared from her dreams. As she had been such a practical girl and afraid of things that could hurt her in real life—this was as close to a real sort of monster as she could get. She could touch him, feel his heartbeat, and experience the pure raw pleasure that came from something as horrifying as his *mouth*. No matter what she did, he was going to hurt her. Not physically. Oh no. No danger there. She sniffed and took a gulp of her own tea, watching the storm clouds approaching. Her heart was the only part of her in danger from him.

Later in the afternoon, as the sun was making its descent, the boys were drying off on the back patio and she and Adrian were helping Leslie prepare the rest of dinner aside from the steaks Preston was going to grill. When the girls shooed him out of the kitchen and out onto the back deck, she watched him through the windows, interacting with her brother easily and without hesitation. Preston interacted well too, she thought. But the others were still wary of him. Kyle and Steven would sit across from him. Never next to him. They would eye him as though he might threaten them or their social standing within the group. Steven perhaps thought everyone a potential bully.

One of them was the killer. One of them had murdered Ben. At least that's what Winston thought. Perhaps she could talk with each of them. One by one. Get them alone and talk to them. They were so rarely caught without each other that she might be able to glean something. Something that Winston might use.

Of course, wasn't it dangerous? She shivered to herself as she prepared the mashed potatoes, putting a bit of garlic powder in with them to give them a slight zing. She would have to consider it just part of her life at this point. If she were going to become a target for the murderer, at least Adrian would avenge her. She bit her lip.

Throughout dinner, she was mostly silent. She was so zoned out that she almost didn't respond when Leslie thanked her for the polish on the wooden surfaces. She didn't even listen to the boys as they went on about how good the steaks had turned out. She only half-heard them when they were teasing Adrian about his courtship of her. She wasn't interested in them together. She was only interested in them apart. She looked around and decided that she would choose one to talk to. Tonight. The first. She eyed each one.

Preston, she thought to herself. *I'll talk to Preston. He's the one who smiles the most and he'll be the easiest to get me into my groove.* She nodded slightly to herself. *He'll be practice.*

After dinner they all paraded into the den and started a fire in the fireplace. The first patter of rain started on the roof and Leslie went around making sure that all the windows were closed before she brought the box of cards for *Cards Against Humanity* which Adrian seemed to be particularly tickled by. The pairing up of politically incorrect cards with other politically incorrect cards seemed to be his strong suit and he won easily, putting the rest of them in stitches with his odd card "haikus" and disgusting pair-ups.

It was easy to get Preston alone. He went into the kitchen for more wine and she followed, leaving the rest of them behind with Adrian as the source of their raucous laughter.

"Preston," she asked as he opened the fridge, taking out the Rosé they had started earlier in the evening. She handed him her glass and he filled it almost to the brim. She didn't know what to ask him. "Where were you when Ben died" seemed like something that was a little too confrontational. She decided on, "What do you think of Adrian?"

"I like him." There had been no hesitation. "I think he's funny and sweet and he's most definitely a keeper." His strong and wide smile was slightly influenced by how tipsy he was but she could tell he was genuine. He really did like Adrian.

"A keeper?"

"Yeah. He's a keeper. Hold onto that one." He didn't bother pouring his own wine. He just gulped it from the mouth of the bottle and she snorted a little at this. "Now I'm not saying that he might not be flawed. I mean, he's a little on edge, but he's better after he has a smoke. Always has them Camels on him I guess." He shrugged. "But if you're into that. He's a bad boy, you know? But inside him. There's good in there."

She nodded. "All this murder business has got me all tired out." She changed the subject a little awkwardly.

Preston didn't seem to notice her awkwardness and shrugged both his shoulders this time. "I try to not think about it. I really don't like considering the fact that this is so close to me. Truth is, I actually try to be a little drunk all the time so I can deal with it better. Maybe that's why I'm such a charmer." He winked at her. "I hate that you're all caught up in this too, Shan. We're not bad guys, the five...er...the four of us. We're just cautious."

She narrowed her eyes at him and sipped her drink to try to mimic him so he wouldn't think she was after information. "What do you mean that you're cautious?"

He shook his head. "What I mean is that there are just some skeletons in all of our closets and it's hard to let them out when the police are involved. We're rich kids and the reporters love to lap up all that press." He put his hand through his short hair and sighed. "I'm not some Kardashian. I don't like being knocked up by Kanye and having my image dragged through the mud. Having a reality TV show all about my life so people can see how stupid and rich I am? That's not how I want to live my life. I don't want all my sex tapes and dirty secrets strung out like some dirty laundry for the world to see."

Shannon sipped her wine a little more.

Preston stared out at the droplets of rain on the window and the darkness outside. They couldn't see the lake, but the dim yellow light on the end of the dock glowed fuzzily through the weather and the streaked windows. "So that's what I mean. By cautious. We just have to stick together through this. And we *will* get through it. Solidarity is key, you know. We've all got something to hide. I mean, it might sound morbid, but we all just need an alibi every so often." He touched the lips of the bottle in his hand with two fingers. "I just don't know which one of us needs that alibi for murder."

"Or any of you at all," she supplied but the look in his eyes when he glanced up at her was enough to tell her that Winston's realization wasn't simply limited to Winston's mind. Preston was convinced as well. *That one of them was the murderer.* She swallowed and followed him back into the den. Adrian was sipping from a white can of beer with a tiny red leaf on it that she thought might have been Canadian. She sat beside him and he slipped an arm around her waist, a gentle touch that comforted her more than any words ever could.

It was an interesting moment. To suddenly understand that Preston was convinced that the killer was among his own friends. To understand that he had accepted that fact and considered it a side-effect of their shared need for alibis. To provide his murderous friend with an alibi with himself in return for an alibi for his own vices—none of which she could imagine being quite so foul as murder. Could they all consider murder a simple given? Acceptable in the face of letting go of their own philandering and gambling? They were all a little sick, she thought, watching them all laugh together.

She leaned her head against Adrian's shoulder. He was sick too. The thought made her want to cry but she held her breath until the tears were gone. His strong body next to her radiated heat and energy, a body and mind capable of inhuman acts. Just like one of the other boys.

The rain was still beating down hard when they wandered, tired, upstairs. Leslie pulled her aside and whispered with a tiny little grin, "I took the liberty of putting yours and Adrian's things in the same room. Don't kill me." She then wiggled her eyebrows up and down and gave her a thumbs-up while Shannon was still processing what had just occurred. Her and Adrian—sleeping together? She was much too tired to experience the same kind of pleasure he had given her earlier in the day. She gulped. Would he expect something like that to happen?

She led him down the hall and to the room she usually slept in. Sure enough, his bag was on the bed alongside hers and his brows popped up as high as they could go. She watched him carefully as he moved his things and pulled off his shirt, throwing it down on the floor. The bandages around his middle just held a piece of gauze to the cut on his side. It was healing well. It would match the rest of his scars, she thought as she watched his muscles move under his flesh. He meandered into the bathroom with his toothbrush and Crest, scrubbing his teeth with extra caution. She waited for him to be done, changing into tight cotton boy-shorts and a tight T-shirt without a bra. Her normal sleepwear. She let down her hair and put her hands through it. She was just taking her socks off when he came back into the room, the top of the band of his boxer shorts peeking over the waistband of his jeans and the belt he wore.

"Are you finished?" she asked nervously.

"Yeah."

She skirted past him and brushed her own teeth, her heart beating faster and faster in her chest while she watched him in the other room via the mirror, catching a glimpse of him shedding his jeans and socks onto the floor, clad only in his boxers. He was most definitely a fine specimen of a man. His chest was virtually hairless and a thin line of fuzz led down and widened just slightly before dipping below the band of his underwear. She'd only seen male genitalia in pictures, and of course, Sean's back when they were both kids, before puberty, when they would take baths together. But Sean didn't *count*. She wondered what it might look like. Thin? Thick? Long? Short? Curiously bent one way or another? Was he circumcised? She was intensely curious. So curious in fact that she forgot that she was staring at his crotch.

"Ahem," he cleared his throat at her and she looked up at his gaze staring at her in the mirror. Her cheeks turned a lovely shade of violet and she immediately spit out the foam in her mouth and wiped her face off with the fluffy white hand towel.

She wasn't sure what to say. "I'm curious about the 'D'" seemed to not be an option.

The yellow light emitted from the old lamp on the nightstand illuminated the hunger in his eyes. The pure animal lust that clouded their icy depths. When he spoke to her again, it was with a careful leashed voice held together as if just by strings. "I know you're tired." It was that low gritty voice that had frightened her before. But now it just sent odd ripples through her body and set goosebumps over her skin. The wind pulsed against the side of the house and the branches of the tall oak tapped over the windows with a small rhythm that sounded like it could have been the beat to an old blues song.

"I don't…I just…" She shook her head. It was as though all

189

tiredness had flown away from her, but her eyes still remained half-lidded and her knees felt weak.

"Darlin'," he murmured, a hint of a southern dialect clear in that word and in his next, "There ain' nothin' I expect from you." He held his hands at his sides with his palms out toward her as if imploring for her to believe some kind of innocence. "I'll be next to you should you ever want somethin' from me."

For some reason she felt a burn at the back of her eyes and she stood like a stick in the mud in the doorway of the bathroom, the sticky linoleum under her feet. She watched him move toward the bed, pulling back the covers and sliding under the cotton sheets. For a minute she just looked at him from where she stood. His white hair was sticking up and was all that she could see of him until she moved around the bed and his eyes looked up at her, warm now. All the warmth in the world, she thought. She pulled back the covers as well and climbed in, the bed already warm with his excessive body heat. *Are all men like human heaters?*

He didn't reach for her and she understood it. He didn't want to frighten her. He spoke to her softly. "You did a little snooping today. You know you should probably keep yourself out of harm's way."

"Are you trying to spook me?" she asked him, twisting around to face him. Their bodies were just six inches apart and his warm gaze was washing over her.

"Take it from me, I think you're safe right now. But you know, you might put the killer on edge. And killers don't take stress very well."

"And you would know?" She smiled a coy little smile at him.

"Who says I wouldn't?" With this statement he grinned and finally reached over her and curled an arm around her, pulling her closer to him until her body was against his. He was warm and his body was lithe and hard, muscular and strong. "I only said I was a consultant. I didn't say for which business."

She kissed him then. Just a tiny little peck on his soft lips. "I think I'll be okay. Let's just watch each others' backs. Is that a plan?"

"I'll be watching something, darlin', and it might be a little bit below your back." He was still grinning and his minty just-brushed breath tickled her lips before he claimed her mouth in another kiss. She could feel his arousal but he kept himself grounded, leaving the kiss as it was, resting his head on his pillow and staring at her through contented blue eyes.

"I should thank you for your concern," she giggled. Then she stopped and looked deep into his eyes. In a softer yet more serious tone she asked, "Adrian, can I trust you?"

His whisper back made her heart skip, "As far as you can throw me."

She punched his shoulder and laughed, "Jerkbag. I'm being serious." She shifted and she could tell she had rubbed him in just the wrong place as he gave a sharp intake of breath and closed his eyes. She held herself still and continued. "I want to be able to tell you things."

He kept his eyes closed and sighed. "Anything you tell me you have to be able to tell Winnie. I'm…I'm just his dog. It must sound odd to you, but I'm always just someone's dog."

"You don't have to worry about being my dog, Adrian."

"I suppose not. But how exactly do you plan on carrying out this new hobby? Just approaching them all and asking them how much they like me as a person?"

She gasped, "How did you...? Is this whole place bugged? Is that what you were doing when you were looking at the rooms?"

"What are you, Jessica Fletcher? Gonna solve all the mysteries now? Who's the killer, old lady?" He was chuckling.

"What else aren't you telling me?"

"Nothing you need to know."

She was beginning to feel irritation rising in her chest and she bit her bottom lip. She didn't want to say anything to him to raise his ire. She could only imagine the type of ire she could inspire in those dog eyes. She wondered if that warmth she saw in them now could morph into a searing heat. Or a searing cold—so cold that it felt as though one were being scorched by blue flame. She closed her eyes against him and tipped her head forward so as to place her forehead on his. She could feel his gaze so close, the flutterings of his eyelashes against hers even. She whispered to him again and this time her voice shook.

"Adrian. Please."

"Eddie Nero followed us here. Followed *you* here. He thinks that you've got something more to do with the murders than anyone thinks."

"*What*?" She opened her eyes but his were closed.

"Winston doesn't know that."

"How do *you* know that?"

His hand cupped her cheek. "I'm observant."

"What else do you know?"

He shook his head lightly and his whisper was imploring. "Nothing I can tell you that will not risk your safety. Don't make me tell you anything else, sweets. I can't bring you closer to what you're looking for. I can only tell you that it will do you no good to play your game."

"I can't be the Jessica Fletcher of this show? You've got to be the only Columbo?"

"I always thought of myself as more of a Magnum P.I."

She laughed, "You can't be Magnum. That's Winston."

"Lucky fuck."

She kissed him then, gently, and then she took a risk and slipped her tongue into his mouth. He accepted her readily and pulled her until she was on top of him, her breasts squished against his bare chest through her shirt. "Not so lucky," she murmured while she pulled up on the hem of her shirt, baring herself to him and sitting up on his stomach. The light from the lamp on the table illuminated her and she felt his gaze roving over her nakedness. He was right, she thought, he was quite observant. His hands moved to her hips, then her waist, and finally both eased up to cup her full breasts, his palms rasping over her sensitive flesh and causing a hitch in her breath.

"Is your tactic to seduce the truth out of me? You won't succeed."

"Won't I?"

"You're too inexperienced for that."

She ripped his hands off of her and held his wrists to his shoulders. "Bastard."

"Is this your new game?" He was grinning again. "Hold the beast at bay and let him have what he wants when he tells you all the secrets? It's a good game. But I am very good at holding myself back."

Her heart was beating faster and faster. The tattoo of it drumming in her ears. "I don't want you to have sex with me," she admitted.

"No?"

She shifted a little and a flash of pain shot through his expression and he groaned. "I'm sorry," she faltered, fearing she had pressed against his wound.

It was a ruse, she realized too late as he easily overpowered her and flipped her so that their positions were reversed. His hands were on her wrists, held by her shoulders while he hovered over her. The sudden movement had her baffled if only for a moment. With a voice that didn't show any sign of exertion at all he chuckled, "You're much better suited to be a house cat than a hound dog, Miss Kingsley."

"Miss Kingsley? When did I suddenly become Miss Kingsley again? When my shirt came off?" She arched her back and gasped when his mouth suckled one dusky pink nipple. She balled her fists and tried to move them but he held her fast. "I thought you weren't going to force me?"

He removed himself from her breast and murmured, his breath grazing her sensitive flesh, "You provoke me, miss." He sat up, releasing her. "But as promised, I expect nothing of you and I will never inflict on a lady any fate which I could not expect her to inflict onto me." He mocked a shallow bow toward her and got up, sliding off the bed and heading toward the bathroom.

"Where are you going?"

"I'm going to jerk it in the bathroom."

A sudden and horrifying idea crossed her mind and she blurted it out before she could think properly about it. "Can I watch you?"

He paused for just a moment at the door to the bathroom, obviously considering her request. "No," was the short reply. The door clicked shut and immediately she was on her knees beside it, her ear pressed against the wood shamelessly listening for those delicious hitches in his breath and maybe, if she was lucky, a groan or two. She waited expectantly to hear those sounds that would ease her curiosity and her want of him but they never came, save a single sigh that she just barely heard over the rain outside. When he opened the door again, he leaned against the door frame and looked down at her with his arms crossed, a twinkle of amusement flashing through his eyes. "I'm done being romantic with you."

"You've been anything but romantic."

"Oh, well then allow me to try this again." He cleared his throat, *"Vous êtes le soleil, ma chère. Vous avez toutes l'amour dans mon coeur."*

"I don't know any French."

"That's what makes it romantic."

"Is it?" *Isn't l'amour "love"?* "Are you lying to me but in French?"

His eyebrow twitched downward for a moment. "I've never lied to you."

It felt as though someone had taken her intestines in their hand and squeezed. "I don't care if you *are* predisposed to violence, Mr. Woods. I want to keep you."

The side of his mouth turned up. "When did I become Mr. Woods again? When my shirt came off?"

He was back in the office. The digital recordings from the bugs that Ren had placed all over the house were tedious to go through and no more enlightening than their dinner conversation had been. Ren had neglected to place a bug in the room that he and Shannon were sharing, much to the detective's chagrin, but he understood Ren's reluctance to allow Winston into that part of his life. He'd get him back. A well-played prank would do justice for such an "oversight." Snippets of conversations moved through his mind as he sat at his desk with noise-canceling earphones.

Was there something you needed to say to me, Steven?

N-no.

Okay. If you ever need to talk to me, you know I'm here for you. We only pick on you because we like you.

Th-thanks Sean.

Goodnight.

Night.

The door to Office 19 inched open and Winston's gaze shifted, finding Rayne Wilson's figure standing in the doorway, hesitant and curious. He paused the recording and took off the earphones to invite him to speak.

"I knew you'd be here late," Rayne said. "I figured you'd still be working on this case."

"I feel like I'll be working this case until there are none. You know what I mean."

Rayne's lips pulled back into a grimace and his brows knitted. "I know what you mean."

"If it helps, I'm thinking your killer has a severe complex dealing with the idea of not being good enough or being wrong. He might have been a mistake baby. He most likely doesn't drink or drinks very lightly so as to retain a sort of upper hand. He doesn't have to cloud his judgment or feelings with any substance to commit a murder. It's very cold and calculated. He might prefer to play games of strategy rather than luck and although he might be considered an extrovert, in reality he's very withdrawn and prefers to learn skills alone. I'm willing to bet that your killer works alone through a very perfectionist mindset."

"Interesting. But only one of our boys doesn't fit that kind of description."

Rayne shrugged one shoulder. "You're right. That Preston gent just doesn't fit the mold. He's too perfect. He's too 'classic rich kid.' He might have his own secrets but none of them would ever even come close to murder. Not to say that he's above it, I'm just saying that guilt would probably eat him alive."

Winston nodded. "Thank you, Rayne. You were right when you said you could help me. I'm sorry I've kept you in the dark for so long. I've been wrong to burn bridges."

Rayne flashed him a rare smile. "You've always been moody and secretive, Winston. It's just the way you are. Be careful driving home. It's raining cats and dogs out there."

"You too, buddy." He switched to a different recording and put the phones back over his head, straining himself to hear the muffled conversation at the other end of the hallway from the bug.

I saw...careful...near woods...-porter.

Fucking...can't even get...-way...madness.

He felt his guts squirming. It wasn't him they were talking about in the woods. Who was it? Valechy? His teeth gritted hard.

CHAPTER 21

His strong arms were wrapped around her when she woke up and she was surrounded by the warm masculine scent of his body as they lay under the covers, two little bed bugs snuggled together, lighted by the soft squares of light coming in through the window. The leaves on the oak made an ever-shifting pattern of light and dark over his sleeping visage and she smiled at him. He was too innocent-looking when he slept, she thought. Too human.

His lashes fluttered when he woke and he stared into her eyes with a kindness that was almost unfamiliar to her. He didn't bother to say anything but squeezed her closer to his body, holding her against him while she twined her arms around his back and pressed herself against him fully. He had never lied to her, he'd said. Which meant that she could trust him—but only as far as she could throw him. He was right. He'd never lied to her. At least not outright. But there were so many things he just hadn't told her—wouldn't tell her. Her heart ached to know if he ever would.

They didn't bother talking while they cuddled. His hand cupped her breast but that move was the extent of his morning fondling and they laid together silently until they heard the noises from the rest of the house rising and moving about. It was easy to hear Leslie downstairs in the kitchen rattling about the pans in an effort to make eggs and bacon for everyone and the water was running for Sean's early morning shower.

Preston had the shuffling footsteps in the hallway and Steven always muttered to himself when he was sleepy. She smiled and closed her eyes, her hand coming over his that was curved over her bare breast. He was one of her boys now, despite his and Winston's insistence on being only a temporary installment in her life. Her boys were her boys and he would forever stay in her heart as one of them no matter where he managed to get himself off to.

He still did not speak when he moved away from her and sauntered into the bathroom to pee and brush his teeth. She lay with the blankets at her hips, the patterns of sunlight playing across her bare skin as though they may have been a thousand lovers' lips. She waited for him to come out and see her. To have his eyes cloud over with lust and something else he could only say in French. *L'amour.* But when he did come out, his glance raked over her just for a moment and then was gone and he pulled on a pair of jeans from his bag.

With cautious fingers, he changed the bandage on his side, discarding the old one. He wrapped the new one tight around himself, the wound facing away from her so she couldn't see how badly he was hurt. She'd seen it briefly and still felt so guilty about it. As if she herself had wielded the blade. The cut on his arm had healed quickly, leaving a darkly-pigmented scar in its wake. The center of it was still a bit pink, the skin fresh and new.

Memories of that night flew back to her while she watched him pull on a thin long-sleeved T-shirt, this one black with a white decal on the front overwritten by the singular band name *Styx*. A list of concert locations was on the back but he was too far away for her to try to find D.C. on it. He had crawled in through her window, a shadowy raven who had made her forget the events that had occurred just a few hours before then. She remembered his blood in the bathtub. The streaks of red that had colored the sides of the tub and the toilet. It must have been so painful, she thought while she watched him put his hand through his tousled white hair. She fancied that she could see his dark roots growing in and she wondered if his hair was black like his little beard or just a dark brown.

She'd just put her money on black when there was a knock at the door and she quickly pulled up the covers to her chin. "Yuh-yes?" she called out.

"It's just me." Leslie's voice came as a wondrous relief. "I'm making breakfast downstairs. It'll be ready in a few minutes. Put some pants on and come on down."

"Sure thing," she called out and kept the covers to her chin while she sat up. Adrian was studying her. "What?"

"Nothing. You're just beautiful as always."

"Shut up, you kiss-ass."

He did shut up, slipping on a pair of flip-flops before opening the door and leaving her to her own morning solitude. She considered him for a little while, reflecting on the night before and the things he'd told her. *Eddie Nero thinks I know about the killings?* It was an odd thought. It was an odd situation. He was an odd person to tell her this. *Even Winston doesn't know.* Was it Eddie who had been watching them? Was he the one she had seen in the woods? A shiver ran through her body and while she got up and dressed, she started looking around the room, trying to find the bug that Adrian may have placed. When she couldn't find one, she shrugged to herself and made her way downstairs.

The conversation at the breakfast table sent her mind into a tizzy immediately.

"Well, just think of all the possibilities." Preston was the only one with a martini in his hand. The rest of them were all sipping orange juice. "I mean, consider the fact that every person on this Earth has a mother and father and most of them have at least some kind of family who's on their side."

Her ears perked up. They hadn't noticed her yet as they were all sitting out on the patio and she was just inside the door to the kitchen.

Kyle continued Preston's thought, "The idea of someone just disappearing into nothingness is almost preposterous. There would always be *someone* out there who knew who you were or where you were. It would be insane to have to think of all the different people and ways to cover up your tracks."

Adrian was quiet and she couldn't see his expression as his back was toward her.

Sean tapped his foot on the patio's concrete. "I'm of the mind that disappearance would be possible, but an unlikely way to escape from a crime. There are too many issues to be dealt with. Too many loose ends like we've been saying. But what if you didn't have those connections? A family? A relationship? What if all of that was suddenly gone? It would be rather easy to just come up with a new name for yourself, although these days with all the government hullabaloo about your social security numbers and identifications—it would be difficult to obtain all the correct paperwork. Although, if anyone was on your tail, you could always just ditch that paperwork and go rogue again, I suppose. Tough on whoever you were dealing with, but that's the way of things."

Steven piped up, a small murmur compared to the rest of them. "There are just so many people though. One would have to be born in such a position as to be susceptible toward an ability to disappear. That is to say that someone like us, or hypothetically *me*, would never be able to fully disappear. To live off the radar is something quite difficult, I would imagine."

Adrian finally said his line. "Having no contact with any human being is a hard thing to do and that is what would be required. To have absolutely no contact with society or civilization for at least several months. An occasional food-run would be necessary, but that is easily controlled by simple disguises and a mind for strategic 'strikes' as you might call them."

Steven's expression darkened and Shannon's belly squirmed. Was he gathering information? Was he considering disappearing? Who had started such an odd conversation?

Adrian continued, "The hardest part would be destroying anyone who had seen you getting away or who would have any information on where you would go. Can you trust them? Or do you have to kill them? I suppose that's just a matter of the mind and of loyalty. Could they let you get away with murder? Do you know if they would?"

There was a silence around the table as everyone thought about their particular circumstances. This was the moment she decided to step out onto the patio and they all greeted her, their collective expressions lightening up as she walked out.

"Well, I see everyone is in rare form this morning," she said.

"At the root of it all, we're intellectuals, you know." Sean smiled.

"Oh, don't I know it." She rolled her eyes and sat down with them right as Leslie came out with a giant steaming platter of scrambled eggs. This was followed by bacon, fruit, toast, and every different type of jam she could ever imagine. But her imagination wasn't coming up with how many possible jams there could have been on the table. It was on something much more dark. Something much more sinister. She was stuck on what Adrian had said.

Do you have to kill them?

There were too many liabilities in Adrian's life. Winston. Avery. *Her*. He wasn't aware that she was a liability, though. At least not yet. But what if he did find out? What if he found out and he needed to get away somehow? She couldn't let him get away with murder if she knew about it—he would have to kill her.

Could he?

He would have to kill Winston and Avery too. It would be harder to kill them, logistically. They were much more strategic than she was. They were the hunters. He was the hunted. Killing Winston and Avery was just something of a chore. Killing *her* was another story. She couldn't tell him. She couldn't risk it. Could she? Did she trust him enough? Even after he'd admitted such a thing in public?

As far as I can throw him.

There was a slight bit of panic in her heart. She wanted to be honest with him. She wanted to be able to tell him. A slow, rising panic was welling in her stomach.

Leslie sat in the single empty chair with the rest of them and beamed at them happily. "It's such a wonderful morning. What a fantastic day. You all are just so wonderful, I don't know what I'd do without you."

Shannon took Leslie's hand and squeezed, trying calm her nerves. "Thank you for breakfast. You're fabulous as usual."

They took to eating and it was just half an hour later when the boys figured that it was time for some good old-fashioned sport in the form of tether ball. They dragged Adrian with them to the pole that was set up a small way from the house and they set to playing. She and Leslie watched from the patio. Her anxiety was waning.

"He is a very handsome man," she stated.

Shannon nodded. "Very."

"How was last night?" A kitten smile came over the cook's face.

"Not as sordid as you're thinking it was," she replied. "But thank you for putting us in the same room. He's a good bedwarmer."

"Is that all he's good for?"

"Unless he's hiding some fabulous fortune," she laughed. "No, he's worth more than that. I'm just not ready for more than that yet."

"Your mother is going to be very disappointed with me if I can't get you two together properly."

She stared at the girl. "Mother put you up to this? I should have known. It must have been her idea to have us share a room as well." She tsked. "Tricky devil woman."

Leslie laughed, a sound that was as delightful as the tinkle of a bell. "You are picking up his language and humor. That is at least a good thing. You won't sound as green as you are."

She felt her cheeks turn pink and she moved again to watch him playing against Kyle.

The grass was slippery with the dampness from the rain overnight. It sparkled in the morning light with a thousand little specks of fairy dust on the lawn and over the tall grass that led to the trees he was camped out under. His bottle of Coke didn't have any Jack in it. He was wearing his hiking boots and the jeans he'd allowed Ren to wear after the night of the wedding. They were stained with those old paint smears and the dark spots where Ren's blood had turned a sick shade against the denim.

The whole world seemed as though the colors were bleeding into one another. A watercolor painting that had used too much water. A melting of sorts and a blending. He put the camera up to his eye and watched Ren jumping to hit the yellow ball on a string. Just a dog and his ball. Nothing out of the ordinary, he thought carelessly. *Why didn't the boys bring some girls with them?* He blinked and tried to focus the rest of the world outside the camera view. *Why didn't they bring some girls to fuck? Don't they have girlfriends?* He took a swig of his Coke and watched Ren again, this time standing on the sidelines, his white hair sticking up at odd angles after he'd tried to get the sweat off his brow.

A small glint caught his eye outside of the camera view and he turned his head. With great discretion he pointed the camera lens in that direction and panned the edge of the lake and the woods surrounding it. He almost passed his mark, but caught himself at the last moment. A shimmering. From the reflection of something in the dark of the woods. He could see a languid figure that almost melted into the darkness of the forest. His teeth gritted hard while he racked his brain for something that made sense.

The tension in his jaw tripled when the thought came to him suddenly. His lip curled upward and he thought that perhaps it was he who was making that odd little animal growl that reached his ears.

Eddie. Nero.

CHAPTER 22

It was after Adrian's afternoon shower. He had changed his clothes, favoring shorts and a short-sleeved T-shirt. She was confused until he turned up with an under-armor type elbow supporter. It was something that any of the boys might have worn had they strained themselves at any sport, and if she wasn't mistaken, she could have sworn Sean had something like it for his knee after he'd fallen off his horse during a violent game of polo.

"When do you think it'll fade away?" she asked him and he shrugged at her. "I think I want a nap," she sighed, laying down on the bed while he messed up his hair in the mirror.

"Okay. I thought I might explore a little bit outside if that's alright with you? I'll come wake you up when I get back."

"Mmmf," was her response as she put an arm over her eyes. "Wake me up nicely."

She could hear his smile, "Will do, sweets."

Her dreams were of him. Cool and sensible and sitting on the back patio on a day with not a cloud in the sky. She was laughing with him about something that they shared together. A secret maybe. The sun shined down upon him as though he could do no wrong and all of his past had been erased by nothing but sweet memories of childhood ice cream and musty old antique shops. In front of him was a book, but the title was obscured by a sheet of paper she couldn't read in sloppy left-handed scrawl that must have been his. His smile was wide and sane and squinted his eyes, making temporary crows feet at the corners that proved it to be as real as the trees and the grass around them.

She wanted to kiss him. She wanted to feel his heartbeat. She wanted to touch any part of him and feel his warmth and the closeness of him. A deep sadness started to fill her heart when she reached for him, despite not even having brushed his skin with her fingertips. He was slowly fading away. The world was still as sunny and bright and colorful and cheery but his form was slowly fading. He was translucent and unaware of it. She couldn't open her mouth to tell him that he was...

Dying.

She gasped in a huge rush of air and the world was spinning. Not the world. The *real* world. She was falling but before she could hit the ground strong arms were around her and she cried out, her body bracing for a blow that never came.

"Hey, hey, hey, come on, shhhh, you're alright. You're alright."

She was confused, panicking, her heart racing in her chest, clutching something—*someone*. It took her eyes a little while to focus completely into the warm hazel ones looking down at her. "Wuh-wuh. What are you doing here?"

He smiled. "Obviously, I'm rescuing you." He gave a light chuckle. "Do you think you can stand or shall we sit here for a little?"

"Sit, sit please." She looked around them and realized that she was in the middle of the lawn near the edge of the lake, the house probably around thirty yards away. "Winston," she breathed, "How did I get here?"

"You were sleepwalking. I recognized the glazed look you had from an old case I worked on back in the day. I'm not sure how long you've been wandering around but from the scratches on your legs I'd say you were probably in the woods at some point." He took a handkerchief from his pocket and wiped at her calf. "You might have cut yourself too, there's blood on you."

The detective looked tired and worn out, like he'd been running all day. What crinkled under his eyes appeared to be more worry than tiredness though, and the feeling of guilt suddenly racked her. The poor private investigator had been busily worrying about her well-being instead of worrying about who the killer could be. "I'm so sorry, Detective." She put the heel of her palm to her forehead and closed her eyes. He was too kind to her. "I should have told Sean I was taking a nap. I should have brought the bells with me. Oh, that doesn't make any sense to you though." She shook her head. "This sleepwalking thing has been going on for a little while. Sean and I had a plan to keep it in check but I didn't think about it when we decided to go on a little vacation. I'd forgotten all about it. I'm so sorry. I've taken up your time."

"Miss Kingsley," he murmured, "time spent taking care of you is not time spent wasted. You're an important part of this investigation and I need you to understand that. Now go ahead into the house and find Ren. Adrian," he corrected with a blink. "Get yourself some *Constant Comment* and gather yourself before dinner."

She pursed her lips while she studied him. "You aren't going to lecture me?"

"On what?"

"My interrogation of Preston?"

He grinned. "You did fine for a novice. If you would like to prod at the killer you're welcome to do so. My telling you not to won't convince you at all. You haven't listened to a word of my advice so far and I don't expect you ever will."

She sighed, "Well that's a relief. I think I can stand now." She did with the help of the strong investigator and she brushed herself off rather nicely. Her shirt was torn at her shoulder and at the hem, her shorts had grass stains on the butt, and her legs were covered in scratches. Her bare feet had taken quite a beating too and she was sure they would be sore by the time she made it back to the house. "You should go back to your cover," she suggested. "before they see you."

He shook his head. "It's blown. Forget it. Your feet are bleeding." He motioned down and for certain her feet were streaked with red. "We should get you back to the house and washed up." He turned around and offered her his back and she reluctantly climbed on. With his hands in the crooks of her knees, he asked back over his shoulder, "Comfy?"

"As ever," was her tentative reply. She could just see her feet bobbing up and down as he walked with her as a human backpack. They hurt but they didn't hurt bad enough to be bleeding, she thought. Her body was against his back, her arms around his neck, resting against his collarbone. He was a strong man, built slender but steady. She rested her head on the side of his neck and rocked gently as he walked, dreading the reaction Adrian would have to her less-than-triumphant return—on the back of his best frienemy no less.

"Shan." Preston's jaw seemed to drop to the patio when he saw her over his book and he pushed his reading glasses up to the top of his head, staring between her and Winston while trying to form words. "How did— I didn't even— Where did you— Does Sean know—?"

"Calm down, Mr. Gregory. She's fine. We're just going to go inside and wash up her feet and make her a cup of tea."

"Detective Winston," Preston's voice had obtained an air of officialism. "I request that you put that task onto me. I'm sure that you're much-needed elsewhere. I'm sure you're here for a reason, of course."

Winston paused for a moment and seemed to study Preston hard. "I assure you, Mr. Gregory, Miss Kingsley and I have a few things to discuss."

Discuss?

He waddled with her on his back through the blessedly air-conditioned house towards the bathroom on the first floor where he set her down on the toilet and twirled her about so that her feet were in the bathtub. They'd left Preston standing on the back porch with a book in his hand and his glasses on his head, staring after them like some kind of abandoned animal.

While he ran the water to get it to a bearable temperature, she looked at him. "How did you know my favorite tea was *Constant Comment?*"

"I know a lot of things about you, Miss Kingsley. I thought that should have been apparent by now. Are you going to ask me how I knew where the bathroom was in a house I've never stepped a foot into before?"

She sniffed when he took the removable shower head off its mount and switched the spray to a dribble, passing it over her achy feet to wash off the blood. "I suppose it's just your business to know things like that. Blueprints or some such. But my favorite tea?"

"Your favorite tea can say a lot about you. Much like some believe that their astrological sign says a lot about them."

"And what is Adrian's favorite tea?"

"*Adrian* doesn't have a favorite tea," Winston ground out, his voice laced with venom, "he's a fictional character made up as an alias to cover for a sick-minded serial killer who preys on the good and innocent people of this world." He lifted an eye toward the doorway and then kicked the door shut with a spare foot.

Her heart was suddenly in her stomach and misery started to well up in her throat. Tears pricked the back of her eyes and her lips were suddenly screwed shut. She felt his gentle hands washing the blood off her feet and his thumbs skimming over sensitive raw flesh.

"You'll need a few band-aids, but you'll be fine."

She sniffled and covered her face with her hands so he couldn't see her cry.

He sighed. "I'm not sorry I said that, Miss Kingsley. It's the truth the way I see it and there's nothing that can be done to change it. What's done is done and he's going to have to live with it the way it is. Same as we all do." There was something off in his voice. Something not quite right.

She couldn't stop her crying and she balled her fists over her eyes while she felt him cautiously drying off her wounded feet and heard him digging around in the cabinet for some band-aids.

Winston must have a heart. He couldn't stop explaining himself. "I'm not a sentimental person, Miss Kingsley," he explained in a low voice. "I've never had much need for empathy or feelings for other people. I don't understand the need for small talk or witty banter. I'm a straight-out kind of guy and I'm not used to forcing a belief of some kind of tall tale. Your life can't be based on a lie. Your romance shouldn't be. It's a balancing act and I simply can't stand aside and watch you try to stay on the rope when you're clearly about to fall."

"It's not *fair*," she sobbed, interrupting him. "It's not *fair* that he should be given to me and then taken away."

Winston's tone was lower and a little more firm. "We're not talking about a *car* or a *pet* here, Miss Kingsley. We're talking about a *cold-blooded killer* who's obviously taken his charms with you too far for my comfort. I took him on with this case so he could find the killer and *kill* the killer. Not so he could try to get laid at every turn and act like some spoiled little rich brat with the rest of them."

209

"Why would he want to help *you?*" she spat out at him, finally taking her hands from over her eyes to glare at him. "You're just some jaded, bitter, *malicious* man who's only out for himself. *You're* the one who's cold-blooded, Winston."

He spat back at her, his eyes flashing with something that scared her. Malice. Violence. Rage. His hissed-out words struck at her like a blade: *"Birds of a feather, Miss Kingsley."*

She was sitting in front of him crying. Great. He'd made her cry. *For the love of Christ, did you really just say that to her, Trent?* He blinked at his thoughts and steeled himself again. It was all true. He hadn't brought Ren into this case thinking for one second the guy was going to start sipping *Dom Perignon* or hanging out with crowds who spend nine hundred dollars on *Armani* leather jackets just to look cool. Ren was *not* the type of guy who even wore a watch much less a *Rolex*. And yet the rich life of Shannon and Sean seemed to grow on him. To turn him into less of a ruthless Rottie and more into a complacent mutt, curled by the fireside with one ear perked.

He very lightly placed the band-aids he'd found over each of Shannon's scratches while she shook with her pent-up frustration that released itself as her tears. She was staring at him, unblinking.. She'd sucked in her lips and her entire body was trembling. Every so often she would make a small squeaking sound as though she thought she might have something else to say but thought better of it and stopped herself. That or they were just choked up sobs she was too proud to let go.

"There. Your feet are patched up. When you find Ren, be sure to tell him to keep an eye on you while you sleep."

She didn't answer him and he didn't look at her. He was aware of how much of a cold bastard he was. He was aware of how badly he wanted to pop a Prozac right this moment just to get rid of the feeling that he was in some kind of flattened world of black and white. He was very much aware of those odd thoughts that just kept popping into his head. *Why not now? You've got a gun. Just do it. It'll be quick.* He almost brought a hand up to flick the side of his head but didn't because she was still watching him. She was still glaring at him through teary eyes and her face flushed with anger. He thought about asking her for a Valium. She had to have one somewhere around this magnificent house. Or maybe one of the boys did. Anything to cloud this mind just for a moment. *Why'd you go and do a thing like this, Winston? Look at what you did. This mess you made. There's no way he won't know it was you.*

"Shut up," he whispered.

Shannon's mouth opened suddenly and she took in a deep and shuddering gasp of air. When Winston turned toward her to see what in the world she was going to say, pain suddenly shot through his face and he found himself on the floor. *She just slapped you, idiot.* He was holding his stinging cheek and staring up at her when she got up from the toilet, standing on her bandaged feet. She kicked him hard in the stomach, knocking the wind clear out of him. He was trying to take in a breath—his diaphragm was to busy saying "nope" to such a request— when she kicked him again in the chest.

"How dare you." Her voice was a murmur. "How dare you even rescue me and come into this house just to berate me and my feelings." She hesitated before she kicked him one more time and then disappeared, her stomping audible even after she'd slammed the door to the bathroom behind her, leaving him gulping for air like a fish out of water on the linoleum.

He rolled onto his back and felt the tickle of tears leaking out of the corners of his eyes as his lungs burned for air. When he was finally able to take in small sips of breath, he lay gathering his strength, his hands rubbing the places she'd kicked him on his belly and chest. They would bruise for sure. At least his head was lying on what had to be a fairly expensive bath mat. It felt as though that single part of him was lying on a cloud while he stared up at the white walls of the bathroom, decorated only by a few photographs of some of America's lighthouses. He recognized Hatteras first. A symbol of his home.

He closed his eyes and concentrated on breathing. *Hatteras. Home? It's been so very long since you've been home, Winnie.* His nose wrinkled. Why did the voice in his head have to be *him*? Why couldn't it be Avery? *Because everyone has a dark side, Winnie the Pooh. And yours just so happens to win every so often.*

When he was finally able to sit up, there was still a deep ache in his solar plexus so he put a palm on it. The door opened behind him.

"You smell like blood."

"Ren. Go make some tea and bring it to your girlfriend. And don't touch her feet."

"Why the fuck would I touch Shannon's feet?"

"Just go. *Constant Comment*."

"Whatever." The door shut and he could hear his dog move into the kitchen.

He took a few more minutes to collect himself and to regulate his breathing before he got up and opened the bathroom door, wandering out into the kitchen where Ren was still in the process of heating up water. "She sleepwalks."

"Does she?"

"Yes. She was out like a light outside just walking around. Could have fallen right into the lake and drowned. She's lucky someone found her."

"Someone being you."

Winston gave Ren a pointed look at the anger lacing his tone. "I suggest you keep a better eye on her in the future. I don't know what you're playing at with this game but you'd better start making sense real quick. I don't want to be on this case any longer than I have to be."

Ren glared at him over his shoulder. "Just stay out of my way."

"I'm not sure I can do that anymore."

Their conversation halted when Kyle stepped through the doors from the patio. "Detective. How've you been?"

"It's been an odd few days."

Kyle grinned. "I'm sure it has been. You've probably been watching us. We're terrifically boring when it comes right down to it. Our whole lives are pretty much a vacation. This is just a change in scenery. Anywho, Sean and I are going to set up the badminton net if you'd like to watch us play."

"Love to," Winston breathed while Ren still glared at him. "But I'm afraid I have some other business to attend to at the moment."

Kyle shrugged. "Whatever suits you." He ambled out into the hall and left the two of them alone again.

The water had started to boil so Ren poured it into a mug and opened the cupboards to find a tea packet. When he'd found one he dropped it into the water and turned around. "I'll be with Shannon," he growled.

"Good."

She hugged him while he sat next to her, her head resting on his chest while his back rested on the headboard of the bed. They breathed together for a few minutes, her tea steaming in the mug on the bedside table. The dapples of light from the oak outside played across her bare legs and the band-aids on her feet. They ached and stung in places. His warm body next to her comforted her, filled her with a sense of belonging so strong she wasn't sure how she ever did without it.

"Adrian?" She called him such a name. Such a lie.

"Yes?"

"What's your real name?"

"Renatus."

She smiled, "You're joking." She knew it was the truth, but he had surprised her by saying it.

"Nope. Winston calls me Ren. It was a pet name my mother called me. My father's name was Leonardo." He played with her hair. "I'm not sure how Winston found out my nickname. But then again, I'm not sure how he finds out any of the things he does."

"What's your last name?"

He gritted his teeth. "I'm reluctant to tell you that just based on the Google possibilities."

"You think I'm going to Google you and get negative results?"

"I *know* that if you Google me, you'll get negative results."

"Then forget it." She traced a circle on his chest. "What's the baddest thing you ever did?"

"I'm reluctant to tell you that as well." He chuckled.

"Murder?"

He was quiet.

"You really can't lie to me, can you?" She sat up and looked him straight in the face. "You're incapable of lying to me. So you just stay quiet. Silence is the answer that keeps you within your status quo."

He was silent again and she could tell she'd used up all of his patience. She leaned forward and kissed him but he pushed against her shoulders lightly to stop her. A confused look was enough for him to respond. "I'm...it's not a good time. I'm not a good afternoon lover."

"You did okay the other day." She frowned.

"That was...that was different. I wasn't frustrated with you."

She felt a tiny prick of offense to his statement but decided to just let it go, resting her head on his chest and hugging him around the middle. "I'm sorry," she mumbled.

"It's not all your fault. It's mine too. And Winston's. And..."

"And the killer's?"

"Mostly the killer's." He sighed. "This is going to be the hardest damn thing I've ever done."

"This case?"

He nodded.

"Ren?"

"Don't call me that."

"Adrian then."

"Yes?"

She tapped a finger on his chest. "We're not going to have sex unless you're going to stay with me. Is that understood?"

"I understand."

She flipped over onto her back, her head still resting on his chest. He put his hand over her eyes and she let him. She suddenly felt a bit guilty laying down an ultimatum like that. She felt like the female counterpart of an odd version of *Paradise by the Dashboard Light* and she didn't like the feeling at all. Women were born to be sensual, strong creatures—weren't they? Wasn't that what her mother was trying to get her to be? A strong, independent woman who could make love with whomever she chose and feel perfectly fine about it the next morning or even the next year? She'd never truly dwelled on her sexuality before. It had never occurred to her that she could be "compromised" like Valechy had noted. It was never instilled in her that it was abnormal for her to become sexual with anyone she pleased—she just hadn't found anyone she'd been comfortable with. Now that she had found that comfortable being, she didn't want him to leave. It seemed inevitable. That he should have to leave her. That he, being what he was, would eventually slip away. It would hurt too much, she decided, to have to live with being so intimate with him and then lose him.

It was perhaps ten minutes later before they both got up and went downstairs. Dinner would be in about half an hour and they spent about half that time watching Kyle and Sean knock the birdie around. It was a rich sport, she thought carelessly, watching Adrian's eyes following the small rubber and plastic birdie. He might have played it as a kid on the beach. Next to the Atlantic with his childhood friends. Perhaps. Or perhaps not. She sat on the patio with a glass of sweet lemonade and her feet propped up on Adrian's lap. He grazed fingers between the band-aids, careful of her scratches and humoring her with small tickles.

When the two boys were done playing, they came over to the patio. Kyle and Preston got up to take a walk around the lake, a small towel over Kyle's shoulder to wipe the sweat off his brow and Preston's reading glasses perched atop his head. Sean decided to sit that one out, sitting regally in his patio chair with an iced tea that Leslie had brought out to him.

Her brother looked around with keen eyes and gave a small sniff. "Where is Steven?" he asked. "I haven't seen him all day. I find that to be a little odd. He at least *acts* a little social most times. Although, it *is* his vacation." He sighed and then looked at her, "Love, why don't you go find him and make sure he's not slipping off to go to the clubs without us, would you?"

She nodded, leaving Adrian with her brother while she went to find the rogue boy.

Winston had said that he had taken Adrian on in this investigation so that he could find the killer and *kill* the killer. Which meant that Adrian's purpose was to kill one of them. One of the boys. That familiar panic was starting to well up in her belly again while she padded barefoot down the halls of the large lake house. The sun was hidden suddenly by a cloud, allowing the house to grow darker in a short moment. The shadows disappeared into larger ones and the haunting silence of the empty place was vast and terrifying. She took in a deep breath.

I'm condemning one of them to death.

One of them would be dead by the end of this. She wasn't sure what she could do. Beg Adrian not to kill one of them? It would give away that she knew what he was. It would give away her position as a liability. He would *know* that she *knew*. What would he do? Destroy all of them? Was he so cold? She wandered into the room she shared with him and sunk down onto the side of the bed with her arms wrapped around herself.

One of them was going to die. It was either her or it was one of the boys. Sean would be devastated once more. With no outlet for his frustration. Adrian would leave and that would be the end of it. And she would have to live with it. For the rest of her life.

I'm responsible for the murder of a murderer if I do nothing to stop it. Does he deserve to die for what he's done? That's not up to me to decide. But.

But.

But if I say anything, I could face the wrath of a monster. Is my own life more important than a killer's life?

Her resolve to find the killer first intensified and she stood up, quickly moving about to find Steven in order to talk to him.

Alone.

CHAPTER 23

"Hello Steven." She smiled at him while he sat on the front porch steps with a book and a bottle of Diet 7 Up. He was sipping it with the book open in his other hand when he saw her with those wide puppy-like eyes of his under his tousled reddish hair. "May I sit with you? I don't want to disturb your reading."

"Oh no, I was at the end of the chapter anyhow. Bret Easton Ellis has a way of creeping me out so I'm afraid I'd do anything to put it down for awhile. Funny how books can get so addicting."

She raised her eyebrows and expected to see *American Psycho* beside him but instead her brows were raised only at *Glamorama*. "Well good. I didn't want to impose on you. Have you been reading all afternoon?"

He nodded his head, "Out here on the front porch. Preston's been on the back patio and Kyle and Sean were together all afternoon playing different sports. I'm no good at sports so I simply decided to stay out of it. It seemed like a wise choice." His voice was fluttering and nervous and he was explaining himself a little too much.

Her eyes narrowed. "That's alright, Adrian and I were together all day until I managed to get myself sleepwalking again." She sighed and sat down next to him, her knee just brushing his and causing him to jerk away. She pretended not to notice. "Speaking of Adrian, how do you like him? Is he kinder to you?"

"Than the other boys, yes," Steven nodded, "but it'll only be a matter of time before he starts to feel comfortable enough to pick on me. That's how it usually is." He shrugged. "I don't take any offense to it. I'm content with it as long as it means they'll be around for me when I need them."

"Like say for a false alibi?"

His head swiveled toward her immediately and his mouth opened. "What—what would make you say that?" He sputtered and his hands went to the front of his sweater vest and then his tie that was tucked neatly underneath. "I wouldn't—I mean I—there's nothing that…"

"Preston let me in on it," she chuckled. "That you guys had provided each other alibis I mean. Who were you paired with? What would you have to hide?"

He cleared his throat. "I hardly think that the things I would need an alibi for are things for a polite society lady to hear. I mean, really, I might appear the lonely little bookworm, but Miss Shannon, I fear you may have underestimated me."

"Oh, and I fear you may have underestimated me as well, Steven." She gave him a coy grin and delighted in the blush that colored his pale cheeks. Or was that merely a sunburn? "After all, I *am* being courted by a scoundrel of the highest order as everyone seems to know by now and for certain he's introduced me to things that a polite society lady should perhaps never see or hear or even experience in her life. Did you know he's tried nearly every drug known to mankind?" She put a finger to her lips. "I've always wondered what it would be like to…how do they say it? 'Drop acid?'" She lifted one brow at him.

He cleared his throat. "I assure you, Miss Shannon, I wouldn't know. I merely meant that I may or may not have required an alibi for such things as some ah…" He looked around them and over his shoulders to assure that they were the only ones in attendance. "Some uh…sordid affairs. I have a weakness for blondes, you see, and there are just so many from this one escort service. But if father knew what I was spending my pocket money on he'd have me cut off for sure. Hence the need for an alibi. Now, I know that you're a very delightful young lady and would hold these confessions to yourself of course."

She lightly touched his hand and this time he did not pull away. "Of course, Steven, I wouldn't dream of divulging such information. Your secret is safe with me." She gave him a warm smile to show him her genuine manner.

"If we're busy telling each other our uhm…secrets. Would you mind a little quid pro quo?"

"Hmm?"

The red in his cheeks became deeper while he apparently tried to put his thoughts into words. "I was just. I was thinking. Since I had shared something so deeply personal I was wondering if you would share something ah…something perhaps that Adrian had shared with you."

"Like what?"

He cleared his throat and put a finger to his lips, studying the sidewalk intently before opening his mouth with a large breath. It was obviously hard for him to get out what he wanted to ask. "Uhm. Uh. Ummm. Such as some of the…sexual things he might have shown you? Please excuse my manners, Miss Shannon, but I am curious to know some of the things I might be able to pick up in terms of practical usage. I am not known as a very smooth lover, I must admit."

"That might be something that he would be better off telling you although…there might be something I could tell you." She leaned toward him and cupped her hands around his ear, whispering a description of the way Adrian had used his tongue on her in enough detail that poor Steven's cheeks had flushed so much she might have mistaken the color in them to be more of a purple hue. "Does that help you at all, dear Steven?"

His mouth worked but not a sound escaped his lips. He was too shocked by her. His wide eyes met hers and his mouth suddenly shut. "That's just…" He shook his head. "All it takes is patience, doesn't it? A good amount of patience."

She smiled. "And if you'd like to be more mysterious, just put down the book you're reading and give the ladies a few more scandalous glances next time we have a get-together. Adrian was getting all sorts of ladies' eyes at the wedding just because he looks like a rake and acts like one too. Why don't you start by messing up that slicked back hair of yours and wearing a T-shirt every so often? I know you're stronger than you look under those stuffy dress shirts."

He nodded, staring at the sidewalk again. "You asked me these things because you think I could be involved with the murders." His expression was suddenly serious. "You're unsure of who the killer could be. Of the four of us I mean. It has to be one of us. Preston said that he saw the detective in the house. That he'd been watching us. They're all unsure of who the killer could be. It's because we've shared alibis. Well, it's true. None of the four of us have alibis for any of the killings. And even if we did, such as myself, we would be loathe to hand them out. In addition, any alibi we had with each other would also become moot since we've lost our credibility. Damn this whole situation and damn ourselves for putting us there." His fist was on his knee, curled hard, the tension in his body mounting.

"Don't blame yourself, Steven."

"I will blame myself because I deserve to be blamed. I'm weak against them, Miss Shannon. I'm weak against all of them. They pressured me into providing them with alibis and like the usual boob I am, I said yes." The wind rustled the trees as the sun sank in the sky. Steven was frowning still at the ground. "I can't believe what we've all done. This web we've woven for ourselves. I can't imagine the kind of mayhem that will come about if the killer thinks we're getting close to finding him out."

She cupped a hand over his trembling fist. "That's what I'm trying to avoid by talking to each of you individually. I need this to stop. Not just for my sake but for our sakes. If we want the status quo to continue, if we want everything to go on normally this has to go away. I'm trying to get that across to everyone in the hopes that whomever the killer may be, he'll find it beneficial to quit while he's ahead. Mostly I don't want anything bad to happen to Adrian."

"So this is a selfish little fishing expedition then," Steven smiled at her. "I admire your pluck, you know. You'd never let them pick on you."

"Oh, they pick on me enough as it is. And Sean can be stifling at times. I'm sure you know."

He nodded.

"Anywho, I'm off to talk to Kyle. Thanks for chatting with me." She patted his fist before standing.

"Of course, Miss Shannon, any time."

She padded her way up the porch stairs and wandered back through the hallways toward the kitchen. The sun was hanging in the western sky and the heat of the day was beginning to subside. She knew that it wouldn't get cold out but she could always count on Adrian's wintery eyes to cool her off. *And his warm hands to heat you up.* She shook off the thought.

Just as she entered the kitchen, she saw Kyle and Preston running through the lawn at full tilt toward the house as if they were being chased by some kind of fire-breathing dragon bent on scorching their toned little butts. They burst into the kitchen in a panic, Kyle slipping on the linoleum with mud-covered sneakers, catching himself on the counter and frantically grabbing for the phone. Preston was behind him and doubled over, putting his hands to his knees and panting out four of the most ominous-sounding words she'd thought she'd ever hear.

"Where is the Detective?!"

She opened her mouth but was distracted by Kyle's frantic dialing and his impatient waiting with the phone mashed against his ear. His voice was strained, hiccuping, cracking like a teenage boy.

"We need help, we need an ambulance, we need the police we need...agh. 1456 Briar Lane, it's down a long driveway near the lake. Please hurry. It's just one guy but he's dead. He's dead, man, we found him in the woods and he's dead." He was getting more and more frustrated, more frantic, his voice becoming higher pitched with each word, "Just get here please! Goddamnit I don't know how he was killed, why is this so hard to get through?! *Just get your asses down here!"* His thumb mashed the hang-up button and he threw the phone on the counter, sending it skittering over the marble and crashing into the tin of flour by the toaster. He covered his face with his hands and then ran them through his hair.

Shannon's voice was just a whisper, "I don't know where the detective is. There's been a...murder?"

Preston stood up, his hand clasping his side as he must have had a stitch there. "Yes," he stated breathlessly. "I don't...I don't recognize him. He looks like a reporter."

"You don't recognize him?" Her hand went to her chest and she suddenly found it hard to breathe. "Adrian. I need to talk to Adrian."

He was there, suddenly with her. He'd come from behind her and his hands were on her shoulders. "I'm here."

She took his hands and led him into the den where it was quiet, the early evening sunlight filtering in through the blinds over the windows, shining on the dust motes that filled the empty spaces. When she turned around, she spoke quietly, "There's a body in the woods."

"I heard."

"You're not alarmed."

"I'm plenty alarmed." His eyes didn't look it. Not at all. They still held their ice. "Kyle called the police. They'll be here soon. There's no reason to panic. We'll all sit down in the same room, be questioned in turn, and then events will run their course."

She whispered back, "Are we in danger?"

One of his shoulders rose. "Maybe."

Tears fell down her cheeks suddenly. She hadn't even felt them coming. "Adrian, how can you be so calm about all of this? How can you just stand here in front of me after a man has died and tell me that maybe we're in danger? How can you be so nonchalant about life?" She could feel her lower lip trembling.

I know why. I just don't want to.

He smiled at her and his thumbs wiped her tears away. "I'm not nonchalant about life, Shannon. I'm just not big into panicking over death. There's nothing we can do now for someone who's already dead. So just relax, keep your eyes and ears open, and work with the police as best you can. Always tell them the truth but never speculate. Speak only when spoken to and do not embellish."

Sirens started wailing a far distance off and she curled her arms around his middle and allowed him to comfort her. They were getting closer. They would turn down the long drive and come to the house and again cause havoc. Police tape and constant tracks would remind her of the ever-present specter that haunted this place and her life. The specter of murder. The thought that behind any corner, even corners in her mind, there would be someone who meant harm. The fact that one of those specters was holding her in his arms was not lost on her. She remembered Sean's words and wondered if one day, it would be true. If she would look at him and not Adrian but *Ren* would be staring back at her. If such a day came, could she forgive him? Could she ignore it? Could she *forget* it?

When the boys managed to find him, he was just looking at his reflection in the water of the lake at the end of the dock. It was rippling constantly from the activities of the fish and the ducks and the wind that rifled through the tall strands of plant life and cattails that jutted up from the water's edge. Preston's hard stomping gait came up right behind him but he didn't bother to turn around.

"Detective. Kyle and I. We stumbled on a body. Kyle's already called the police. It's the same as the others."

He didn't turn around when he said it. "I'd like to see it."

"It's this way." His hard stomps moved away.

His reflection almost gave him a longing look. As if pleading him not to go. Was it so painful in reality still? Was he still searching for a way out somehow? A way to escape into that dull grayness. Another murder. Life truly was the only hell, he thought as he turned away from himself and moved to follow the distraught young man toward the woods. It was off the path a little ways and he pulled out a Marlboro and started smoking it to ward off the slightly-off smell that was wafting from the body.

Preston stood stock straight and still, watching Winston as he leaned over, examining the corpse a bit, eventually kneeling down to peer at the dead man lying face down in the forest duff, blood speckling the surrounding leaves, sprayed there by antemortem wounds.

"Interesting," Winston mused.

Preston didn't say anything at first but waited a few minutes with his head tilted toward the sirens that were approaching. "What's interesting?"

Winston stood up fully and took a drag before answering. "I thought he'd left."

"Who?"

"That little fucker journalist. Valechy."

He motioned toward the body. "Is that who that is?"

"Yep." He took another deep drag from his cigarette and started to walk away.

"Aren't you going to…you know…detect?"

"I can't touch the crime scene. Blaze will no doubt be here and he'll be able to actually look around the scene with his team. I'm already close to finding out who the killer is and it turns out that he's done me a favor by killing so close to his friends." He smiled at Preston and he could tell that he'd creeped him out a bit. "He's set the ball rolling so to speak. A killer who's stressed out is much easier to spot."

Preston was silent as he followed Winston away from the scene to the edge of the woods. They stood there a small while, Winston smoking calmly and Preston fidgeting in the leftovers from his anxiety. When he finally spoke, it was not the question that Winston was expecting. "Is Adrian going to leave once all this is over?"

He didn't answer right away and merely watched with the other man as several squad cars and an ambulance raced down the long drive. When they had stopped and the cops were rushing out of them, Blaze included, he stubbed the end of his Red on the tree next to him and dropped the butt in his pocket. Blaze was halfway to him when he murmured his reply. "I don't know."

The police inspector was curt. "Winston. Fuck you. Where is it?"

"About ten yards in, straight back," he replied. "I didn't touch it. Would you like me to gather everyone for questioning?" He didn't bother to hide his smug little smirk.

"In one room," he said brusquely, taking Winston's offered cigarette and planting it behind his ear for later. "Keep them from talking to each other. There will be no made-up alibis for this one."

"Sure thing, Blazed."

"Get fucked," he muttered before he took his men in through the brush.

"Well," Winston murmured to Preston, "let's get to it."

It only took them a few minutes to gather everyone into a single room, Ren sitting with Shannon on the loveseat, their fingers intertwined, while the rest of them milled about the room, only Steven sitting with his book next to him on the arm of the chair. They were silent at Winston's request. When Blaze came in with sweat on his brow, he called each of them one by one. Leslie, Preston, Steven, Kyle, Sean, Shannon, and Adrian. The sight of the dining room door closed while Ren was sitting inside made his mouth itch for a Marlboro. He tried to hold his anxieties back. It was difficult to imagine Ren looking concerned, innocent, modest. He closed his eyes and tried to will Ren to quit looking so smug all the time.

When the young killer emerged, he flashed Winston a tentative smile, probably the warmest that the detective had ever received. Winston made sure that their arms didn't brush when he slid past him and clicked the door shut behind him, Blaze sitting at the table quietly. His reading glasses were perched on his nose while he was scribbling things in his notebooks.

"Funny," he mused in his deep voice.

"What's that?" His heart was pounding.

"I always knew you were too big of a dick to have friends. That Adrian fellow referred to you as his 'frienemy.' I just thought that was a polite way of putting it."

"Putting what? That he can't stand the sight of me but puts up with me for self-serving reasons?"

Blaze grinned, "That just makes him look like the bad guy. We both know the truth." He chuckled before he flipped through the pages. "Winston, I have a problem."

"What's that?"

"Not a single person here has a solid alibi."

"Truth," he sighed and he put his red and white pack of cigarettes on the table, spinning it in a nervous tic. "Tell me where they were."

"Preston was on the patio, Leslie was in the kitchen. Those two remember seeing each other and don't remember either of them being missing. So that's tentative. Steven was on the front porch reading by himself, and Kyle and Sean were playing badminton."

"That one sounds like an alibi."

"Except for one thing. Sean left the court for a pit stop in the middle and they don't remember how long he was gone. Leaving Kyle or Sean able to leave for long enough to whack our guy." The older police investigator tapped his temple with one finger. "Shannon was sleeping. Or should I say sleepwalking outside and doesn't even know where she was. Hell, the girl could have witnessed the murder and she wouldn't even know it. Said you rescued her." His bushy brows raised.

"Before you start thinking that was uncharacteristic of me, I then proceeded to insult her until she slapped me and kicked me multiple times on the floor."

"Sounds more like it," he nodded. "Adrian, that charming little frienemy of yours, was taking a walk. Which leaves him as the most likely candidate for murder. However, he claims he was walking along the drive and Steven claims to remember him there. Said it was how he knew what time it was."

"Let's not forget me, Blaze," Winston smiled. "I don't have an alibi either. I was stalking all these rich little fucks and missed the murder completely. Can't help it when they spread out like they do. I also got distracted by Shannon, who ended up bumping right into me in the woods. That would have been around four-thirty."

"Medical examiner put the death around then," Blaze noted. "Liver temp indicated that T.O.D. would have been between four and four-thirty. So you're saying Shannon bumped into you around four-thirty, you rescued the damsel in distress, got the shit kicked out of you and then what?"

"Adrian found me writhing on the floor in the bathroom. Before that though, when we came back to the house. Preston was on the patio. He didn't look winded or sweaty so he hadn't exerted himself at all. He couldn't have run out and killed anyone and come back. Who's not wearing their original clothes?"

"For blood spatter," he grunted. "You tell me."

Winston shrugged. "I feel as though someone would have noticed something like that. I didn't. As far as I know, you wouldn't change your clothes half way through a badminton game." He opened his cigarettes and pulled one out, rolling it between his fingers absent-mindedly. "I'd look through Kyle and Sean's rooms if you ask me. Maybe you should rifle through Adrian's too. Just to make sure the bastard's on his toes. I kinda wanna make him nervous."

"You're a dick."

"I know." He put his feet up on another chair. "What's the plan, hotshot?"

"There's no plan that I'm going to tell you. You've got no alibi and this Valechy character was supposedly writing a book about you."

"Who told you that?"

"Adrian."

Winston growled, "That dirty suck-fuck. I suppose that makes me a suspect."

"Not quite."

He raised a brow and stopped twirling his Marlboro. "I don't understand, Blaze. I could have recreated the crime in the exact M.O. as our killer just to keep this a-hole reporter from writing this book about me."

Blaze shook his head. "This book wasn't an exposé, Trent. It was some hero worship bullshit. That's what Shannon said anyhow. I'm going to have the guys start going through Valechy's files at home and see what we can come up with. Do you want copies of his manuscript as it is? I'd be willing to bend the rules a bit just to see your face when he describes how warm-hearted you are."

"Just keep it to yourself and fuck off already. Now tell me the plan or I'll make up my own."

"Make up your own, kid, I'm gonna let the crime scene guys sift through the evidence on this one. If you've got a move to make you'd best make sure you make it soon if you want your money. And try not to get any other innocent people murdered while you're at it." He paused for a bit and shuffled his papers together. "You *could* just let *yourself* get whacked though...that'd be a bit of a favor."

Winston stood and popped the cig into his mouth. "In your dreams," he muttered before opening the door.

CHAPTER 24

She was trembling when Winston came out of the dining room, wiping his upper lip with his thumb. He had a cocky expression and for some odd reason that didn't make her feel any better. She linked her hand with Adrian's and squeezed, reassured just a bit from his answering one. They had been curt and formal with her. Asking her where she had been, what she had been doing. When she had told them about her sleepwalking, they had raised their eyebrows at her. She was sure that Sean and Winston could set the record straight. That she did indeed have a history of parasomnia. The detective had simply nodded.

She knew Winston and the police investigator knew each other. They had a history. She watched Winston's face when his gaze met Adrian's and it was one of knowing and conspiracy. A slight lift of one eyebrow and the side of his mouth. For a few seconds Winston just looked like a devilish cat as he slunk through the den and took his seat on the couch armrest next to Kyle.

"So what do we do now?" came Steven's unsure murmur.

"Get on with our lives and don't go anywhere," Winston replied. She finally noticed that he had a cigarette in his hand and he raised it toward Adrian as an invitation. Adrian took it and stood, brushing a hand against her thigh before wandering outside with the P.I., pulling out his own pack of Camels as he went.

She watched them out the window, standing at the edge of the patio smoking. They didn't even look like they were talking at first but the irregular puffs of smoke showed her otherwise. Adrian crossed his arms. They were calm. There was no tension in their shoulders. *What are they talking about? And what are they really talking about underneath that?*

She turned back around and looked at her brother. He was staring at the floor, a frown on his handsome face, his lips tight together. He was thinking. Hard.

It was later on in the evening. The police had left and they were all solemn and quiet, staying close to each other by watching movies and eating dinner together. Just sandwiches. Leslie hadn't been feeling well so they made their own. It was late and she was sitting at the small table in the kitchen reading when Sean walked in. A scowl had been firmly set in his features since his interview with the inspector.

There was clunk on the table and when she looked up from her book she gasped at the item on the surface in front of her.

"It's a nine millimeter. I want you to take it. For protection." His voice was firm and unwavering, the frown still in place. "This situation is dangerous and I want you to be protected. I want you to be able to hold someone off if the need arises."

"And who exactly would I be holding off?"

The bottom lid of his right eye twitched and his teeth gritted only for a moment. "I'm sure I don't know. But this is for your own protection. I don't want to take any chances. Not with your safety. You're my only sister and you cannot be replaced. If anyone were to harm you. I would kill them. Kyle, Steven, Adrian, any of them."

She opened her mouth to protest that Adrian would most certainly not harm her but he held up his finger.

"I don't want to hear it. You should never underestimate anyone. Do you understand me? I know you want to trust everyone. You want everyone to be worthy of that trust. But listen to me now." He knelt beside her chair so that he was looking up into her eyes imploringly. "He does not deserve the trust that you give him. He is dangerous. If the time ever comes that he becomes a threat to you, you need to understand that it is imperative that you protect yourself against him."

"Sean, I know you liked Adrian. What makes you think this way now?"

He shook his head. "I can appreciate a man without turning my back on him. He's not my friend, Shan, and I would never put it past him to deceive."

Neither would I, her careless mind provided. She blinked the thought away. "I understand. Do you think he can help solve the murders? Like father does?"

"I think he has no motivation to do so," Sean grumbled as he stood. "He's a fool to try."

She almost asked him why but decided against it when he sighed and turned around to leave. She watched his back as he left, his once proud shoulders slumped as if in defeat. The gun was still on the table and she made no move to touch it until she had finished her chapter and she thought it was time for bed. It was heavier than she expected and it felt foreign in her hand but she took it upstairs and put it in the bedside table drawer before Adrian walked in behind her.

The next morning, she found Kyle alone in the kitchen eating a bowl of cereal and reading the newspaper. The details of the crime were on the front page, of course, as was anything that involved the Kingsley family and murder. She wrinkled her nose when she saw "Eddie Nero" as the by-line for the biggest headline. She could hear Sean in the dining room through the wooden door talking to Mother trying to convince her that everything was under control and that she shouldn't cancel her salon appointments just for a little murder business that she couldn't change anyhow. She heard him assuring her that he would take care of "Little

231

Shan" the best he could.

"Kyle," she said and he looked up at her with tired blue eyes.

"Yes?"

She sat down across from him and smiled. "What do you think of all this murder business?"

He shrugged, "Inconvenience really."

"Let me get right to the point—"

"You know our alibis for the other murders were false and you'd like to know where I was at those times and why I would provide a false alibi for the others?"

She was taken aback.

Kyle grinned. "Steven told me what you'd asked him. As for my answer to that question, it's rather like a loyalty thing. I scratch your back, you scratch mine. You want an alibi for something, I give it to you. When I need help hauling a body—" he stopped and put up his hands, "Theoretically speaking of course, and in light of the circumstances in poor taste, but you understand. We do things for each other because we want to."

"So where were you really?"

"One of my alibis was true. For the second murder, I was with Preston playing gin rummy and drinking the night away. Did you know he can down an entire bottle of scotch by himself? He's a closet alcoholic, I swear."

She hummed a bit to herself and looked down at the table. The spot where the gun had been. Heavy, metallic, frightening. She thought of it upstairs in the drawer. Waiting like a snake to kill its prey. She wondered what would happen if Adrian found it. Would he look at her differently? Would he assume the intent was that she should point it at him?

"I know there's nil credibility for that alibi, but at least I know it's true and nobody can take the truth from me."

"Would you take the conviction if it came down to it or would you give up who you think the killer is?"

He took in a deep breath and looked out the windows toward the back yard, watching the cool wind passing through the trees and causing small ripples in the surface of the lake. He put his hand to his mouth and thought. "My friends are all I have in this whole world. If one of us is the killer though, he can't go free. He shouldn't go free. I can't value him over strangers. If the choice were to save ten strangers or one friend I would have to choose the strangers merely to settle my conscience. It would haunt me forever if I allowed a killer to go free. We were just being cautious. But now the game is different. The game is real. And one of us is the murderer. I wouldn't take the conviction…but I also wouldn't know who to point out as the culprit. I have no evidence."

She nodded and licked her lips before getting up and pouring herself a cup of coffee. When she came back down after having fixed it up with three spoonfuls of sugar and no cream she asked bluntly, "What do you think of Adrian?"

"What about him?"

"Just in general."

Kyle tilted his head. "I think he's okay. A little rough. Didn't really think you'd be the type to go for the bad guys, but if he caught your eye, more power to him. What does he do again?"

"He's a consultant. I'm assuming for Winston. It seems like he consults on behavior patterns. I wouldn't be surprised if the rough outward appearance is a ruse."

The man seemed shocked by such a revelation. "A ruse? Well that's an odd speculation. You are right, he seems rather charming and experienced. I suppose you're right. He could be showing us just what he wants us to see. Do you feel wronged by that?"

She shook her head. "No. I see enough of him that I'm sure of what I see and what I don't." She scratched the back of her neck during the silence that followed that statement and sipped her coffee while she watched him take spoonfuls of *Life* into his mouth. He was still looking out the back window at the serene scenery that surrounded such horror in their lives. She somehow wished that the blue skies would darken to reflect the way their lives were turning out. Rich and spoiled, they had never really matured. They acted as though they were still thirteen without a single care. She wondered at the way Adrian had grown up too soon.

"Do you think we're bad people for doing what we did?"

She frowned. "No. I think you all did what you thought you were supposed to do. For each other. It doesn't get much simpler than that."

His voice was forlorn and soft when he replied. "No. I suppose it doesn't."

CHAPTER 25

He was napping when she wandered into the room, his body curled on top of the covers as if he were some kind of animal. *I'm always just someone's dog.* She watched him breathing.

She jumped when he spoke without moving. "Like what you see?"

"I always like what I see when I look at you."

"That won't always be."

She crossed her arms. "Maybe. But for now that's all I've got."

"Fair enough," he supplied as he turned over and looked at her with a content expression in his half-lidded gaze. He gave no indication that he knew about the gun in the bedside table. He was blissfully ignorant that Sean had given her something that she was expected to point at him. He put out his arms as a request for her to come to him and she did.

She cuddled into him and slowly fell into a light sleep for a while before there was a knock on the open door and Winston's low tone floated past her ears. "Hey guys, supper's ready."

"Mmmf," was Adrian's response and it quite mirrored her own sentiments.

"Mmkay."

She blinked her eyes open and realized that she was famished. Had they really slept through lunch? She rolled to look out the window at the tall oak's branches and was shocked to find the sunlight as having a hazy sort of quality indicative of a later time in the day. "Adrian," she murmured. "We should get up. I'm hungry."

"I'm always hungry," he replied and those words suddenly struck her. He had told her about shooting up heroin. How he had sometimes been laying in trash. He had been homeless. He had been starving. He had been desperate.

"How would you like to never be hungry again?"

"Is that an offer?"

"It's always been on the table. You've just been reluctant to look at it."

He was quiet and searching her face for something. "I'm not entirely sure of what you're asking right now."

"Think about it." A warmth spread through her belly when she got up and straightened out her clothes. "I'm going down to supper." He watched her leave and joined her on the stairs with a few bounding steps through the hall. She expected him to bring up the subject again, but he was silent as they walked down into the dining room where Leslie had set up the table.

Leslie greeted them when they walked in. "I hope you had a good nap. I set up dinner in here tonight because it looks like it's going to rain soon and I didn't want us to be caught out in it on the patio."

They all heartily agreed that this was the best course of action and sat down together to eat. She noted the way the boys looked at each other. Suspiciously. Anxiously. Driven apart by their own curiosity. *Who is the killer?* She almost lost her appetite when she realized that one of them must be thinking the opposite. *Do they suspect me?* She had to have tensed up because she felt Adrian's palm on her thigh, a reassuring touch.

The storm came as they were finishing up dessert, a strong wind whipping about the branches of the oak next to the house and whistling around the edges of the structure. When the rain came, it was hard and heavy and they sat through it silently, eating their pudding and trying to ignore the unease that had settled around them.

She started when there were three loud knocks on the front door. Winston was the first to stand, his chair skidding backward over the hardwood and his hand instinctively on the butt of his gun at his hip. For a few seconds he looked like a quick-draw gunman in modern times with his black T-shirt and faded jeans.

"Stay here," the detective told them all as he made his way to the door.

There was a hushed but tense conversation that she couldn't quite make out before Winston came back into the dining room followed by a slightly soggy snake-like reporter. Eddie Nero.

"I think we all know who this is," Winston stated, his posture bristled like an annoyed feline.

Sean stood from his seat with his fingers still on the table, leaned over and intimidating. "And I think he should know that he's not welcome here."

Nero's ugly grin spread across his face like a plague. "Oh, I know how unwelcome I am but I feel strongly that I have some information about this case that I'd like to get some reactions for. You know. To improve the quality of my writing, of course."

Shannon gulped.

The reporter was a nuisance at best. The idea that he could have any thoughts on the case that would be better told to the suspects than to the public at large was suspicious and almost laughable. He pushed Nero closer to the table with a hard shove, relishing the angered expression he got in return. "Let's hear it," he invited. "Let's hear what you have to say before we toss you out on your ass."

The reporter seemed to have to collect himself, breathing a few times in and out. "Jim Valechy was murdered in the same fashion as the other victims," he started. "There were six parallel lines on his palms. Twelve in total."

The dining room was silent.

"Shannon Kingsley has no alibi for any of the murders. In fact, she claims that she was sleeping throughout all of them. Coincidence? That she was sleeping during every single murder? I suggest that Shannon Kingsley was indeed sleeping throughout every murder. I simply suggest that she was *not* in her bed." He pointed a dramatic finger at the wide-eyed girl. "The police found her hair on Valechy's body. She is your killer. Your *sleepwalking* killer." He laughed a little. "And if you find that impossible because of what happened with Mr. Avery—that he was attacked by a *man* then think again." He shifted his thin finger toward Sean with a strange grin spreading on his face. "I propose that *you*, Sir, attacked the detective. To *protect your sister!*"

To this Steven stood, his chair falling backwards with the force as his hands came down on the table hard. "*That's completely preposterous!*"

Winston carefully studied the expressions around the table in that matter of seconds. Most everyone was looking at the reporter, anger in their eyes. Kyle was still sitting but his jaw was down and his fists on the table. Shannon merely appeared anguished and frightened. Steven was seething. Ren appeared amused.

But Sean. Sean wasn't even looking at Nero. He was staring angrily at Shannon, his teeth gritted together hard in a grimace. Something inside Winston's chest started squeezing his heart and lungs. It was as if he couldn't breathe. His hand came up and his palm flattened against his sternum. The past few months began to flash before his eyes as he took Nero by the back of his shirt and very nearly dragged him backwards to the door, throwing him out into the rain as hard as he could. He ignored the cries of pain from the little rat as he tumbled down the steps of the porch.

When he turned back around and went back to the dining room, everyone was staring down at what was left of their pudding. Everyone but Ren who had a smug little expression that Winston just wanted to punch right off his fucking face.

Kyle shook his head. "What the fuck kind of an accusation was that? That's ridiculous. Miss Shannon could never do anything like that. Sleeping or not. And Sean? Really?"

Shannon's meek trembling voice piped up. "What if he's right?

What if it was me? What if I'm the killer?"

"Pure speculation." Ren patted her hand. "The guy's insane."

Winston's heart started beating faster in his chest. "I think it's about time we all retired to our rooms. This has gone far enough for tonight." He couldn't have said anything more opposing to what he felt. This had not gone far enough. But he didn't have time to think of the rest of a plan. This was not what he'd had in mind for the night.

Everyone complied easily, the boys meandering up to their rooms, Steven still trembling from his outburst and Sean's shoulders tense. Shannon was crying into Ren's chest and Ren gave him a strange look. One that begged Winston to come upstairs.

The detective put a steady hand on the girl's shoulder and he murmured, "Why don't we all go upstairs and we'll talk this out with you? It's highly improbable that you would sleepwalk your way through murder."

She nodded but she was still sniffling. When they got her upstairs and sat her down on the bed Winston knelt between her knees and looked up at her while she wiped tears away from her eyes.

He handed her a tissue and sighed and repeated, "Highly improbable."

"Why?" Her voice sounded defeated.

Winston smiled up at her. "Because that's absurd. For you to sneak, unnoticed, in the dead of night to offices, to homes?"

"Oh." Her eyes grew wide and surprise filled her features. "But it seems so likely. I'm the only one without an alibi for all the murders. I came back from the woods with blood on my feet but I swear to you that those cuts weren't deep enough to bleed. What if, this whole time, I've been wandering far and wide?"

"The chances of that, Miss Kingsley. They're astronomical."

Her face fell. "But what if—"

Ren put a finger to her lips and her eyes looked up at him. "No 'what-ifs' or 'buts' around Winston, sweets. They drive him crazy."

He nodded at her and then stood, facing Ren with his hands on his hips, his back to the open door. That was his mistake. The open door. It was just for a moment. Just for one single moment. A sharp, sudden pain shot through his back and he gasped and tried to take a step back but someone caught him. He barely heard Shannon's voice when she yelled out. He was stumbling backward as he was let go. He hit the wall hard, his head snapping back with the force and his legs had turned to mush so he slid down onto the floor. Ren was poised but couldn't move, his hands out at his sides, anger in his expression.

The room gained clarity as the pain turned from sharp to strong and dull. "The fuck, Sh-Shuh-Sean?" he asked.

"Shut up," Sean kicked him hard in the thigh and Winston's hand curled up toward his gun but Sean was too quick. He disarmed him easily, tossing the gun across the room and holding a long blade to the detective's throat. He spoke to Ren next. "I suppose this fucker isn't all that important to you considering he's your equivalent of a grim reaper. Did you really think he was going to let you walk away from all this? But then again, I'm not sure you really think much at all, do you, Mr. Rockey? Yeah, that's right. I know you."

Ren's angered expression turned into something more akin to rage and Winston was sure he could feel the room getting colder.

Sean continued, his calm voice filled with malice, "Did you think I'd just let it go? Just let you all figure this out without intervening? Did you think I'd let you ruin what we have?"

Shannon finally began to speak in a trembling odd little tone that was higher than her normal voice and seemed out of breath. "Sean? I don't understand."

"You don't have to understand, Shan. Just shut your mouth. That's all you have to do. Nobody's going to find out. Not anyone important, anyway. You don't have to understand me. Nobody really does. Except *Adrian* here. I knew he was different from the moment we met. That he was *capable,* I should say."

"That's crazy," she whispered.

"Don't say that. It's perfectly logical." His voice was still calm but the blade pressed a little harder against Winston's neck. "Tell me why you killed that fat little asshole the way you did."

Ren shook his head. "I would if I'd killed him."

"Don't lie to me."

"I'm not that uncreative," Ren growled. "If I'd killed him, I would have at least been artful about it." Winston wanted to laugh at that statement but he was pretty sure the pain would have been unbearable. He could feel the warmth of his blood spreading under his bottom as he sat there in it. It would stain the nice carpet. He felt guilty.

Ren continued, "As it is, it seems as though the tricksters have been tricked. It's your move, fox. Would you like to answer a question for me? Why didn't you get rid of Winston?"

Sean took the blade from Winston's neck and stood straight and still, pointing it at Ren, his outstretched arm was completely still without a single hint of a tremor. "I'll answer your question merely because it's only common courtesy to do so before I gut you and recreate *your* kind of murder."

Ren's smile spread across his face. That toothy grin that only the devil himself could have produced. *All those fucking teeth. All those horrible fucking teeth.* He couldn't, despite his will, close his eyes against them. "If you really wanted to be authentic you wouldn't use a knife."

Sean paused only for a moment. "That other detective, Avery, was...*predictable.* He was easy to track. I would have gotten Mr. Winston eventually. I would say that I *have.*"

It was when Sean shrugged that Shannon made her move, quickly jerking open the drawer to the nightstand and pulling out a sleek black pistol. She pointed it at her own brother with a sureness in her grip as she cocked it. *Where did she learn how to cock a pistol?* "Stop it, Sean." Her voice was still breathy and light and unsure.

"Little One." Sean put out his hands to either side of himself, the knife still shining in the light from the lamp. A deep roll of thunder interrupted them and Sean waited until it was done to speak again. "You're pointing that in the wrong direction. *He's* the one who's deceived you. He's the one who's always had the intent to leave you in the dust after taking what he could from you. *He's the one who doesn't deserve to live.*"

"I already knew."

Ren broke his glare at Sean and his head jerked toward Shannon.

She looked at him as well, her gun still on Sean. "I knew you were a killer. Winston told me. You never lied to me. That's what...that's what's important."

"Is it?" Sean brought their attention back to him. "How cute. But you won't shoot me Shan. I'm trying to *help* us. You wouldn't. You *couldn't*."

There was a soft click he just barely managed to hear over the sound of the rain pounding on the roof and window. It took him mere seconds to realize that Shannon Kingsley, sheltered rich girl, had pulled the trigger. But the gun wasn't loaded. The sound of Sean's chuckle made chills run up Winston's spine but it was the icy glare that Ren was giving him that put fear into the soul. Shannon merely appeared to be confused, tipping the gun so she could see what she'd done wrong.

Sean's voice was simply a wisp, all laughter gone. "Brave Little One. Did you ever love me?"

The rest of it was almost a blur, so confusing that Winston almost couldn't follow it. The two men lunged at each other but never touched. One single gunshot rang out in the cramped room and Sean fell into a heap on the floor next to the bed. The knife was lost from his hand and Ren was bristled but still standing. Shannon fell to her knees on the carpet, staring at the body that had been her brother only seconds before.

Avery holstered his gun in the doorway and looked at each of them in turn, taking in their shocked gazes. He was soaking wet from head to toe, his black hair plastered to his forehead and every bit of his jeans and T-shirt clinging to his body. He dripped all over the carpet when he shrugged.

"How's that for predictable?"

Ren was the first to reply. "How'd you know?"

Avery straightened his gun straps and adjusted his T-shirt before kneeling down next to Winston. "I'm a clever motherfucker, that's how."

Steven and Kyle were in the doorway when Steven spoke. "We heard a...oh my god. S-Sean?"

Winston allowed Avery to help him to his feet with an arm around his shoulders. "The bastard stabbed me. Call 911. I'm starting to feel light-headed."

CHAPTER 26

They were sitting together with that fake wood surface between them that was meant for meals. The cards were down. Birds chirped out the window of the hospital but Winston wasn't paying attention. He flipped through the possibilities. There were flowers all over the room, fresh and new that had come with cards wishing him well. He had no idea so many people cared about him. One set had even come from someone he hadn't expected to hear from for the rest of his life. A specific blonde Senator, actually. He put a card down into the discard pile and narrowed his eyes at Avery.

"Interesting," Avery supplied. "I could have sworn you were collecting twos."

"And I thought you said you were a clever motherfucker," he scoffed.

Ren chuckled where he sat cross-legged on Winston's bed. "Silly Avery, Winston's not collecting twos. He's collecting kings. Where have you been this whole game?"

Winston kicked him hard and Avery laughed, the sound music to the ears. For so long he had been unable to do such a thing. Laugh, talk, function even. It was so good to have him back. It was strange to have his two partners in the same room with each other. The two of them were so different and he studied them while they stared at their cards. He had done much to bend each of them one way or another and they had done much to bend him.

"One thing still bothers me," mused Ren while he tapped the top of his cards with a finger.

"What's that?" Avery asked without looking up.

"Who was really the killer?" He shook his head. "Sean was absolutely livid because he thought I had killed Valechy but if Shannon was the killer, wouldn't he have immediately thought that *she* had done it? There had to have been someone who'd done it, if none of us did." He looked between the two detectives for any sign of knowing.

Winston shrugged, "Beats me." He lifted a brow at Avery, who lifted his own in return.

"Beats me? That's all you'll put in?"

"Beats me," he repeated.

Ren's eyes narrowed and a demon grin passed along his face. "You're a sly little kitty, Winnie."

Winston glared at him over his cards. "*Beats. Me.*"

"Anyways," Avery interrupted, "I saw you got flowers from all the families involved in the murder case just like I did. Although I can't help but notice that the Kingsley's aren't exactly filled with gratitude. You guys kinda came in like a tornado. And do you think they'll be content with the idea that Sean was the killer the whole time?"

Winston sighed, "Well, you can win the war without winning some of the battles, I suppose." He put down his cards on his lap and leaned backward on his pillows. The flowers to his right, the lilies, were from Grace. He reached over and touched them. They bounced merrily back at him. She'd written the card herself in that loopy adorable handwriting he'd loved so much.

Dear Trent,
Stop taking those dangerous cases
and spend a little time

spoiling yourself on the beach.
Love, Grace

Was that an invitation? He closed his eyes and could smell summer and the ocean on the Outer Banks. He could catch a whiff of her lilac perfume and the way her blue eyes shined with the hope of another summer. She was much better suited to hope than he was. Worlds away in mindset. Maybe it was time to stop taking such difficult cases. Maybe it was time to take the reward and invest it. Maybe it was time to get himself right out of the game. He opened his eyes and Avery was staring at him while Ren was looking out the window over the skyline of the city, his cards forgotten in his hand. Avery would help him in any way possible. Ren would wander forever if he could.

A young, familiar voice rang out in the hallway, mildly distressed. "No, I promise. I'm serious, I'm his...I'm his cousin. I swear. What is with that stupid policy anyway? If you would just *ask* him, he would approve me." She stumbled in wearing bright red peep-toed wedges and a flowing black dress with a tight red ribbon about her middle, the bow resting in the small of her back. Her blonde hair was long, at least to her waist, and it was pulled to the side and braided over her shoulder, daisies threaded through it artfully. Her bangs were to the tip of her lovely thin freckled nose and her nails were painted a pearly pink.

Every man in the room was silent, staring at her in complete disbelief.

She stopped fussing with the nurse and she suddenly appeared to have seen a ghost. "What...what are *you* doing here?"

Ren gulped.

They both could do nothing but stare at each other so Winston broke the silence. "Tomi, good to see you. Didn't quite expect you. You can put those flowers you have on the side table over here, they're very lovely. Avery liked his too. I understand you own a floral shop near Buffalo, that must be exciting."

She didn't move. Her eyes had glazed over while she stared at Ren and he stared back at her. There was abject terror in his expression. As if he expected her to hit him, yell at him, curse him, hate him. When she did speak, it was with a breathy monotone. "Yes. I have a...a flower shop. It's kind of boring sometimes though. I took up knitting. The ladies are very dramatic. But they're nice most of the time."

Ren's mouth opened and Tomi's eyes widened but he couldn't seem to make any words in response. It was a hard task and he tried valiantly before all he could do was whisper at her. "You look...beautiful."

Winston tsked and said a little louder, "Why don't you two go catch up by the vending machines? It would get all this weird shit floating around out of this room." It would also give him some time to just sit with his real partner and reduce his stress. He decided he could use a vacation and he might just take Grace up on her offer.

She almost passed them but the white of his hair caught her attention. They didn't see her when she stopped in the middle of the hallway entrance. The vending machines were down a short little segment of corridor decorated with a few potted plants and a bench at the end in front of a large plate glass window. They were sitting together. Sort of looking at each other. Not really. They weren't touching. Not even their knees were touching in that odd kind of way that knees touch when you're sitting next to someone you kind of like. But she could tell there was something else touching. An aura. Something intangible. Something they shared.

She was stunning. Her tiny body was curled perfectly, her pale knees together, her feet tiny and pointed in those blazing red shoes. She had precisely curved collarbones and her strawberry blonde hair was decorated in its loose braid with perky white daisies. Her bangs nearly hid her wide, curious blue eyes. Even the curve of her ear looked perfect and delicate.

Shannon quickly hid herself around the corner of the wall and peeked out at them, her ears trained for any words they might utter. She waited for a long time. They were just sitting together in a comfortable and strange sort of silence. She recognized that this must be Tomi. The ethereal mythical girl in Ren's past he'd left before her. The girl Shannon reminded Winston of. *How? She's so much prettier than me.* Her heart dropped down into her bowels. How could she have ever thought to keep Ren? When he'd left such a perfect little woman?

Her ears perked when she heard her speak. A soft melodious voice that was mesmerizing.

"Aren't you afraid?"

Ren replied at once. "Of what?"

"Getting caught."

He reached into his pocket and pulled out a few slips of paper and cards. "Winston got me these."

She took them and examined them, leafing through them with a slight frown marring her features. "These are very well-made."

Is he blushing? "I guess that's what you get when you're a P.I. You know some folks who know some folks." *His hands are trembling. He's nervous?* She was trying to remember if she'd ever made him nervous.

"How did you end up working for him?"

He was looking at her knees. "It was just. A chance. And...he...I mean...it's Winston."

She was smiling suddenly. "He scared you into it. Didn't he? That's Winston."

"You're right. That's Winnie. Of course. He threatened me with you."

"Of course he did." She was giggling. As if it were some inside joke and he was supposed to be chuckling along with her. "That makes sense."

One of his brows cocked. "How's that?"

She raised one perfect white shoulder. "I just mean that it makes sense because I was the one who hired him to keep an eye on you."

Shannon's heart was beating hard against her sternum and her hand was against her chest. It was as if she were witnessing the reveal of some criminal mastermind. The sinister last monologue before the bullet passed through her body. The image of her brother's body as a pile on the floor flooded back into her mind and tears welled up in her eyes. None of this would have happened. Only one thing would be sure. The murders would have continued. But her brother would have stood by her side.

She'd almost forgotten that she was holding a magazine in her hands. One of those supermarket tabloids that were printed on low-quality paper with watery, blurred photographs that took up most of the front page. It was a picture of her. Upset. Without any make up. With her hair in a mess. It was a picture of her the day after Sean's death. When Nero had snapped a photo of her. The legitimate news sources were more interested in what the police department was saying rather than some quirky theories that a journalist might have had.

The police had determined that it was just like Winston had said. It was *improbable* that she would have killed anyone while sleeping. They had no real evidence and had decided that Sean was the most likely culprit. They had assured her father that the investigation would be closed pending a review of the circumstances and evidence of the case.

In large white letters, the paper declared that she was the true killer. That Sean was the scapegoat. That she was evil. It had made her cry. Mostly because her brother was gone.

Some because she still wasn't so sure she *wasn't* a murderer.

Ren spoke again to Tomi, drawing Shannon's attention from her problems.

"You're a little fox, aren't you?"

"I didn't know he was going to make you help him. I just wanted to make sure you were okay. Not self-destructing. You know what I mean."

"Winston told me about your boyfriend."

"Mmm," she replied; a careless response as if she didn't want Ren involved in that area of her life.

He took the hint and scratched the back of his neck. He was quiet for a little while before he obviously couldn't hold it inside any longer. "I'm sorry."

"Don't apologize."

"I can't help it."

"I know." She appeared as if she wanted to touch him but couldn't. "You're one of a kind, you know."

He smiled. It was genuine and sincere and it spread from ear to ear. It gave Shannon goosebumps but for positive rather than negative reasons. When the two of them stood up and started walking together back down the hall, she panicked. She had no idea where to go, what to do, how to look like she hadn't been listening to every bit of their sparse conversation like her life depended upon it.

She probably looked guilty as sin when they walked around the corner and saw her.

"Ummmmmm," was her immediate vocal reaction. She was holding the magazine up against her chest as though it could protect her.

Tomi came to her rescue. "Miss Kingsley. Tomi Balekowski. I'm sorry for being forward but I've read all about you in Winston's reports. You're far prettier in person and I hear you have a good kick." Her grin was like that of a careful little coyote.

She laughed nervously with tears welling in her eyes again. She couldn't help it. She looked at the floor to avoid Adrian's gaze. "Well you know. I'm a bit like hot sauce that way. Get in a good kick or two." *What am I saying?* "Ummm, umm, uh," she swallowed convulsively, unable to think of a single thing to ease her anxiety.

Tomi seemed amused, the corners of her mouth twitching a little. "I have to get back to Buffalo by tonight and my plane leaves in two hours from Baltimore so I must be off. I left my shop with my significant other and he's wonderful, but his communication skills are sorely lacking. I'd hate for all the old biddies to get sore over his oddness."

Adrian smiled. "You're a might bit odd too, I should say."

Tomi elbowed him in the side and continued to smile at Shannon as if nothing had occurred. "It was wonderful to meet you, Miss Kingsley.

I look forward to our paths crossing again." Tomi gave her a coy glance as if to ask, *Will you be keeping him?*

"Perhaps in the future," she nodded. "Since we have so many mutual acquaintances, it seems inevitable."

"Good," the blonde stated in way that implied finality. It was settled. They would meet again. The question truly was—did Shannon *wish* to see the pretty little woman ever again? Questions about her origin, the real manipulation around Winston's shenanigans, and how much the girl actually *knew* whirled about in her mind.

She and Adrian were suddenly alone in the hallway, standing together while they watched the tiny Tomi tap away in her stunning red heels. The big bow that was perched in the curve of her lower back bounced as she swayed her hips.

"Okay," Shannon found her bottom lip trembling slightly.

Adrian gently touched her hand and she jumped backward from his touch. He tried again, putting out an offer for the paper in her hands. She gave it to him, lamenting on how crushed and crumpled it had become from her panic.

"Nero's still on that, huh?"

"What if he's right?" Her tears spilled over.

Adrian shook his head with a lopsided smirk. "You could ask yourself that until the end of your days and never know. It's no use now. I'm sorry about your brother. And I'm sorry about me."

"Oh my god," she gasped, falling forward and wrapping her arms around his middle, holding him as tight as she dared. "Oh my god," she repeated. "Please don't be sorry for you. Please don't regret being with me." She sobbed into his shirt, feeling pathetic and useless. "Please don't be sorry. Please. *I love you.*"

EPILOGUE

PART I

He was sitting in her father's study in a chair off to the side of the room. It was off center of the front of the large cherry wood desk upon which sat papers and books all centered on the study of African birds. Sunlight streamed from the glass of a solitary window, shining beams of light down upon the essays and texts. Dust seemed a foreign thing, the place being absolutely spotless in that regard. The books on the tall, dark shelves around the room had been meticulously cleaned and there was not a single speck of dirt to be found anywhere. The dark wood flooring was covered under him by an area rug of a deep forest green and the walls matched the color flawlessly.

He was nervous though he didn't know what for. It was only that her father had asked him here.

What could he want? What could he want? What could he—

One of the books was open to a picture of an African Grey parrot. Its yellow eyes stared at him while he peered over the papers, curious about them. The birds attracted him. The different labels and terms and the overall science was fascinating. Not just the parrots. All of them. The mechanics of birds was an intriguing subject. Their flight, their diseases, their overall appearances and evolutionary molding. He looked over his shoulder to make sure that the professor wasn't going to walk in just that second. He then pushed very lightly on the edge of the book to make it easier for him to read.

It would be nice to meet a smart bird. Smart bird. Smart bird. It would be nice...

"Adrian."

He nearly jumped out of his skin. Immediately, he gathered his poise and tried not to give away how disgruntled he was at being surprised.

The professor moved from the door behind him after shutting it and took his place at his desk. "Good of you to come. I'm sure you're wondering why I've asked you here to speak with me and I won't hold you in suspense. You see, it's been a few days since...well." Dr. Kingsley paused and put a finger over his lips, drawing in a tight breath in, his eyes shifting to the ceiling and then back down again. He removed his finger. "Since the funeral." He cleared his throat as if he were trying, somehow, to remove himself from that memory. "I was under the impression that this was a temporary affair."

It suddenly dawned on him that the man was talking about his relationship to Shannon and Ren straightened in his seat, pushing backwards on the floor until his bottom was flush against the back of the chair.

"Now," Dr. Kingsley continued, "I cannot force you to stay. But I can guarantee that you will not find anything out there that we cannot provide for you. That is to say, I think you have plenty of reasons to stay, even if there are compelling ones to leave. Within that particular thread of thought, and don't stop me, I must get it out: You cannot hide that you've experienced the darker side of life. Of human nature. I can see it every time I look at you. But, contrary to that, you also remind me of my son."

Ren swallowed. He vaguely recognized that he had been holding his breath.

The professor nodded to himself and continued. "You're much like him in that you would never hurt her intentionally. Shannon. I believe that of you. She deserves to be loved." His tone grew darker and he stared Ren in the eyes without blinking. "If you think you're incapable of that then I urge you to leave. Now. Do not string her along. Do not play a game. Do not give her false hope. If you do, you will be no better than her brother. She doesn't deserve any more heartbreak than this.

"So I give to you this warning. If you do not leave now. If you choose to leave later just to build her up and then destroy her—I will stop at nothing. I will find you. I will eliminate you."

There was a silence that filled the room with a sharp ringing in his ears.

Dr. Kingsley asked, "Do we have an understanding, Mr. Woods?"

Do we have...? Do we have...? Do we have an understanding? Mr. Woods?

He took a moment to compose himself. His heart was beating hard in his chest. There was something inherently frightening in the way the man was speaking. The tonality of his voice that chilled him in a way that he'd never before experienced. He swallowed again, gulping back the slight terror that had gripped him.

Ren nodded. "I understand, Sir."

Dr. Kingsley smiled. "Good man. You don't have to tell me what you're going to do. I will simply assume that if you're here tomorrow, you'll be with us for a long time."

He sat still and silent while the professor straightened some of the things on his desk and cleared his throat.

"That's all I had to say to you. I'm sorry if I've shocked you."

He found his eyes snapping harshly toward the older man and his thoughts racing in wild force. They were drowned out.

An ultimatum? What are we going to do? What are we going to do? What are we going to...?

He stood suddenly, the large chair skidding backwards just a slight bit. Dr. Kingsley did not flinch but watched Ren as he moved toward the door. He could still feel the professor's gaze on him until he was fully out of his sight.

He found himself outside, sitting in the yard, getting his khakis dirty. His hands were in the grass, petting it and pawing through it over and over. As if to remember how it felt to sleep on it. To not have a comfy bed. To be free and wild and running around the countryside in fright for his very life. As if that was some kind of golden age. Being lawless and untamed. He found his breath coming in quick, short pants and his chest constricting. He gloomily recognized this emotion. A strange one. One that didn't usually come to him so strongly. Something that kept to the distant reaches of his mind.

Fear.

"Adri—?"

He quickly turned his head.

She plopped down next to him with a serious expression. She was wearing one of the sweaters that Winston had given to him. It was too big on her and bagged around her slight frame. With a great sigh, she said, "I saw you come out here. You seemed upset. Are you hungry? Leslie made some snacks; they're in the kitchen."

"I'm not hungry."

"Me neither."

He wanted to touch her but he didn't. He turned his eyes to the scene around him. The too-vivid colors of late summer and the slight chill that signified the coming of autumn. The trees blurred in his vision and became softly swaying blobs of color. He felt dazed and out of control. Numb and fixed to the spot. What Winston had made him promise came back to him in a rush. *No one gets hurt...* He reflected on the way things had turned out. Odd and distorted. A family of sorts. A broken one. A healing one. He'd never healed anything. He'd only ever destroyed. He glanced at her. A chance. A chance for what? Redemption? The fear that had plagued him in the professor's office wasn't the fear of losing his freedom. It had been his mistake to assume that. As she sat next to him, he realized what he was truly afraid of.

"Shannon?" he asked.

She responded with a soft murmur. "Mmm?"

He whispered so softly that it might have simply been taken by the wind. But from her reaction to it, her sweetest kiss, he knew she'd heard him.

"Will you marry me?"

PART II

Sometimes he could still feel it. That nagging tingle in his muscles that reminded him of the nerve damage from being stabbed in the back. Sometimes he could still feel all of it. Even the pain in his heart. Especially when he had the nightmares. Those horrible dreams that plagued him. Even when he was wrapped in Grace's warm arms.

He was sitting by the pool with his feet up in front of him on another green plastic pool chair. Even after five years he could still feel that odd sensation of pressure where the thin scar was. He leaned forward and rubbed at it through his T-shirt before he was again reminded that it would never work to just touch it. His Rottweiler was curled up beside his chair, sleeping in the hot summer sun. His *real* Rottweiler, Rock.

He dropped a hand down and managed to tickle one of the dog's ears with the tips of his fingers. He couldn't escape his past, he thought morosely. It would always be there. Tingling in his back and in his subconscious mind. He closed his eyes and covered them with one hand.

"Boo?"

"Yes, dear?" he replied. Fury welled up in his throat at the sickening pet name. It made him so angry he could spit. That *fucking* name she called him.

"Could you do the dishes while I'm gone? I have to run to the store to pick up some stuff for dinner tonight."

He couldn't see her but he knew what she looked like. She had that rainbow beach bag she used as a purse over her shoulder and her ridiculously huge sunglasses perched on top of her head. Her blonde hair was pulled back from her face and her eyes were squinted in the sun. She was cute...but, as they say: Behind every cute blonde there was some guy who was sick of her shit—and that was him.

"Yes, Grace," he said.

She didn't respond. She just turned around and headed toward her little fucking Pontiac Solstice that he had partly paid for. It was red, of course, and she'd gotten about five speeding tickets in it so far.

He took his hand away from his eyes and he squinted at the

newspaper beside him.

Rapist Claims Second Victim in Home Invasion.

What the fuck was wrong with this world? He sighed and tickled his dog's ear again. What the fuck was wrong with *him*? He read the article and somehow wished for a few moments that he'd done what Avery had done and accepted the invitation to work with the F. B. I. Maybe it could have been just for a few years. Then he wouldn't be sitting here wasting his time trying to snatch at clues in a newspaper, waiting for the mysteries to be solved by someone else. He wouldn't be tied down by Grace's idiotic ultimatums that he stop working so he couldn't be in danger.

His life had slowed down—but *he* most certainly hadn't.

The question was—where was he supposed to go from here?

ABOUT THE AUTHOR

A. Sleeper lives in the small Western New York town of East Aurora with her African Lovebird, Beebs, and a plethora of incredible friends. Send all questions or feedback to asleep19@mail.com

Like this book? Check out some of these titles from A. Sleeper:

Dog Days of Winter
Three Dog Days

www.ingramcontent.com/pod-product-compliance
Lightning Source LLC
Chambersburg PA
CBHW020551180626
46810CB00007B/2457